The EYE
of the
STORM

STUART K. KIMBALL

From the Author of *In Search of the Lost Light & WOW! Shift Happens!*

This book is entirely a work of fiction. Names, characters, places and incidents are either the product of the author's imagination or are used fictitiously, and any resemblance to actual persons, living or dead, business establishments, events or locales is entirely coincidental.

The author of this book does not dispense medical advice or prescribe the use of any technique as a form of treatment for physical, emotional or medical problems without the advice of a physician , either directly or indirectly. The intent of the author is only to offer information of a general nature to help you in your quest for emotional and spiritual well being. In the event you use any of the information in this book for yourself, which is your right, the author and publisher assume no responsibility or liability for your actions.

Cover design by Rich Carnahan (www.publishpros.com)
Author photo by Glyn Cowden (www.glyncowden.flavors.me)

This book is dedicated to the greatest gifts I will ever receive:
My children—Cecile, Robert Forrest and Taylor

ACKNOWLEDGEMENTS

This book would not have been possible
without the following people:

Marj Wentworth, Nancy Straight, Renee Johnson, Lee
Hunnicutt, John, Bill and Bob Kimball, Mom and Dad,
Bert Keller, Steve Hoffius, Bret Lott, Kelly Fowler, Jack
Hurley, Mark Antman, Hillary Hutchinson, Dennis
Jarvis, Caroline Ilderton, Richard Almes, Jeff Pulley,
Mike Richmond, Jeanne Barreira, Jack Owens, Heather
Sjostrom, Angela Fox, Byron Waldman, Susan Dunn,
Chuck and Ashley Wile, Drew Clearie, Nancy Tyler, and
Mary Semsar.

Very special thanks to Sarah Nichols.

1

"Tide's gettin' ready to change. Put in over there and let's finish this."

Darkness cloaked the harbor as the skiff turned easily towards a small island. The air was still, thick with the smells of the sea. The only visible marine traffic was a distant pilot boat slowly headed out to greet an incoming ship. A flash from the nearby Sullivan's Island lighthouse sliced through the night-sky.

City lights rippled slowly across the water, barely illuminating the island and the ruined brick walls of a long abandoned fort as the skiff nudged ashore.

A short, stocky man jumped effortlessly onto the land. He easily dragged the boat further up the beach with one hand before securing an anchor deep in the mud of the deserted island's shoreline.

"Grab his arms" called the voice of a hook-nosed, taller man as he also stepped onto the beach. The two hauled the seemingly lifeless body of another person out of the boat, carrying it halfway to the tide line. They carefully placed him on the muddy sand. A third man stepped quietly off the boat. Watching, he carefully slipped away from the next lighthouse beam that swept through the night. He remained in the shadows.

"He's not moving. Think he's already dead?" asked Shorty.

"Nah, I just put a little extra in that iced tea or whatever he was sippin'on. Sit him up a little and hold his mouth open so I can get this down his throat."

Shorty easily did as he was told. The third guy stood nearby, quietly observing as he glanced around the harbor.

Hook pulled a large glass bottle out of the skiff, which he quickly opened and connected to a long, thin rubber hose. In the same motion, he started sliding the tube into the mouth of the still motionless man, who gagged slightly as it was pushed deeper into his body.

"That damn light is coming again. Get down," warned Shorty.

"No one can see us, who cares?" snapped Hook, ducking nonetheless as the shaft of light again passed over the beach, and them. "Just keep his mouth wide open," he added while hoisting a half-gallon of Jack Daniels above his shoulders, and then watched the liquid as it began to trickle down the tube and into the guy on the beach.

"Shame to waste good bourbon on a turd like this one. I'm just damn glad this isn't my liquor," he said as he turned on a flashlight with his free hand to be certain the whiskey was still flowing.

"Drink up, you asshole. The next thing you'll be tasting will be seawater."

"You sure this is going to work?" Shorty asked, watching closely.

"Hell yeah. It sure worked on those other two guys, didn't it? It should do really well on a fine gentleman like this dingle berry."

"Crap, here comes that damn light again, duck down!"

"Will you cool your jets? There ain't nobody else out here! No one can see us. Just keep holding him. We're almost done."

But someone could see them. Not thirty feet away, a young man was crouched deep in the shadows behind one of the crumbled walls. He was trying to figure out what these two were doing to the fellow half-lying on the beach. The boy watched them closely as each sweep of the lighthouse beam illuminated the scene. He tried to hear what they were saying.

He stood up, raising himself higher on the wall, trying to get a better look as the next shaft of light crossed over the two strangers and revealed their faces. The third man was a silhouette against the city lights.

Just at that same moment, the young man's foot suddenly slipped, noisily knocking loose an old chunk of brick.

The hook–nosed guy instinctively responded to the sound. He rapidly swung his flashlight; its blaze landed directly on the face of the teenager.

"Holy Hell!!" hollered Shorty, instantly running towards the youngster, who had already begun to scramble away as fast as he could. The boy knew the island well and, even in the deep darkness, had no trouble circling quietly back behind a different broken-down wall as Shorty stumbled in the nearby ruins, turning on another flashlight, searching frantically.

"You better get that dude!" bellowed Hook. The third man backed quietly towards the boat at the harbors edge.

The young man had already slipped gently into the dark waters. The tide silently took him away from the island as he disappeared into the night.

2

A slow trickle of sweat began to descend down the left lens of Jacob O'Leary's eyeglasses. Charleston in late July does that, even to a man who likes to believe he doesn't sweat a thing.

But Jacob was heading to an extraordinarily important appointment. He wore a suit and tie on a summer morning that was unusually warm even by South Carolina standards. He carried a briefcase full of important papers. So maybe it was OK for him to be sweating just a little.

As he ambled along the shady side of Queen Street, Jacob wondered why he wasn't feeling especially excited at this moment. This particular deal meant so much to him right now. Yet somehow, this meeting seemed anti-climatic.

Jacob was a stockbroker working for Hamilton Brothers, one of the nation's largest financial services companies. He was on his way to see Edmund Capers, the CFO of Southern Shipping, a 280 year old family-owned business.

Amongst his other responsibilities, Edmund oversaw 750 million dollars of various company retirement assets which he believed had been very poorly invested by another financial institution. After having met with Jacob on numerous occasions over the past several years to discuss investment alternatives, Edmund had come to believe the funds would be better directed by Jacob and Hamilton Brothers. This meeting was to finalize an agreement transferring the assets for Jacob to manage.

This would be the deal of a lifetime for most anyone. The fee from this one transaction would be in the low seven figures. It would transform Jacob's financial future.

Instead of mentally preparing for this major moment in his life, Jacob was enjoying, as he always did, the beauty of Charleston. He was walking beside a high wall with bits of fern and small budding plants growing out of the moss-covered centuries old brick. Across the road, well tended window boxes sprawled in thick midsummer purple, blue, orange and white floral displays that perfectly accentuated the faded pink, yellow, and white stucco walls of the three-story eighteenth century houses that lined the street. The palmetto trees he passed under were still, waiting for the sea-breeze that would inevitably arrive and blow them into joyous frolic. Aside from a horse-drawn carriage full of tourists, the popular street was nearly deserted. In the distance he could see a bit of the harbor, and, beyond it, a bright blue sky over Mt Pleasant.

It was the middle of a southern summer and Jacob guessed most people were either smart enough to be indoors, or more likely, out of town enjoying cooler weather, which he soon planned to be. As quickly as possible after this deal was settled, he intended on taking an extended vacation to Alaska, a place he'd never visited. He was looking forward to being somewhere far more refreshing than the summer heat in South Carolina's Lowcountry. But first, he had today's business to finally attend to.

Arriving on the street corner next to the Dock Street Theater, Jacob stopped for a moment to clean the sweat on his glasses with his necktie. *"At least these things are good for something,"* he thought. Jacob despised wearing neckties at any time of the year, but especially during the summer. He thought wearing them during those months should be against the law as they clearly posed a major health risk. However, this was the conservative South, and he was a supposedly serious businessman. He was expected to look like this. Plus, the New York based securities firm he worked for had a very strict dress code, which included suits and ties at all times. Image was apparently much more important than substance to those far-away executives that created this policy.

Jacob felt that neckties were a leash of some sort that those distant corporate bosses could use at any time to jerk him around. To him, a tie seemed a red flag, warning everyone that the wearer was a salesman. He didn't care for wearing suits either, but considered them to be a form of camouflage as he worked his remaining days in Tie-Land.

He wondered why he was spending so much energy being bothered by trivial things like clothing. He knew it was well past time for him to get out of this business. He hadn't enjoyed working in it for years. In the early days of his career, it had been exciting for Jacob because it was something completely new. He had been able then to use his creative energy writing interesting articles and delivering financial seminars all over South Carolina. At the time, he had received a great deal of support and encouragement from Hamilton Brothers.

But that was then. The industry's objectives had long since changed completely. Now, the firms stated mission for the year was solely focused on increasing its profit margin by 1%. They had at least been honest enough to not include some meaningless malarkey about dedication and outstanding service for their clients that included providing unparalleled support for employees who did the actual work for the firm. Hamilton Brothers objectives and new policies were steadily sucking the souls out of all the people who did the day to day work that made the gigantic enterprise run smoothly and very profitably.

Jacob's relationship to the industry had gradually soured. And along with it, his enthusiasm for securing the new business relationships that had been his primary source of considerable income. He continued to work hard for his clients and they had done reasonably well, especially during challenging economic times.

If this meeting went as planned, Jacob would probably never wear a necktie again, let alone dwell on what was wrong with the securities industry. He had stopped thinking about what was good with it long ago.

Jacob's cell phone rang. Glancing at the caller ID, he wasn't surprised to see it was the Collections Dept at US Bank & Trust. They called frequently these days. With this deal, that was all about to change. He didn't answer, but did change the phone's setting to silent, to simply vibrate should there be an incoming call.

Just as his arrival in Charleston more than a dozen years ago had been really an accident, Jacob becoming a stock-broker was even more unintentional. Twelve years earlier he had been sailing north and was blown way off course by a tropical storm. Luckily, he was close enough to Charleston Harbor to find safety. He hadn't intended to stay longer than it took to do the necessary repairs to his sailboat *Pearl*. He needed some cash and was able to quickly land a bar-tenders job at the marina's restaurant, The Dancing Marlin, where Jacob got to meet and talk with a wide spectrum of Charlestonians.

Charleston took Jacob totally by surprise. He had known how captivating the city could be from earlier visits when he was in college. He had been vaguely aware that many histor-ical events had occurred in the old seaport. But, this time, he quickly became enchanted by just how many interesting and significant events had actually occurred in this beauti-ful old city. What totally hooked him was the vibrancy of the community. Over the years, many sizable businesses in a variety of industries had relocated to Charleston, bring-ing more jobs and greater wealth with them. Charleston's unique dynamics of a progressive city joined at the hip with the old walls of the elegantly antebellum city by the sea cre-ated fascinating opportunities.

Jacob easily saw that Charleston was a place where some-one could have a great life.

One evening at the bar, he had met Peter Madison, the local branch manager for Hamilton Brothers Securities. Pete had recognized that Jacob possessed a variety of capabilities, which prompted him one evening to surprise Jacob by suggesting that he might have a very successful career as a stockbroker. It had never been a job that Jacob had remotely considered. Pete had finally persuaded Jacob that he would not only be really good at it, but that he could also make a serious amount of money, adding that he might even really enjoy the work. Having no other big choices open to him, and no other ideas even just over the horizon, Jacob decided to give it a try. He spent his remaining cash on some new clothing and plunged into the work.

Pete had been right on all counts. Jacob had surprised even himself by being especially good at it. Only a few years after getting started, he was one of the most successful brokers for Hamilton Brothers Securities in the entire country. Now Jacob thought he would advise people to never go into a line of work that required a totally different wardrobe from the one you had.

Life for Jacob as a stockbroker had been very good for many years, at least until the last couple of years when it had seemed that suddenly the wheels had gone completely out from under his business. Almost instantly, he had gone from making lots of money to not earning much of anything. Undoubtedly it was because Jacob had lost interest in almost every part of the business except for the great income he thoroughly enjoyed.

His life now seemed even more off course than it had been during the storm that had originally blown him into Charleston. Maybe the real storm he had been running from had finally caught up with him. If it weren't for this one deal he was heading to close right then, Jacob would have left the industry several years earlier.

He desperately needed this deal to happen, and to happen today. The proceeds would create a dazzling array of opportunities for him.

This morning's appointment was scheduled to follow the previous evening's annual meeting of Southern Shipping's board of directors, at which Edmund was to propose the transfer of the entirety of those retirement assets from Broad Street Bank & Trust to Jacob and Hamilton Brothers. Edmund had indicated repeatedly to Jacob that this presentation to the board was simply a formality; that he had discussed this transfer frequently with his cousin, Buddy Capers, who was CEO of Southern Shipping, and that Buddy had agreed completely with the decision. After all, both cousins not only owned the company, but each of them also had plenty of their own money in those retirement accounts.

Arriving at the corner of State Street, Jacob waited as another horse-drawn carriage filled with tourists crossed in front of him. He watched a pelican above him glide lazily towards the harbor.

He continued on his way.

Jody's Studio and Gallery was down the street to his right. He fantasized that she was there, perhaps leading an art class or working on one of her portraits. Jacob could resist anything but temptation, and even thinking of Jody had been so tempting, right from the first time he had laid eyes on her.

She was the love of his life.

Proud of himself for not stopping, he continued on, staying as deep in the shadows of an old cotton warehouse as he could. Nearing East Bay Street, another drip of sweat began running down his glasses. As he cleaned them again, he wondered if Edmund would recognize that he was wearing the same shirt and suit as he had the last several times they had met and that it hadn't been to the cleaners for quite a while. Jacob ran his fingers over his chin and cheeks, hoping no stubble showed. He was still having a difficult time adjusting to how desperate his personal finances had so quickly changed. He was now reduced to re-using razor blades and ironing his own work shirts.

Suddenly, the importance of this meeting rose up and almost overwhelmed him.

In his time with Hamilton Brothers, there had been a number of large deals, each of which had paid Jacob very well. Some had been game changers. But this deal dwarfed all of them combined. The payout to Jacob would be enormous. It would allow him to not only pay cash for his Sullivan's Island beach house, but he would also have a considerable sum left over that would give him many new life choices.

This meeting could not be more significant to Jacob O'Leary. He stopped walking for a moment to gather his thoughts. *'It has to happen today. Why wouldn't it? Isn't this meeting just a formality? Isn't Edmund going to greet me with his easy smile and essentially ask-'where do I sign?* 'Of course', Jacob thought *'How else could it possibly go?'* He felt a cold trickle of sweat descend down his neck.

The briefcase filled with all the paper work specially prepared for this meeting suddenly felt very heavy. He knew there was a lot more than just his enormous fee riding on this deal closing.

Jacob thought back to the send off he had just received by Pete Madison back at the office, the encouragingly proud smile on Pete's face as he gave Jacob a big thumbs up at the doorway. His relationship and regard for Peter Madison were extremely important to Jacob. Pete had been more than a mentor to him. When they had met, Jacob's life was floundering; he had no sense of direction as to what to do with his future, no idea at all of anything that might matter to him. That changed when the two met that night at The Dancing Marlin. Pete had helped guide him back to a strong belief in himself as a person. It had been a major turning point for Jacob. Standing there in the shadows, he suddenly acknowledged that the magnitude of this new transaction and phenomenal new business relationship were also extremely important to Pete in his career as a Hamilton Brothers branch manager. There was no way Jacob would let him down.

Jacob's pace increased as he stepped out of the shadows of Queen Street and into the boiling sunlight.

This is it,' he thought to himself, squaring his shoulders as he quickly crossed East Bay and entered the red brick five-story Southern Shipping building that had occupied this entire block for several hundred years, dominating the waterfront of Charleston. Jacob strode through the glass entry doors into the coldness of Southern Shipping's lobby. His glasses immediately fogged up due to the air conditioning.

As he was clearing them and enjoying the cool air dry air, Jacob did as he always did upon entering this building. He stood before the commanding, life-sized statue of Capt. Anson Capers that stood in the center of the wood-walled entrance hall. With its solid oak flooring, walls and timbers, as well as moldings resembling thick ropes, the room gave the immediate sense of being in the cargo hold of one of the old schooners Captain Capers had started this business with centuries before.

An English sea captain at just 24 years of age, he was one of the first to begin regular trade between Charleston and England. The marble statue showed his beard and hair blown by the wind; his face, brow and eyes tight in a look of fierce determination. His strong hands still guided the wheel of his famous ship *The Wind*.

Starting with that one ship, there was soon a second, and before he died at the age of 92, he had a vast fleet of ships, all of which bore the Capers flag, the image of a golden falcon on a royal blue background. Each Caper's ship name began with *The Wind..* . This was the beginning of Southern Shipping's empire.

Jacob also knew the rest of the story. Edmund Capers had shared it with him late one afternoon.

The Wind was actually Capt. Caper's second ship. The first was named *Mary*, and it was on *Mary* that Captain Capers had brought his first cargo to Charleston with great success. But as Capers was outward bound back to England with a second cargo, his lookout had spotted a smaller vessel nearby, apparently on fire. Responding quickly to be of help, Capers brought *Mary* alongside the smaller ship. On deck was a woman, seemingly alone, frantically trying to put out a fire that was threatening to burn down the ships mast. Anson Capers himself was the first to swing aboard the ship to help extinguish the blaze.

It was a mistake. This wasn't so much a lady as it was Anne Bonny herself, one of the few female pirates of her day, and she had laid a perfect trap for Captain Capers. Quickly, Anne's pirate crew had rushed from their hiding places around and below the decks, taking Anson Capers captive. He was wrapped in chains and they threatened to put him over the side if his crew didn't immediately put down their weapons and surrender *Mary* to them. In exchange for his life, Capers was not only forced to swap vessels with the piratess, but she demanded his sea coat and hat as well. As she sailed off on *Mary*, Anne Bonny came back to her stern, and with the jacket open, laughed as she revealed and shook her breasts at Captain Anson Capers and his crew.

Losing his ship and his cargo had been bad enough, but losing them to a woman was too much for the man.

Standing on the shabbily kept deck of the much smaller and poorly equipped vessel, he watched her sail off on his ship wearing his coat and, by damned, his own hat! Anson Capers then swore eternal vengeance on Anne Bonny and on any of her descendants.

All these centuries later, Captain Caper's business had become Southern Shipping, one of the largest shipping companies in the United States. The business employed well over 1000 employees who were located in 50 seaports in the United States, the Bahamas and beyond. The headquarters have always been located on its significant corner of the waterfront in Charleston, adjacent to Capers Wharf, where the original ships had tied up to load and unload their cargo so long ago. Southern Shipping had always been owned and managed by descendents of Captain Capers. Now, the business was run by the cousins Anson Andrew (Buddy) Capers XXI, CEO and President, and Edmund Capers, CFO.

Looking about him, Jacob wondered how much financial history had gone through this very hallway. Now it was time to add his name to the list. Jacob looked into the stone cold eyes of Captain Anson Capers.

"Alright, you old bastard," declared Jacob. "Now it's my turn."

The look in the statues eye seemed to reply "Try me."

Jacob pushed open the tall glass doors before him and walked into Southern Shipping's corporate headquarters.

"Hi Mr. O'Leary, it is so nice to see you today," boomed Nancy, the long time receptionist whose always enthusiastic greeting was a lingering echo of the Old South. Jacob had never thought the word Hi could have three or four happy extra syllables, but Nancy always made it so.

"Good morning Nancy, how are you today?" Jacob genuinely looked forward to seeing her. He was sure many of the other people who called or came by Southern Shipping did so in part just to be momentarily uplifted by her unique warmth and sincerity. "I'm here to see Edmund."

"I'm told Edmund won't be available to see you today and that you will be meeting with Mr. Buddy instead. I'll let his office know you are here."

As Nancy called Buddy's office, Jacob felt a sudden and intense pressure in his neck and shoulders.

'What?? This wasn't right. I have a meeting with Edmund. This is the appointment we have been talking about for months. How could Edmund Capers not be here, waiting for me?' Jacob felt his recently dried skin cascading with new sweat, despite the coolness of the building. *'This is impossible. And I am meeting with Buddy? I barely know Buddy and he doesn't know this deal like Edmund. Maybe it's Okay-They did have the Board Meeting last night, right? Wouldn't the CEO need to sign off on it? I guess this is just fine, I hope,'* thought Jacob as he stood there wishing he was already back home with this business all signed and done.

"Mr. Capers can see you now, Mr. O'Leary. You look so nice in that gray suit and yellow necktie. You go on up to the fifth floor and he will meet with you there. "

Jacob tried desperately to remain calm and focused. As the elevator doors closed, he looked at his reflection in the mirrored doors. He almost didn't recognize himself in the suit and tie, with his graying hair a little too well combed and his face looking way too full. He especially didn't like the strained, worried expression on his face and wondered where the relaxed confidence had disappeared to.

'*When did I start looking like every single sales-guy in America?*' he sighed. '*Just focus on this meeting. This is going to go well. He's meeting with me personally in the board room. Stop worrying. Just relax, take a deep breath and be cool. Act like the guy who has just signed a $750 million deal, because that is who you are. This is your day and this is your deal*' he tried to assure himself. Jacob then thought of the cold eyes of Captain Anson Capers. Those denying eyes had seemed to look right through him.

'*Where the heck is Edmund?*'

Looking again at his reflection in the door, Jacob could see he wasn't smiling.

'*Smile, man, Relax-loosen your shoulders, take a deep breath. Relax, this is your day, this is your deal, go get it. Be cool and be glad to see this man.*'

Jacob tried to remember the last time he had actually spoken with Buddy Capers. He recalled it had been just a few months before, at the annual spring party held at Morgan's Bluff, the Capers family plantation up the Wando River from Charleston. Their extensive property covered more than 10,000 acres of riverfront, farmland, woods, marsh and creeks that led all the way from the Wando to Bulls Bay and then on to the Atlantic Ocean. It had once been a smugglers paradise, when first the British imposed heavy tariffs on any imported goods the colonial merchants needed, and then many years later when the Union navy had blockaded Charleston Harbor during the Civil War. Bootlegging goods into Charleston had been a very profitable business during each of those historic eras. The Capers family had always excelled at it. Edmund had once told Jacob that his ancestor, Captain Seth Capers had consistently smuggled significant weaponry through those creeks and into Charleston to help the Confederate Army.

Morgan's Bluff had a number of Capers family country homes. Buddy's was the largest, an enormous three-story classic Southern mansion with a live oak lined road leading to the columned front porch and steps. The centerpieces of the plantation were the magnificent gardens surrounding Buddy Capers home. There the wide deep green lawns sprawled in all directions with towering magnolias, crepe myrtles of every hue as well as magnificent live oak trees, all interspersed with vast arrays of azaleas, camellias and oleanders. Wherever one looked, flowering shrubs sprang into view across the property. Something was in bloom every day of the year at Morgan's Bluff.

In April, there were huge, flamboyant azaleas with perfect white, pink and red blooms accented by the purple wisteria blossoms whose vines trailed from the surrounding trees. Yellow daffodils and white jonquils lined all the paths and driveways. Spanish moss hung in profusion everywhere, its ghostly presence offered a subtle reminder of old times not so easily forgotten.

It was in this garden where the Capers hosted their annual spring party; it was one of Charleston's most important social events. To be invited was considered a very big deal.

Even Jody, who was usually not interested in such things, was thrilled and impressed that they were there.

Jacob remembered how Buddy and his wife had presided over the occasion, showing off the new polo pony they had recently purchased for one of their sons. Jacob also remembered that, other than a quick handshake, the only thing Buddy really had to say to him that day was that they should talk some time, which seemed to be a polite way of saying "get lost." Jacob hadn't really thought much of it at the time because Edmund had been happy and gracious to see Jody and him, introducing them to many of his friends. It had been a really nice party.

Jacob hadn't been concerned then, but he cared now as the elevator door opened and whatever was going to happen was going to happen now. *'This is your moment'*, he assured himself as he stepped forward, being sure that he was smiling, trying to relax his shoulders and taking a slow deep breath as he stepped forward.

The fifth floor of the Southern Shipping Building was exclusively Buddy Capers domain. His office was there, adjacent to the board room, as well as an apartment he used when he chose to stay in town. The elevator doors had opened to a well-appointed sitting room, its wooden paneled walls hung with paintings of various sailing vessels.

As he stepped into the room, Jacob found himself drawn to one painting in particular. It was of a schooner wrecked on a shoal. The scene was at night with lightning flashing; the ship's masts were broken, her sails in the sea.

A huge wave was poised to crash over its stern. The ship was doomed.

"That's the wreck of the *Queen Anne*, the bastard Marshall's ship. She went down at Cape Fear in 1827. May all their ships do the same! "

It was Buddy Capers standing in the doorway next to Jacob. Jacob was always surprised at how different Buddy and Edmund were, especially in appearance. Where Edmund was tall, dark- haired, slender, and usually attired in horn-rimmed glasses, a conservative suit and bow tie, Buddy was shorter than Jacob, but broad in the shoulders. His neck was thick beneath prematurely white, close cropped hair. Jacob quickly saw the image of Captain Capers in Buddy's dark, fierce eyes above his cold professional smile. Buddy wore a blue golf shirt with white trousers, his forearms bulging with muscles. His skin was dark from many years either out on the water or in the saddle of one of his polo ponies. His casualness seemed to mock Jacob, who now felt even more uncomfortable in his suit and tie.

"Good morning Buddy. It's good to see you again," began Jacob, extending his right hand in greeting.

"Thanks for coming up. Why don't you come in and have a seat," replied Buddy as he abruptly turned and entered the adjoining room, not seeming to notice or care about Jacobs offered handshake.

'*No handshake, this is not good at all,*' thought Jacob gloomily. His briefcase was beginning to feel extremely heavy and conspicuous as he followed Buddy Capers.

Having never been in Buddy Capers office before, Jacob quickly looked around as he entered. To his right, a large wall of windows over looked Charleston Harbor. Even from where he was standing, Jacob could see well out to sea, beyond Fort Sumter, out to the jetties leading the shipping lanes from the harbor to the Atlantic Ocean. He imagined the view out the opposite windows would be of beyond the Cooper River Bridge up to the shipping terminals further up the Wando River.

Buddy was already seated behind a massive desk with little on it. His office was simply furnished, with just a few chairs. A telescope pointed at the harbor facing one of the windows. A painting of his Morgan's Bluff house framed him perfectly on the wood paneled wall behind him. On another wall hung an oil portrait of Anson Capers at the helm of *The Wind*, far offshore under vicious clouds with threatening seas all around him. There were none of the usual brag walls of photographs, stuffed marlins and diplomas Jacob usually found in the executive offices were present.

Jacob was still standing as Buddy began to speak.

"Thank you for coming over. I'm seeing you today, Mr. O'Leary-Jacob-because, frankly, we don't know where Edmund is. We know he was scheduled to meet with you this morning" said Buddy quickly, looking directly into Jacob's eyes. "It's unusual. He also did not attend last evening's annual meeting of our Board of Directors. He has not called or emailed. At any rate, his secretary knew of your appointment on his schedule and notified me. Frankly,

I have been expecting you. I am aware of your financial proposal to Edmund regarding our various retirement funds. I put it before our board on Edmunds behalf last evening. I assume you are here today to follow up on that proposal," Buddy paused, his eyes never wavering from Jacobs, awaiting a response.

"Well yes, of course," Jacob immediately replied, his heart pounding.

"Yes, I know you met frequently, and obviously, both of you have put considerable effort into those recommendations. We discussed your proposition at length last evening. You may know one of our board members, Joseph Browne of Broad Street Bank & Trust, who took particular interest in your suggestions. Our family has dealt with his bank for more than 200 years. Mr. Browne was quite taken aback and offended, as you can imagine, that Southern Shipping would even consider talking with an outside investment institution, especially one from New York City. Mr. Browne has convinced the board that Broad Street's trust department is more than capable of providing the very services you have offered. To be perfectly candid, we are also aware of your association with the Marshall family. For many of our board members, that makes it impossible for our company to do business with you. I know Edmund felt very differently about that, but his is just one vote. At this time, we thank you for your interest and time spent making important investment recommendations to us. But we will keep our money with Mr. Browne's bank."

And then Buddy simply stood and came around the desk. The meeting was over. Jacob said nothing, not knowing what to say, what to think. Buddy extended his hand, and for the first time, he smiled. "Thank you once more, Jacob, Nice to see you again."

Jacob was in such a daze, he was barely aware of leaving Buddy's office or entering the elevator back to the lobby. *'Did I manage to shake Buddy's hand?* 'He wondered. Jacob wanted to believe this meeting hadn't just taken place; that somehow the deal could still be saved. *'This couldn't possibly be over after all the time spent on it and all the promises made! How could it possibly be that he really hadn't gotten the Southern Shipping business?'*

His briefcase, which on the way over had felt so light and so full of hope and promise, was now unbearably heavy. It seemed to be carrying everything that was going wrong in his life.

As gracefully as he could, he said goodbye to Nancy and started to leave the building. Heading out the door, he stopped for a moment before Captain Anson Caper's statue in the lobby.

"So you beat me after all," was the best that Jacob could say as the cold eyes seemed to mock him. He slowly pushed open the door back to the street.

3

A blast of thick, wet, hot air greeted Jacob as he exited the Southern Shipping Building.

He imagined he had just stepped into hell. He didn't know what to do right then, where to go, how to deal with this brutal rejection.

'Where in the world is Edmund right now? Why wasn't he there?'

He stood for a moment on the top step as he tried to gather himself. While waiting for his eyeglasses to un-fog, he became aware that a crowd of people was standing below him on the sidewalk. They were all looking in his direction.

As one of Americas most historic and beautiful cities, many people from around the world came to Charleston year round to walk its beautiful streets, admiring the multitude of beautiful homes and gardens as well as learning about the stories that make up the cities remarkable history. These tourists often took guided tours to get all the details they could. As Jacob was standing on the steps of Southern Shipping, a tour group had stopped directly in front of the building. Jacob impatiently waited for them to move on so that he could continue down the steps.

The group's guide was a tall, attractive, animated woman wearing a tri-cornered colonial era hat over her cascading brown hair. With a truly engaging smile, she was enthusiastically telling this group about Southern Shipping's enormous role in Charleston's history. The woman started pointing out architectural details of the building. Jacob's immediate reaction was that she was pointing directly at him. He imagined her saying to the group *"There he is. That's the guy who just lost the biggest deal of a lifetime! It's not polite to stare."*

Not knowing at all what to do at that moment, Jacob fell in with the crowd as they continued further down East Bay Street towards the Battery. He simply couldn't think. Totally devastated by what had just transpired and having absolutely no clue as to what to do next, he found himself drawn along by the energy of the group. As unobtrusively as possible, he removed his necktie, depositing it in a street side trashcan.

His briefcase banged against his leg. It was too big and heavy to be as empty inside as it actually was.

His cell phone, still set to vibrate, buzzed in his jacket pocket.

'*Great,*' he thought. He didn't have the energy to even look at his messages.

'*Where the hell is Edmund? What just happened up there?*'

Jacob began listening to what the lady was saying to her group. Her passion and grasp of Charleston's history was a momentary distraction for him. He knew about the horse drawn carriage history tours in Charleston because they were impossible to miss; however, he had never stopped to think that there were also guided walking trips on which people could amble along and be right there with a piece of history as they were learning about it. The tourists could take their time absorbing all the information that surrounded them. And in downtown Charleston, there is history everywhere you look.

His desolate and leaden briefcase eventually became too distracting for him to continue listening to the woman. The realization that the Hamilton Brothers office complex was not especially far away began to dominate his thoughts. Jacob drifted away from the group after walking several more blocks.

At that moment, he only wanted to get in his car and disappear. As far as Jacob was concerned, whatever those voice mail messages were on his phone, they could wait a little bit longer.

When he finally returned to the Meeting Street office building, he didn't go upstairs, not even to discard his briefcase somewhere where he would never see it again. He didn't want to face anyone. He didn't have a clue as to what he might possibly say. The confusion of the situation overwhelmed him. Instead, Jacob went down to the parking garage beneath the building and quickly walked towards his faded silver Honda hatchback. He couldn't help reminding himself about the new BMW he had decided to reward himself with after the deal was done.

Now, all he hoped for was that he had gas money for the Honda.

Jacob drove out of the garage as quickly as he could. He had no particular destination in mind. Turning on the radio, Bruce Springsteen was singing 'You spend your life waiting for a moment that just don't come. Well, don't waste your time waiting.'

'You got that right, Bruce,' Jacob said to himself.

He left the radio on as he drove, hoping for more great music to completely distract him. He really didn't want to think. A weather report came on, announcing that Tropical Storm Danielle was now approaching the Leeward Islands, and that a new storm seemed to be forming off the Cape Verde Islands near Africa. The radio weather man promised he would follow these storms closely and would warn everyone if there was anything remotely worth worrying about.

'Today's just full of good news. Is there anything else I don't want to hear about?' Jacob screamed in total frustration, banging his fist on the steering wheel.

Jacob pulled out his cell phone and gave Edmund a call, but only got his voice mail. Jacob left a message, asking Edmund to please get back to him as soon as possible.

'You never know,' Jacob thought glumly.

Jacob's mind was blank. He was filled with a total sense of defeat unlike anything he had ever experienced. His neck began tightening with anxiety. He had no earthly idea of what to do. Instinctively, he drove south on Meeting Street, heading towards The Battery. He hoped to find Edmund at home and to get a better answer on Southern Shipping than the one he had just received.

'Wasn't success all about working hard and being persistent, never giving up?' Jacob hoped. He wasn't clear in his thinking. His thoughts were clouded over with everything that had gone wrong.

His thoughts drifted to that storm 12 years ago that had blown him into Charleston Harbor for the first time.

He could still feel those oh so heavy winds. His sailboat, *Pearl*, was totally at the mercy of the seas and the huge waves coming at her from every direction. The horizontal rain made visibility nearly impossible. Steering and handling the boat were extremely difficult. The radar and most of the other electronics had failed. The dark, swirling rain cover that encompassed him was more frightening than anything else. He had especially feared that a huge wave might suddenly appear, capsizing *Pearl* and tossing him into the hungry, swirling abyss below.

'If only that storm hadn't come along right then, I'd never have been in this mess.' The thought did not comfort him.

Jacob felt suddenly ashamed of himself, an emotion he found very unusual.*' Hadn't he had the biggest deal ever in his hands? Wasn't it there just for the taking? How could this deal not have happened? How could this be? Why had he stayed in this business so long, spending his days working at things that meant nothing to him except the reward of lots of money?'*

His body began to tremble. He felt dizzy, weird, slightly out of control. He slowly inhaled and exhaled. As he drove along, he made every effort to relax.

He continued south on Meeting Street. Anger began building within him. It burst as Jacob started screaming again at the top of his lungs. Exploding with frustration, every single obscenity he had ever known erupted from deep within him.

Losing sight of what he was doing, he nearly drove right through the red light at the intersection of Broad and Meeting Streets. His brakes squealed as he left a trail of black rubber on the street behind him. He narrowly avoided running down a group of startled tourists, as well as a pair of black suited lawyers who where hurrying to the nearby courthouses. Jacob took a deep breath, hoping the Honda wasn't too far into the intersection to earn him a traffic ticket. While the tourists glared at him, he took several more deep breaths, slowly exhaling his feelings. He turned off the car radio.

He kept the Honda below the speed limit the next few blocks south as his body began to tremble again. A feeling of light- headedness slowly crept up from his spine.

Finally, he turned right onto South Battery. Jacob could see that White Point Gardens was filled with tourists. The large live oaks covered them in a heavy shade. The palmetto trees lining the sidewalks waved in the breeze, frolicking as if a party was going on that Jacob hadn't been invited to. He drove slowly by Edmund Capers house, hoping his old black Range Rover would be parked in front of the two-story brick home.

The circular drive was deserted.

Jacob drove on, guided only by his intuition. He needed to stay in motion. He was not yet prepared to stop and to fully accept the devastating result of the morning's ill-fated meeting.

He found himself heading to the Crosstown Expressway, automatically turning on to it and then he continued on to the Cooper River Bridge. As he drove, Jacob was increasingly feeling overwhelmed with a fear he couldn't recognize. He sensed the energy of a huge oncoming wave he could not see, rising up behind him, chasing him as his car climbed higher and higher up the span of the bridge. Perhaps this was the wave that he had most feared would show up one day.

He felt totally spent. His body was shaking and the daylight seemed too bright despite his sunglasses. A feeling of dizziness was returning. He didn't understand anything. He was confused by all of these sensations. Despair crashed all over him. He tried to hold it back, to just keep on driving and leave it behind him. He had never before felt this depth of sadness within him.

At long last, he arrived on Sullivan's Island. He didn't go to his house, but instead drove to a special place he often visited when he had a lot on his mind.

Jacob's hands trembled as he opened his car door. He was shaking so much he could barely close it. He saw almost nothing before him as he stumbled forward on his quivering legs. He went blindly to the particular spot where he felt a strong connection to a reality he couldn't possibly describe to anyone. He sat clumsily on a huge boulder which was part of the huge seawall before Ft. Moultrie. For Jacob this day, this moment, that huge rock was his only anchor against the inner storm overwhelming and consuming him.

There was something special for him about being at this place with its views of the harbor and of Ft. Sumter. He found there a sense of peace and focus he did not find anywhere else, a strong sense of being connected to something he couldn't name. Being there, his thoughts had a sense of completion. He often felt as though he were in conversation with an incredibly positive force that he couldn't name.

Sitting on the rock, he absently watched the tide flow past. He observed a dolphin nearby schooling some fish as a flight of pelicans eased across the surface of the moving water.

Jacob suddenly started sobbing. It came out of nowhere. The wave of despair he had felt closing in on him while in the car now crashed over him. It was like one of those huge swells that seemed to be waiting for him during that tropical storm that had first brought him to the very waters before him. His anguish was uncontrollable, gushing from a deep well of sorrow. He wept and wept.

Finally, exhausted by his outpouring of grief and utter sadness, Jacob softly but passionately said "God, I am really in trouble. I need your help."

A quieting voice, calming and assuring, immediately replied. It seemed to gently roll across amidst the harbor breezes, riding the tips of the waves coming his way.

It whispered to him, "Jacob, don't be afraid. Put your mind on your work, and everything will be Ok. Just don't be afraid."

Jacob did not at all consider himself to be religious. He did not go to church. He thought of himself as perhaps spiritual, but he didn't spend much time on that concept either. He had never knowingly spoken to God and hadn't come to this place to do so. What Jacob said had spontaneously poured out of him, as if it was the most natural thing in the world for him to do. And then, amazingly, a voice had instantly responded! Jacob didn't know what to make of this. Yet he felt instantly assured and calm.

He didn't know if he had just heard the voice of God or if he had heard a voice from inside himself. Maybe it was some wiseguy in the bushes near him making a bad joke.

It didn't matter. All that mattered was how Jacob was responding to this. He suddenly felt at peace. He felt a sense of purpose. He felt a warm glow and sense of joy filling his body. *'Everything will be OK! But what does that mean? Does it mean anything? What is my work?'* he wondered.

He had no relationship that he knew of with God. *'Surely God didn't see his work being as a stockbroker. Wasn't it more about how you did what you did? Could it be something else?'*

Jacob got back to his feet and walked steadily back to his car. He was still feeling shaky, but buoyancy was returning to his step. A sense of joy and excitement steadily spread through him. He was not going home. He needed to take a step forward right now. Jacob needed to find his work, his place in the middle of this.

He looked about him. He inhaled the breeze coming towards him from across the harbor. He suddenly noticed just how blue the sky was. He could feel the textures of the tall grass he walked through. He could hear children laughing, waves crashing on the shoreline, gulls calling to one another. The oaks, palmettos and wax myrtles all around him blew gently in the breeze that seemed to pass completely through every pore of his body. In that moment, he felt a part of the rich red brick walls of the fort, with the colors of the flags flying above it, with the vastness of the blue sky.

A flight of pelicans again soared above him, headed towards the harbor and downtown.

Jacob saw them as a sign of what to do next.

He got back into his car and returned to Charleston.

4

Jacob was looking for a miracle. He needed one desperately.

He drove back down to South Battery, hoping Edmund had returned home. As he cruised slowly by the house, Jacob only saw the white Mercedes station wagon that belonged to Julie Capers, parked in the rear of the Magnolia shaded driveway. He continued on to the High Battery seawall, and then up East Battery.

'Maybe Edmund was at the Yacht Club,' he hoped. If Jacob saw Edmunds car, he intended to go in to find the man, and get to the bottom of all this. At least that's what Jacob thought he wanted to do, but as he got closer to the Yacht Club, he wasn't sure he could actually do it. Upon arriving at the clubs parking lot, he found it to be nearly empty. Jacob was relieved to find that the Range Rover was no-where to be seen.

'If Edmund was in there, what was he really going to say to me that Buddy hadn't already said? What was that Buddy had said about the relationship with Oliver Marshall? Edmund had assured me that had no bearing on this deal. This was business. The proposition was so favorable to Southern Shipping that it's benefits where all that mattered.'

Jacob parked for a moment in the Yacht Club's parking lot and reached for his cell phone. It was time to at least look at the messages he had accumulated. Scrolling, he saw there were several calls from his office, one from Tadpole Gaillard and, of course, US Bank & Trust collections. Although he did not want to actually speak with anyone, Jacob decided to at least listen to the messages.

The first was from his assistant at Hamilton Brothers.

"Hi Jacob, it's Carol. Hope you are out celebrating after landing your big deal. Can't wait to hear all about it! Don't forget about your hardworking and loyal assistant when you're trying to decide how to split up that gigantic commission check. Ha ha. You have a couple of messages-a Mr. Nathan Goldstein called. He said he's a friend of Tadpole's from New York. He would like you to give him a call at the number I texted you. Also, Tadpole called. Finally, Pete asked if I'd heard from you. Give me a call when you get the chance, OK?"

Tadpole Gaillard was one of Jacob's oldest friends. They had met long ago on their first day in the South Carolina Tech locker room. Jacob had just begun to don his new football equipment and uniform when suddenly, someone truly massive took his shirt off while standing right in front of him. Jacob had been around some large guys, but never this kind of big. At 6'5" and nearly 290 lbs, this man was gigantic. Not an ounce of fat appeared to cover enormous muscles that were nearly as large as his grin.

Looking right at Jacob, he had said "What, you never seen a midget before?" Jacob replied "I'm just trying to figure out how all that hair is going to fit in that helmet of yours." Tadpole had a major Afro in those days.

They became friends right then.

That all seemed like another lifetime or two ago. Tadpole had gone on to become a star left tackle, first for Tech and then professionally for the New York Giants. Tadpole eventually retired back to his home town of Charleston.

Jacob had been the Tigersharks punter and was a very good kicker, often creating bad field position for the other teams. Jacob had also been a decent open-field tackler. The two were good friends during their college years, not only rooming together occasionally on road trips, but also spending lots of time together off the field as well. Jacob had been one of the groomsmen for Tadpole when he married his high school sweetheart, Rosie.

Tadpole had been the first person Jacob interviewed as a new sports writer for the college newspaper. This became the first of many such interviews Jacob conducted with other athletes, coaches, cheerleaders, trainers, equipment managers, announcers and even the bus driver who drove the teams on all their road trips. His stories were about the entire world of South Carolina Tech athletics; not just the star players, but everyone who played a part. Jacob's relationships in the locker room along with his talent and love of writing had combined into what had seemed a perfect career for him as a sportswriter.

Tadpole liked to occasionally remind Jacob that it was simply that first interview with him that had made Jacob so famous and gotten him his first paying newspaper job.

They had happily re-united shortly after Jacob had arrived in Charleston.

Sitting in the Yacht Club parking lot, Jacob decided he would just drive over and see Tadpole. It was a good time to see a friendly face.

As he drove through the city and then crossed over Calhoun St, Jacob barely noticed how quickly the mansions, huge oaks and manicured lawns that Charleston was known for transitioned into the East Side, a rundown , impoverished neighborhood perpetually ramshackled to a history of generational poverty. Single-story cinderblock apartment buildings grimy with neglect stood surrounded by lots so barren of grass the summer heat radiated a white pall over all it touched. He passed by broken down and burned out houses. Litter filled some of the empty lots. People stood idly on street corners. Others walked slowly across the road, seemingly oblivious to any oncoming cars that might run them over. A large young man rode a very small bicycle for a few moments next to Jacob's car, asking him something Jacob was glad he couldn't hear with his windows up.

Palmetto trees struggled to stay erect under the weight of seemingly decades of neglect as huge cascades of dead branches threatening to topple them. The late summer afternoon sky baked the area with heat, beating down relentlessly on a community worn down by the constancy of poverty and indifference.

Young people of all ages were prowling the broken sidewalks. There were old, rusty beaten up cars and abandoned shopping carts. Elderly people sat on chairs in what little shade that could be found.

Jacob turned on to America Street. The sun seemed even brighter but the atmosphere all the more drab and bleak. A collarless, three legged pit-bull hopped down the dirty sidewalk as a guy in a wheelchair rolled by.

Jacob was able to find a parking space near the entrance to the building that was home to Charleston's #1 All-Stars. Beneath a shady spot across the street, two old men sat on wooden chairs under a ragged beach umbrella.

As Jacob climbed out of his car, one of them called out a cheerful greeting.

"Hey, Mr. J, you got some you can lend me till next week?"

The man was Hucklebuck, a neighborhood icon. He held his 'office hours' on this corner, entertaining a 'client' by sharing a bottle of fortified wine wrapped in a paper bag that they passed back and forth.

Huck had been a fixture on that corner since long before Tadpole's creation, Charleston's #1 All Stars, began stirring up the East Side. Everyone in the hood knew that Huck was a man you had to respect. When he was growing up on the East Side, Huck was the baddest guy on the street, someone you did not dare mess around with. Having semi mellowed with age, he let his multitude of offspring do the dirty work for him. One phone call from Huck got done what needed to be done. Despite his reputation, he was reasonably likeable and totally reliable. The Stars had become his personal responsibility because of his high regard for

Tadpole. He kept his eye on the place. He knew who was hanging around the block, who belonged and who didn't. Huck especially knew who the truly bad boys were. This was a Godsend. If you got on his wrong side, you would pay the price, East Side style. Hucklebuck was a funky cross between a Guardian Angel and The Godfather.

Jacob waved and shook his head. "Hey, Huck," Jacob hollered back across the street. "If it weren't for bad luck, I'd have no luck at all. Maybe you could lend me ten? It's been a rough day."

Hucklebuck slapped his thigh. "Man, I know's what you be saying. You a lucky man, Mr. J. You help me out next time. I know's your luck will come back. We be counting on it."

Jacob waved and walked towards the building. *'I sure hope so,'* he said to himself.

After a knee injury had ended Tadpole's NFL career, he and Rosie had returned to their childhood hometown of Charleston. Tadpole had been very careful with his NFL money and had felt a need to contribute to the kids in Charleston who most needed help. He knew how important this was, especially because of his childhood friend Marcus.

Tadpole and Marcus had done everything together that kids growing up in downtown Charleston did. They had been football and basketball teammates in high school. Marcus had been the star tailback running through gaping holes Tadpole had blown wide open in every defensive line they faced. But Marcus spent his nights out on the streets while Tadpole was home with his family. Eventually, Marcus was arrested, and later convicted after he had been involved in an armed robbery while still in high school. That was his second offense and meant jail time. He was still in prison when Tadpole returned to Charleston for good.

The thought that his friend was still behind bars for all those years had pained Tadpole greatly. He knew Marcus was an otherwise good kid who was just never shown any options other than life on the streets. Tadpole felt an obligation to try to help as many street kids as possible. He wanted the children growing up on the East Side to become aware of the better choices that could be available to them. Tadpole did what he could to help them see that a more interesting and fulfilling life was just down a different road than the streets they normally roamed.

Tadpole made a deal with the city to buy and renovate an abandoned building and playground in the midst of the neighborhood. His plan was to turn this into a place where lots of kids who had nothing could hopefully find a center for their lives. But those were bad streets in Charleston. Crime was rampant, as it was in neighborhoods like this all over the country.

The Center, as it was initially known, covered an entire city block. It had two outdoor lighted basketball courts surrounded by a rusted old fence. The building itself was a large cinder block gym containing another basketball court, which was joined to a one story brick building.

Tadpole had both buildings painted a deep-sea blue with red trim, to match the South Carolina Tech colors. Thriving palmetto trees were planted throughout the grounds. The torn up, rutted dirt playground was re- planted with sod and regularly mowed by some of the kids as a way for them to pay for their time at The Center. A red tipped photinia hedge lined the interior of the fences. Tadpole wanted The Center to be an urban oasis; a special place to reflect the greatness he knew was present within each of the young people who came there.

The East Side was primarily a basketball oriented culture. The Center built on that enthusiasm. But Tadpole's vision was it would be more than just a place to come to shoot some hoops. Tadpole's brother Jeremiah, who everyone referred to as Jaybird, was a teacher at the downtown high school. After school let out for the day, Jaybird was at The Center every afternoon to help coach the kids on how to read, and how being good students would open doors for them. At first, the kids hadn't shown much interest in being better students. As most of them and their families could barely read, they had never seen the point of being good in school.

One day, a team from The Center that called itself 'Charleston's # All-Stars' had won a city-wide basketball tournament. Their name had been quickly adopted for the center itself. After that victory, lots of kids in that area wanted to be a part of The Center. They dug being part of a winning team and the recognition that came with it. It was an identity that Tadpole hoped would define the future for all these kids. Tadpoles deal with the young East Siders was that if they were passing all their subjects in school, they could play at the 'Stars' for free. They would even get a Charleston's #1 All Stars T- shirt. However, if they weren't passing, they had to spend time with Jaybird. When their grades improved, they could actually play on one of the 'Stars' teams.

It had been a success so far. High school graduation rates for the kids who were on those teams had increased. Some of these young people were starting to get attention from colleges throughout the South. At first, there had only been boy's teams, but many of the East Side girls had begun showing up as well, playing good ball, pulling down better grades, and all proud of their Charleston's #1 All-Stars shirts and identity.

As he approached the entrance, Jacob looked fondly over at the mural which covered the cinder-block building. This was the result of an East Side community project he was especially proud of. Jacob had secured the funding to sponsor a citywide competition to design the mural. Many local artists had submitted entries. All the 'Stars' teams voted on which design they liked the best. The winning artist was then responsible for developing an outline and organizing the volunteers who would paint the mural over the course of one week. The winning artist was Lakisha Brown, a 21 year old Charlestowne University art student originally from the East Side.

Jacob got sponsors from all over the city to contribute. Painting contractors offered their scaffolds, ladders, skills and paint. Restaurants made sure that everyone was well fed with pizza, hot dogs and burgers. Soft drinks and water flowed. It was a memorable week for all involved. Even

Jacob had donned paint spattered clothes and pitched in. Charlestonians from all walks of life worked together on the project. Local politicians, East Siders and South of Broaders all worked together painting the mural at the 'Stars.

The finished painting depicted a basketball just leaving the extended fingers of an out-stretched black hand. The ball arched high into a bright blue sky filled with hundreds of white stars. A rainbow curved over the scene with one end of the rainbow ending above the entrance door. Painted on either side of the door were images of Tadpole and Jaybird linked arm in arm with well known national and historical figures such as Martin Luther King, Malcolm X, Maya Angelou, Charleston Mayor Joe Riley, Michael Jordan, Darius Rucker and Muhammad Ali, as well as inspiring local heroes including the teacher and civil rights activist Septima Clark and Charleston's Jewish Black police chief, Reuben Greenberg. Painted behind them was the internationally famous Jenkins Orphanage Band, widely credited for putting Charleston on the world's musical map in the late 19th century. Each of these heroes was pointing their arms upward to the stars and beyond.

Jacob spent a lot of time at the 'Stars He had never been married and had no children of his own that he knew of, but he really loved kids. He especially enjoyed being around young athletes, because they reminded him of not only some of the happiest days of his life and but also of so many of the wonderful people he had gotten to know well through sports. Because of the time he spent at The Center, Jacob had also come to appreciate just how fortunate he had been all his life. He could clearly understand how truly stacked the deck was against these mostly fatherless and sometimes motherless children of the streets.

Jacob's love of Tadpole's vision motivated him to contribute as well. He did so primarily by going to all of the area's civic organizations and giving presentations that eloquently presented the case for how supporting Charleston's #1 All-Stars helped the local business community. After the success of the mural project, Jacob sponsored several golf tournaments as fundraisers for the 'Stars. Those proceeds had purchased additional equipment, basketball shoes, shorts, shirts and socks. The tournaments also raised funds to pay for well known coaches to travel to Charleston to hold basketball clinics for the kids.

One year the tournaments paid for two industrial washers and dryers that were installed in The Center. Tadpole let the community know they could use them for free if they needed to. And they did. This started bringing parents and grandparents around, and they started watching the kids play, something that had rarely happened before.

Rosie Gaillard had the idea of asking folks if they wanted their mail delivered to the The Center. Since most of those folks couldn't read, the 'Stars' would help them to do so. Many of the families began to take advantage of that as well.

What no one expected was what happened. Many of those families had never been what most would consider really functioning families. As they spent more time together at The Center, they found themselves growing together into an extended family community, committed and caring for the success of the participating young people. Now The Center had a big Thanksgiving meal every year, but for regulars only. The number of regulars had steadily increased each year.

Most of the night time basketball games drew enough of a crowd who were watching and cheering the players that Tadpole had paid for some bleachers to be installed next to the courts opposite the team benches. There were a number of teams organized through the 'Stars that competed in city tournaments and for AAU teams.

Jacob sponsored a team which he called 'Whozup?' He found he really liked talking to the kids who would speak with him, which weren't that many. He didn't care. He just smiled at those who wouldn't speak to him and watched them develop into better student-athletes.

As he entered the building, Jacob walked through the aqua blue painted lobby. He stopped to admire the over-stuffed trophy case that displayed the ever-growing recognition that the various athletes playing for the Stars continued to earn.

Seeing Jacob in the lobby, Tadpole waved him into his office while finishing a phone call. Jacob sat in front of Tadpole's desk and, through the office-wall window looked out into the gym, he watched a basketball game in progress.

One of the players was Tadpoles 15 year old son, Robert Smalls Gaillard. Everyone referred to him as Smalls but he was almost as tall as his father and still growing. Jacob marveled at the athleticism on display out on the court, at how fast the kids were, at how high they could jump. He fantasized that maybe he could entice Smalls to join 'Whozup?

Looking back at Tadpole, Jacob could easily see the massive number of scars on the tops of Tadpoles hands, permanent reminders from the years of blocking and colliding violently with other huge guys.

Jacob thought back to the first game in college the two of them had played against their arch rival. Tadpole had so severely broken his little finger that it bent sideways. But he hadn't noticed how bad the injury was until later in the locker room when he was having trouble getting his jersey off. It was at that moment when Jacob realized just how physically tough Tadpole actually was, which was sometimes difficult to recognize because his off the field nature seemed to be so easygoing and caring.

Tadpole's giant Afro was long gone, replaced with very short hair beginning to gray. As usual, Tadpole was wearing a sea blue polo shirt with the Charlestons#1 All Stars logo: a silhouette of the extended black fingers with the basketball sailing upwards surrounded by white stars.

"My man, you look like you need some alley cat to finish dragging you in here. You havin' a bad day on Wall Street? Your favorite stock down an 1/8th of a point or something? What's up?" Tadpole's grin was bigger than he was, and Tadpole was one big guy. People often mistook him for Charles Barkley, the NBA player, especially when Tadpole was traveling.

"You got it, T. Just having a bad day. What's been going on here? Hey, did Smalls just dribble right through those three kids?" Jacob asked, still watching the basketball game over Tadpole's shoulder.

"Yeah, he is getting some serious air time these days. He got 40 points earlier today. They are getting ready for the big game here tonight. Our East Side Slamma Jamma is getting started."

This was one of the summer nighttime basketball tournaments at Charleston's #1 All-Stars that attracted high school summer teams from throughout the Charleston area. It now offered trophies and, on occasion, some college coaches were known to come by to look for new talent.

"You playing tonight, Tadpole? You ought to."

"You're out of your freaking mind, Jakie. That computer you sit starin' at all day must be making you crazy. Sides, even you can get higher off the ground than me these days, and that's pretty sad. At least I can still dribble circles around you. Not these kids. We got a new kid who's been coming around who is amazing. Name's Demetrius somebody. You should be here tonight to watch some very serious hoops."

Leaning forward, Jacob asked: "Who is this Nathan Goldstein?"

"Damned if I know. The dude just came walkin' in here this morning. Looked like he got off the wrong subway stop in the City or something, comin' in with his dark suit and tie and everything. Said he met me several times at those big parties in New York back when I was playing. Might have, 'cause we sure met lots of people then. Anyways he said he's just moved here to Charleston and wanted to come by and say hello. Says he's a lawyer and a philanthropist and wants to invest in the community and who should he be meeting? Just like that. Not lot's of how have you been chitchat, just he's here and who should he talkin' to. Said he wondered if the 'Stars could use an outside, no strings, cash infusion, which we always do. Asking me 'cause he doesn't know anybody here. And then he asked if I knew a good local investment guy. I couldn't remember Warren Buffett's number so I gave him yours. He's probably just another Mr. Full-of-Shit dressed in a new suit, but I don't usually say no to someone else's dough. He seemed real enough, though. I guess he called you?"

"Yeah, he left a message. I'll call him later."

"You should. He did seem like money. How's that big deal going?"

"Don't ask. It isn't. I better go."

"Ok, I won't. Oh, Charlie came in earlier and wondered if you were going to be around. He's a funny kid. Usually, nothing sticks to him, but today he seemed really nervous about something. Wants to talk to you but didn't say why. Ok if I give him your number?"

"Sure, how is Charlie?" Jacob asked, realizing he hadn't seen the boy in several weeks.

Charlie Mack was a new kid in town, a friend of Smalls from school. Jacob had met Charlie not long after he came to Charleston when Tadpole had brought him out to Jacob's house one afternoon. Jacob's first impression was of a tall, thin, athletic boy with an Afro, almost a throwback look. Charlie had recently moved to Charleston from Baltimore. His mother, Bessie, had been a police officer there and had been killed on the job. Tadpole had told Jacob several times that Charlie never would talk about his mother, not with him or with Smalls. Charlie had to come to Charleston because his only living relative was his Moms half sister Berthie, who lived in an East Side public housing project.

Charlie had met Smalls at school and they became instant friends. It didn't take Charlie long to become a regular at the 'Stars'. He was a terrific athlete and a good student who said he liked football best of all, even though he was really good at basketball. Charlie had been so excited to receive his Charleston's #1 All-Stars   t-shirt, he had vowed that he would wear it all the time, which he did.

Jacob had never met Charlie's aunt. He didn't want to. He had heard enough to figure Charlie's Mom would have arrested Berthie any number of times had Bessie been a Charleston cop.

"You OK, Jacob? Rosie wants you over for dinner, you know? You heard from Jody?"

"Like I said, bad day, man. Lucky for you, otherwise, I'd drag you outside and kick your ass on that half court."

"Anytime, Mr. Big talk."

Both guys rose. Tadpole came around the desk, and sat on the edge of it in front of Jacob. Even sitting, he was still taller than Jacob. Tadpole looked carefully into Jacob's eyes.

"Seriously, you alright? You want to hang here for awhile?"

"Got to go, man. But later, you and me, outside. Better start warming up. Have Charlie call me. Please tell Rosie hi and I will be over soon. I love her shrimp and crab cakes better than anything. Say hey to Smalls and the girls too, OK?"

Jacob and Tadpole bumped elbows like always.

Jacob said "Later man, tighten your shoes, I'll be back."

~~

Jacob called Nathan Goldstein as soon as he got the air conditioning going in his car.

"Mr. Goldstein's office. May I help you?"

"Nathan Goldstein, please. This is Jacob O'Leary, returning his call."

"Oh yes, Mr. O'Leary. Thank you for getting back to Mr. Goldstein. He is not available but wondered if you might be able to join him for dinner tomorrow evening? He is in Charleston this week."

"Dinner tomorrow night is fine, actually. Did he have a restaurant in mind?"

"Yes, Mr. Goldstein hoped you were familiar with The Creek in Mt Pleasant. Do you know it? He said he would be happy to meet you elsewhere if you had a preference."

"Well yes, I know The Creek well. That's a very fine place. Would 7:00 be a good time for Mr. Goldstein?"

"Yes, he can meet you then. Thank you for calling right back, Mr. O'Leary. May I give Mr. Goldstein your number in case he needs to reach you? I see it here on caller ID."

"Sure. Please thank him for the dinner invitation. I am looking forward to meeting him."

'*What in the world?*' wondered Jacob. '*Was that a little too easy? I'll give the guy credit for not beating around the bush. The Southern Shipping deal is a disaster and now this guy calls me out of the blue and wants to meet me? And why meet at The Creek?*'

The Creek was a favorite restaurant of Jacobs. Curiously, it was also directly across Shem Creek from the headquarters of Coastal Traders, Oliver Marshall's business.

5

Later that evening, Jacob was restless. Finally giving up on trying to relax, he left his house and took the short walk to the dock where he kept his 32 foot sloop, *Pearl*. Jacob had bought this sailboat when he was still living in Key West. Jacob had visualized a boat just like this one for many years, and it had been love at first sight for him. Jacob paid cash for her, using his share of the only pot smuggling trip he had been involved in. He named the sailboat *Pearl* in part because the fiberglass hull seemed to be that shade of white, and partially because he loved just how full of life Janis Joplin seemed to be when she sang. The boat had been his home for a year while he still lived in the Keys, and then again for many months after arriving in Charleston.

The night breeze was thick with the familiar, abundant aroma of pluff mud. Pluff mud is the dense, gummy organic remains of centuries of decomposing marsh grass and the remains of all the creatures which have lived and died in the marshes. The resulting nutrients are the fertile substance for the endless cycle of much of the natural life in the South Carolina lowcountry. To some people, it seems like its distinctive smell is of rotten eggs ; to most, it is an intoxicating aroma of life and renewal.

Jacob did a quick inspection, making sure all the lines were secure and that everything was in good working order. He lay down on *Pearl's* forward deck, resting his head on a boat cushion, looking up at the night sky. Just a sliver of the moon was high in the west. It was his favorite, coming just after the new moon, because it made him think of a big wide grin. He liked to believe it brought good luck. He definitely needed it now. He was very tired, worn out by the emotions of the dreadfully strange day he hoped was now ending. Settling into the deck, Jacob wondered for the hundredth time what could have happened to Edmund.

'How could that deal not have closed?'

Jacob worried about what might be next. He had assumed this to be a done deal; in fact, he had so counted on what the proceeds would do for him financially that it had not occurred to him to make backup plans for his pending obligations. The option to buy his house was going to end soon. He was deeply in debt for the first time in his life, and his financial resources were steadily depleting.

But , despite all of that, Jacob wondered where Jody was right at that moment. He wished she was there with him right then.

He looked further into the night time sky. He could see that at least her star was still there, the one he had given her that first night they were together.

Jacob thought back to the first time he had seen Jody Pickens.

The wind had been blowing so hard that day that he was afraid he was going to lose his hat. It was a mid-October Saturday morning. Jacob had been walking barefoot on the sandy path from his house to the beach, carrying a mug of coffee in his right hand, a beach chair with his left, a book tucked under his arm and his hat not especially snug on his head. This wasn't just any hat. Jacob had won it years before in a bet with Juke O'Bannion. It was a Boston Red Sox hat from that time back in the '60's when Boston had almost gone to the World Series. Now it was Jacob's favorite. Plus it fit him. Jacob could almost never find hats that were quite big enough for his head, but this one was. At least it fit when he bothered to put it on right. This time he hadn't. But it was such a perfectly beautiful day, Jacob had been anxious to get on the beach. He loved to walk along this old, windy path through the cedars and wax myrtles, a trail that twisted so much you never knew what you might find around the next bend.

The wind was blowing harder than Jacob had supposed. His hat suddenly blew right off his head, disappearing over a nearby small dune. Jacob carefully put his things down to retrieve his wayward Red Sox hat. He walked carefully to avoid any unseen stickers, and slowly went over the top of the dune.

It was almost like she had been waiting for him there.

She was watching the ocean, her arms were up, raised before her. Her long brown hair blew wild in the wind as her blue jeaned legs gracefully moved sideways below a long sleeved un-tucked white shirt.

Jacob stopped. He knew she was special just by the way she moved. She seemed like a dancer just beginning a movement that only she knew the rhythm to.

Jacob realized that she was holding a camera with a long lens just before eyes focused somewhere in the distance. All of her energy seemed to flow into her hands and eyes as she was looking for just the right picture of the ocean. She kept moving slowly, her body turning and twisting, the camera snapping, and then quickly snapping again and again.

She had seemed to suddenly sense something nearby. She quickly turned and looked right at Jacob. For just an instant, she slowly lowered the camera. He could see her deep brown eyes. Her left eyebrow seemed to arch just a bit, as if she were communicating a message he would never understand. Then, just as quickly, she raised the camera and took three very fast shots of him.

She lowered the camera. Now he could see her whole face, especially those eyes that seemed to see everything, eyes a little more widely spaced than usual. She was smiling, a big very proud of herself smile that Jacob felt pounding right into his heart, an ancient message he thought he had long forgotten.

Their eyes met briefly. She seemed happy, curious, very sure of herself. But then her face seemed to flush. She turned suddenly, walking rapidly away towards the beach. She waved her right arm and someone in a crowd on the beach waved back.

Jacob was going to run after her, at least to ask her name and how could he reach her. But, he didn't move. His feet felt firmly entrenched in the sand beneath him. He hadn't felt anything like this in a remarkably long time. His heart hammered. His energy level was way up. He had felt a sudden sweetness deep inside, an echo from some distant and unknown place. Jacob had never been married, not that he had anything against marriage. There had been plenty of relationships, but never The relationship

Something big had just happened then. He longed to know what it was.

He watched her stride across the sand. The way she moved, the way she looked, the way it had felt to simply look into her eyes. It all told him that they would meet one day. Just not that day.

Jacob watched until she entered a group of people standing on the water's edge. She was obviously expected. Jacob prayed she wouldn't walk up to one of the men there and be enveloped in a huge embrace. But Jacob couldn't see what happened next. She had just walked into the group of people that started to walk closer to the ocean. But then he saw her turn slightly. She looked back in his direction. He hoped seeing him still standing there watching her would bring a smile to her face.

Jacob, with his hat firmly planted on his head, returned to get his chair, book and coffee. He continued on to the beach, hoping she might return, but he didn't see her again that day.

Rain drops landed on his face. Lost in a wondrous dream, he had woken suddenly on the deck of *Pearl*. Jacob looked quickly up towards Jody's star, but it was hidden somewhere behind the clouds.

Jacob stirred restlessly. His sleep had been disturbed by troubled dreams of dark alleys and of floundering ships run aground on stormy seas.

It was still early in the morning and yet he was awake. From his bed, he could see white caps in the shipping channel entering Charleston Harbor. The cedar trees out near the dunes in front of his house were moving in a rare summer morning breeze.

Jacob sat straight up in his bed as he painfully realized that this was going to be a very different kind of day for him. He needed to make some very quick decisions about what he would actually do now that the long anticipated proceeds from the enormous Southern Shipping deal were not going to materialize. This was the first day of a new life, and just then he had no clue as to what was next for him.

He slowly dressed and went downstairs, not bothering to shave. After getting his coffee started, he walked in to his living room to continue waking up.

His eyes were drawn to a painting of Jody's that hung above his fireplace. One rainy, stormy afternoon, she had drawn the initial sketch from this room while looking out through his screened porch and over the dunes to the harbor and beyond. The painting depicted dark clouds filling the sky above gray, marbled waves. In the distance were brighter clouds hinting of sunshine and the storm clearing. It had taken Jacob many looks at this painting to finally notice that what appeared to be one of the white clouds was actually Jody's profile looking down towards calmer waters. It had seemed to be a promise of brighter days ahead.

'Brighter days ahead, my ass! Damn it all, damn it! What in the flip am I going to do? The option is coming due very quickly, my investments are in the tank. Damn, damn, damn it! How did that deal not happen?'

Jacob thought about his meeting the day before with Buddy Capers and how Buddy's eyes seemed to twinkle just a little as he delivered the bad news to Jacob.

'Asshole! Buddy had to know what this meant,' thought Jacob. *'What could have happened to Edmund?*

Jacob recalled all the details of the meeting, how broken he had felt as he left the building. But then he thought back to his visit with Tadpole.

'Who exactly is this Nathan Goldstein?'

Curious, Jacob got up and went to his home office. Turning his computer on, he did a Google search for Nathan Goldstein, and quickly found a good deal of information. A bit older than Jacob, he was a graduate of Fordham University and NYU law School with a professional specialty in estate and tax related law. Jacob was surprised that there were many references to this one man. As he read, he found no photographs, but did find many articles about charitable functions mentioning Goldstein, including a golf tournament Goldstein and a famous New York Jet's football player had co-hosted. A few of the stories did refer to legal matters, generally estate related issues with Nathan Goldstein as the attorney of record.

But on page three of the Google search, Jacob was startled to find a link to a Charleston related story from the local newspaper, The Post & Courier. Jacob started reading closely. Ten years earlier, Nathan Goldstein had represented the estate of a Charleston lawyer named Harvey Ross who, along with his wife Victoria, had disappeared and were believed to have both drowned in the Bahamas while on a fishing trip.

'*Why would he have been involved in that?*' wondered Jacob, who had been in Charleston a few years by then and could still vaguely remember the stories details.

Finding no further references to Nathan Goldstein's involvement in the Ross matter, Jacob started a new Google search, this time on Harvey Ross. He began recalling the rumors he had heard at the time. He had never met Harvey, but did remember occasionally seeing the burly, long gray- haired man wearing a three piece suit as he flamboyantly drove his classic silver Mercedes convertible around Charleston's downtown area. The gossip then had been that Harvey Ross had been somehow involved in drug running down in the Islands and later in Charleston. During the years after his death, stories occasionally surfaced that Harvey had been spotted several times, very much alive; once in a hotel lobby in Costa Rica and another time in a

Panamanian bar, and had apparently disappeared rapidly in both instances. The new Google search also revealed some additional stories about the incident from The Post & Courier. There were articles initially reporting the disappearance of the Ross's, and then police interviews of the fishing boat captain and his mate, both claiming no sight of the either Ross after the boat had struck something while cruising near Abaco's and gone down quickly. Even the Ross's poodle had not been found. The stories ended with official reports declaring the couple deceased, and that their adult children had received an inheritance and a substantial insurance settlement.

'Interesting' thought Jacob. 'And now Nathan Goldstein is in Charleston!'

'So, Why does he want to meet me, again?' he wondered.

Jacob called Carol at the office, knowing it was too early for her to be at her desk. He left a message that he would not be in that day, and to only call him in case of an emergency.

As he passed through his living room to get his coffee, he glanced at a photo of himself back in college, wearing what became his trade mark tweed vest, interviewing a South Carolina Tech basketball coach on the arena floor after a game. Jacob looked a little closer at this picture, at his own eyes sparking with excitement, his posture leaning in to the coach, the way he was really listening to this man, working as hard as he could to draw the guy out of this normal postgame interview into a place of revealing something of his passion for coaching, what it meant to him to see his players performing at their personal peak level. It was a place from his heart that the coach could share with Jacob's readers; to revel to his fans more of who he was a person and to maybe make their own lives just that much more special. Those moments had meant so much to Jacob at that time in his life, and did so even now as he thought back to them..

Looking more closely at himself in the picture, he could see how alive, how excited and how alert he was, how just filled with passion he had been with what he was doing at those moments.

Jacob wondered how in the world he had gotten so far away from that person to the one now that often did not like to look closely at himself in the mirror.

Jacob wondered if he had even noticed when he had stopped writing. Even in Key West, he had generally kept a reporter's pad with him in a back pack, because he overheard so many remarkable things people actually said in the most casual of conversations. He wrote as many of them down as he could, thinking one day he would turn all of them into a collection of stories like those he had started writing at Tech. He had accumulated quite a number of those little notebooks. But during the tropical storm he had been caught in that sent him into Charleston for the first time, the box containing all those pads was totally immersed in the deluge of seawater that had nearly swamped *Pearl*. All he had been able to do was deposit them in a large trash container in the marina.

It was time for him to get real about just where was he now in his life and what was he going to do next. He grabbed his coffee and headed to his screened porch. He did some of his best thinking there, in the wind and the light; in touch with all the elements around him.

Next to the door leading to the porch was a truly fantastic photo, a lucky shot taken by a Tuscaloosa, Alabama sports photographer that showed Jacob making his famous game saving tackle that led to that great upset victory for the Tigersharks. The picture centered on Jacobs face mask planted into the guy's chest, his eyes focused and excited, driving the running back into the air and onto his back at the feet of the Alabama football coach.

He spent most of the morning on his porch, using a legal pad to write down whatever thoughts he had about his immediate future as he searched through his mind, wondering just what could he do right then while also asking himself what he was prepared to do.

The porch overlooked a small, fenced yard and garden. It was bordered by dunes and old, thick cedar trees bearing their summer-blue berries. The beach and harbor channel lay just beyond.. He relaxed into his favorite chair, an old wooden rocker he had found one long ago day, just sitting alongside a country road as if it were a gift waiting for him to drive by and take with him.

Jacob suddenly remembered the voice that had spoken to him the day before. It had not been one he recognized, but the words stayed with him.' *Keep your mind on your work and everything will be ok. Just don't be afraid.*' He felt again the effect the words had on him. He was instantly calmed and focused, his mind momentarily emptied of all his concerns.

'*What is my work, really?*' he wondered.

He thought back to one afternoon, to a moment that changed his life. In high school one day during football practice, he had happened to pick up a bouncing, incomplete long pass and had just mindlessly punted it back to the passer. The ball had arched high into the sky, hanging there before coming down well beyond the quarterback. An assistant coach ran quickly over to him with another ball and excitedly said, "Do that again!"

Jacob had, and then quickly became such a good punter that this natural gift had led to him coming to South Carolina Tech. He had already done some sports writing, and had inquired at the college newspaper about continuing on with his reporting. The response was to come back with something unique. So he interviewed Tadpole who was a true freshman but already starting on the varsity team, and that story got him a place with the newspaper. His access to the football players and staff gradually led to all of the athletes at that college, and he had begun a weekly column for the newspaper entitled 'Inside the Tigersharks locker room.' It had been a big hit. After graduating, he had gotten a job with the large local newspaper, primarily to continue with that weekly series of inside articles. If it hadn't been for that inadvertent kick long ago, none of what happened next would have.

While he was in college, many of his friends began dropping out and moving to Key West, especially Matthew Marshall. Eventually, Jacob had followed. Upon arriving there, he had been able to meet many people right away and was quickly able to get his first bartending job.

When he had become a stockbroker, Jacob had created his own good luck through lots of hard work, calling lots of complete strangers who hopefully had investment capital. He had to do that because there was absolutely no investment business automatically heading his way. He was not only new in town, he quickly came to be frequently reminded that he was also a Yankee in the city where the Civil War had begun and seemed to have not quite ended. It was often stated that Charlestonians were like the Chinese in that they revered their ancestors, liked rice and didn't cotton much to strangers. Jacob had to go out, find the opportunities and make the business happen. He had started writing articles about investing and was able to get some published. That had led to public speaking engagements. He still carried an old reporter's pad almost everywhere with him, as well as a small tape recorder that also fit in his pocket so he could quickly record any sudden ideas that came along. It had proven to be extremely useful habit.

Now he had no plan whatsoever. He thought briefly about finding a job with a small newspaper somewhere, wondering at the same time if he really wanted to go back to sports writing. He knew he didn't, not now.

After college, he had been hired as a sportswriter for the local newspaper with statewide distribution, and was able to continue writing his weekly column. Jacob had done some very good writing, won some awards and achieved a good deal of success. But he had been fired from his job after writing a series of investigative articles about an out-of-state coach who had committed not only many recruiting irregularities, but had also been looking the other way on steroid injections for his players. Jacob had felt strongly that no matter how famous the man was, he was cheating and shouldn't be able to get away with it. No matter how true the articles had been, Jacob had failed to recognize how influential that coach was throughout the Southeast. As a result of those articles, Jacob's name had become tarnished within the collegiate athletic community.

At that time, Jacob liked to believe that if his stories were all about how important athletics were and what they did for the wider community. He needed to write them as authentically as he knew how to. He hadn't realized that newspapers were a business first and foremost. It was all personal to him. He wanted to believe it had been about writing the best stories possible. It hadn't ended well.

Despite offers of writing jobs elsewhere, he had gone to Key West instead. Initially, it was just to visit Matthew Marshall., Juke O'Bannion and some other friends who had drifted down there. But the lifestyle in Key West was pretty easy to like. It had been a great change of life for him. There were no daily deadlines, no long road trips and no corporate politics. He was just pouring drinks, listening to people and having way too much fun. His old friend Juke had often said that Jacob's greatest gift was not only in getting other people to talk, but to really listen and help them to keep getting deeper into their own stories.

But living in Key West for several years began to be way too much fun. Jacob grudgingly finally acknowledged to himself that he needed something personally more gratifying. He had sailed away, headed north to see his family for awhile, to get grounded and to find his next big thing.

It all seemed so long ago.

A thought was clawing its way into Jacobs mind, climbing all over him and was not going to let him go. These old photographs were triggering something deep in his memory that was now rocketing directly into his reality. Jacob knew he thought best on his feet and decided to go for a walk.

He was happily surprised at how deserted the beach seemed to be that morning. He couldn't remember the last time he had been out there during the week, let alone at mid-morning. With the breeze in his face, Jacob walked on the edge of the sea, looking at the shells and various kinds of sea weed and other stuff washed ashore; for a moment just enjoying the magnificent day. He hoped some good ideas would start to arise, but he thought again of Buddy Capers eyes as he told Jacob the deal was off.

Jacob began feeling angry again, and, taking advantage of no one else being in sight, he began screaming again, just putting his body completely into it, expelling all the bitter feelings he could.

He suddenly felt ashamed of himself. He had become a complete sellout. He was only in this business for the money now, and he knew it was completely hypocritical of him to be upset with the brokerage industry. They were a business, responsible to their shareholders to make as much of a profit as possible.

Wasn't that all Jacob was doing as well?

'Why was it so much easier to point the finger at someone else than it was to point it back at myself? Apparently it was. After all, it was me, Jacob, who had gotten all fixated on owning a Sullivan's Island beach house, on purchasing a BMW and then on taking an extended Alaskan vacation, no one else. When did I even start thinking this way? When had all these things become suddenly so important?'

He had always taken great pride in having what he called the three-finger rule, which said never point at someone else for being wrong about something because you always had three fingers pointed back at yourself.

'How could I even try to blame the securities industry for any of this? I sold out, plain and simple, or at least had tried to, and the deal not working was maybe what I deserved happening. The sooner I acknowledged that, the better.'

He knew long ago he had stopped looking for ideas and interests that excited him. He had started coasting, living the dream. Several years before this, he had been in at least a comfortable financial position. He had even known then how uninspired he was. That was when he might have acknowledged the truth and moved on with his life.

But, then he had met Edmund and had made the choice to continue pursuing the deal, wanting to believe it wasn't that much of a long shot. Now he was responsible for getting himself into this place of diminished economic options and it could only be him who could solve this.

But as to what exactly he could do, right now he didn't have a clue. So, he continued his walk, absently watching some shrimp boats out near the horizon.

As he continued on down the beach, Jacob thought back to the pictures of himself back at his house, especially remembering just how excited he had been back then about everything. He could see it so clearly in his eyes, how just lit up they were, glowing it seemed from deep within him. Those were some of the best days in his life simply because of how into football he had been and how immersed he was in his writing, in conveying some truth to his readers in each of his articles. Why had he really given it up?

The painful truth of the real reason he had just walked away crashed at his feet along with a large wave. He had never been able to talk about it with anyone; not then, not ever since.

He hadn't been fired for writing the articles about that coach. His editor had been very involved in the whole series all the way. But after they were printed, the coach and his university had raised a big stink, denying all of it and threatening to sue the newspaper. Jacob had been called to a meeting with the publisher and her staff. They had wanted him to write a graceful retraction of some sort. Jacob had refused. When they insisted, he told the group to shove it up their collective asses. When the words came out of his mouth, his young male ego had gotten the better of him and he stood his ground. And then he was fired.

He was embarrassed by the entire incident, an emotion he had no way of dealing with at the time. He had loved doing the writing, as well as all the accolades he had been receiving. He thought he was bullet proof. He couldn't admit then, even to himself, that he was the one who had screwed up, and no one else. Rather than either attempting to make amends or to go elsewhere and start over at something he deeply loved, he found it easier to just walk away than to let his ego be damaged by admitting what he had done.

It was something he had not wanted to acknowledge for many years. He just couldn't find a way to tell anyone what had actually happened. The fact was that his ego had gotten the best of him and done him in. The truth of that had been his constant shadow.

He thought then how gratifying it had been for him to have achieved the success he had as a new stockbroker. The work he had done both writing investment articles and seminars had been interesting and satisfying. The level of success he had achieved had been completely unexpected. The financial rewards were amazing. The secret truth was that he had especially loved the accolades he had begun receiving, as if they were some form of long overdue recognition.When his business had started slipping, he was ready to walk away from the business, to go out on top.

But that was when he had met Edmund Capers, and that opportunity had appealed massively to his ego. It was the chance to not only do something major, but to also to become what he considered rich. His ego completely went for it.

That was really it. Jacob never would have described himself as having been on a massive ego trip. Yet he finally acknowledged to himself that yes, a lot of his motivation in life was some form of external-gratification, first as a writer and later as a stockbroker. He loved being thought of by others as successful. Why that was he couldn't even guess.

But then he thought about Jody, and then of Tadpole. Their work was doing what they simply loved doing, what they loved sharing and giving to others. That was one of the things Jacob so especially admired and envied about both of them. They were doing the work they simply and uncompromisingly loved, just as he once had.

'*So now what? Do I start over again as a stockbroker, become a writer again? What do I really want to do now?* '

Part of the answer was as clear to him as anything. He wanted to be truly immersed in something simply because he loved it and it excited him. Jacob wanted to feel fully engaged in something worth putting all of his energy towards. '*What would that be?*' No easy answers presented themselves.

He continued to walk, feeling tons lighter, happier, as if there was a destination, some new source of light to find somewhere just ahead of him, perhaps just around the next bend.

He returned to his house, still without any ideas, and decided to go for an early lunch; perhaps he might come up with some inspired thoughts at one of the two Sullivan's Island restaurants. With a tremendous amount of luck, maybe he would come across an opportunity of some sort.

Stepping into his open garage, he was startled as a pick-up truck suddenly and noisily sped off from the front of his house. Jacob didn't know what that was about so he quickly forgot about it.

As he backed the Honda out from under his house, his car radio was on. Chrissie Hynde and the Pretenders were just finishing a song and then the news came on. The lead story was that 'a prominent Charleston business executive has been reported missing. J. Edmund Capers, Chief Financial Officer of Southern Shipping, Inc has been reported missing by his wife Julie. In a related story, Charleston Police have reported locating a fishing boat believed to belong to Mr. Capers washed ashore on James Island. The Police are not denying reports a boating accident may have occurred.'

'*You mean Edmund is actually missing, as in officially missing? The kind of missing when his wife really doesn't know where he is? Or anyone else? Oh, my god! What could have happened to him?* '

As he entered Bert's Bar, just a few blocks from his house, Jacob had to wait a moment for his eyes to adjust to the dim lighting. The place seemed nearly deserted, which was surprising because it was lunchtime and Bert's had the best cheeseburgers anywhere in Charleston. An older guy Jacob didn't know was seated at the far end of the well used wooden bar.

As he was settling on to a bar stool, Jacob greeted the bartender.

"Hey Tom, how goes it?"

"So what would you like today, Jacob'

While he was waiting for his cheeseburger and fries, another guy who Jacob knew was named Gus came through the front door. A bright shaft of piercing light slashed across the bar, which caused Jacob to need to re-adjust his eyes again.

Gus said "Man, it is so hot out there the bumper stickers are falling off my truck."

"Great," Tom replied. "It's so hot today everyone's a comedian. The usual, Gus?"

Jacob ate his cheeseburger and fries, glancing at the TV in the corner behind the bar, watching the noon broadcast of the local news. Suddenly, a photograph of Edmund Capers flashed on the screen. "Tom, could you turn up the volume please? A local newsperson was finishing the report, repeating that Edmund was missing and if anyone had any information, would they please contact the Charleston Police.

"Have they checked the Appalachian Trail yet?" yucked the older guy at the bar. 'Hey Tom, it's so hot out I need another cold draft."

Jacob wondering about Edmund and what might have occurred. He had to think for a moment, wondering when was the last time he had spent any time with Edmund away from the man's office discussing the retirement accounts. Jacob realized it was at the spring party at Morgan's Point.

He and Jody had been walking through one of the gardens and came across Edmund, his wife Julia and some other folks gathered near one of the bars set up to keep the party crowd properly lubricated. Edmund was dressed very casually, at least for Edmund, in a blue blazer, blue shirt, red bowtie and khakis. Jacob waved and Edmund signaled for them to come over and say hello.

Julia Capers greeted them. "Jacob O'Leary! It is so nice to see you again! Jody, I so enjoyed our nice chat at our Christmas party! You look very lovely in that beautiful peach dress! Thank you for being here today!"

"Thank you Julia" replied Jody. 'Lavender is really your color. Your dress is stunning. What a lovely garden this is. I have never seen as many blooming azaleas in one place. It is gorgeous here! Hello Edmund, so nice to see you as well. Jacob often mentions how much he enjoys knowing you.'

"Good afternoon to you both. Jacob, it's great to see you away from the office. "

"You too, Edmund. Thanks again for the invitation. This is quite a place."

A waiter came by, offering to freshen up everyone's drinks.

"Nothing for me," Edmund had said to the man. "I never drink alcoholic beverages. I'll have just my usual glass of club soda, thanks."

At that moment back in the spring, a call had gone out for everyone to gather before the house. Buddy Capers had an announcement, which was that the new polo pony for his son had arrived.

Jacob felt very sad for Edmund and his family. A boating accident could happen to anyone, no matter how careful you were. Jacob also thought about how ridiculously bad the timing of this was. He knew it was selfish of him to be thinking of his own apparent loss at the moment, but that was what he had thought about. He also thought again about what Buddy had said about Jacob's relationship with the Marshalls.

'Could it have always been true that this was a deal that never was going to happen?'

Edmund had assured him that he and Buddy didn't care about that; they just wanted a better return on their money

Jacob knew he shouldn't keep dwelling on this, that it was over, but he needed to know why he had apparently wasted two years chasing something that didn't exist.

7

Jacob felt tired and sleepy when he returned to his house. He went straight to his favorite place to take a nap, his hammock. As he settled in, he could see a couple walking together hand in hand out on the beach.

Jacob immediately thought of Jody, remembering that first night they had been together, when they too had been just another couple walking together down that same beach for the first time on a moonlit night. He would never forget the moment when he had finally met Jody Pickens.

It had been at a bonfire on the beach at Sullivan's Island one fall evening. Jacob was sitting on a log, talking with a friend when he happened to glance across the fire.

All he really saw was just an eye looking right at him, suspended above someone's shoulder. He recognized it instantly, knowing it was that woman from the beach. Then she had disappeared from sight. He rose, circling behind the crowd, searching for her. Then she appeared before him, her eyes shining in the firelight, looking closely at him. Her long brown hair was in a partial braid falling over the shoulder of a red-fleece jacket.

Her smile glowed at Jacob, and he had said, "I know you.'"

And smiling deeply into his eyes, she responded, "I know you too. So, how are ya?"

They introduced themselves and started talking. Under a quarter-moon, they went for a long, slow walk down the length of the island, ending at Breach Inlet. Jacob wondered how many footprints just like theirs were buried deep in the sands of this beach; how many lovers meeting for the first time had also stepped on those same moonbeams as they walked and talked for the very first time, drawn together by the same forces the moon had on the tides.

Jacob learned that Jody was a portrait artist from the foothills of South Carolina; a little place called Tamassee, where her Momma and Daddy still were, along with her sisters and brothers as well as lots of other cousins, aunts and uncles. She had a small portrait studio downtown on an alley off of State Street.

They stood near the waves and before the moon at Breach Inlet. He looked into Jody's eyes and she smiled deeply back. Jacob reached his arms around her, pulling her closer. Their eyes locked and Jacob bent forward to kiss her. But Jody very slowly moved her head backwards so that he couldn't quite reach her lips. Yet her eyes stayed glued to his eyes, the smile never leaving her moonlit face. She reached her arms around his neck and they stood there for another moment or so, looking into each other's eyes.

Jacob said, "I have a gift for you."

Jody seemed to slightly raise her right eyebrow, her eyes curious.

"Look up there, Jody. Do you see the Big Dipper?" And she could. He pointed to the top star of the cup. "That's your star now, Jody. Now it belongs to no one but you. It is the most important star in the sky. Without it, there would be no Big Dipper, no way to really identify the North Star. Without that star, all of us sailors would be lost."

Jody looked deeply into Jacob's eyes, saying nothing, but her smile somehow changed to a deeper level of joy and serenity.

"Let's head back, "he said.

"You gonna carry me?" she had asked, smiling.

"Sure," and he had scooped her up, staggered forward a step or two before slowly falling gently to the beach, turning so that he ended up landing on his back. Jody's face was inches above his. He could feel her energy as she leaned her forehead into his.

"Are you real, Jacob? Where have you been all these years?"

Jacob suddenly rolled her over onto her back, facing down on her. Jody looked back up at him curiously, and then he rose, pulling her with him as he stood. He laughed, and she laughed with him.

Arm in arm Jacob and Jody had then walked slowly back down the beach.

8

Walking into The Creek restaurant, Jacob tried to imagine what meeting Nathan Goldstein was going to be like. He only knew what Google had revealed, which was probably very little about who this man really was. So he had decided to just enjoy the evening, to listen closely to whatever this man had to say when Goldstein revealed the reason for meeting Jacob.

"Jacob O'Leary! It is so good to see you again," enthusiastically greeted Carl, the long time host of The Creek.'

"Good to see you again too, Carl," replied Jacob."I am meeting a Mr. Nathan Goldstein. Has he arrived yet?" Jacob was 10 minutes early, his normal time to arrive for a meeting.

"No, but we have a table reserved for you upstairs by the windows, where I recall you prefer to dine. Misty, would you show our friend to his table. Enjoy your dinner, Jacob. So glad you are dining with us tonight. Enjoy your meal!"

Misty led him upstairs to his window table. Jacob didn't recognize any of the other diners in the oak walled dining room, which displayed several local paintings depicting life in the marshes of South Carolinas Lowcountry.

Jacob declined Misty's offer of getting him something to drink while he waited, preferring to see what would happen next. He looked across the creek and marshes before him to the distant city, which was silhouetted against the late afternoon sky. His eyes were drawn to a massive container ship coming across the harbor, headed out to sea as it passed a number of smaller boats gathered in the water near Patriots Point. He could see a large flight of white ibis flying towards the creek. His eyes followed them as they crossed the nearby marsh and then Jacob noticed a large, wooden classic yacht he didn't recognize tied at the dock just below him. It seemed freshly painted with a white hull and teak cabin and bridge.

'*Wow, easily a fifty-footer!*' Jacob guessed. He figured Humphrey Bogart and Lauren Bacall must be aboard. He could not quite make out the name painted on the stern.

Jacob raised his eyes to look at the Coastal Traders building nestled amidst an ancient forest of cedar trees just across the creek. A two-story building, it was one of Mt Pleasants oldest, dating back to just after the Civil War when Oliver Marshall's ancestor, Rodger Marshall, had rebuilt it on the site of the original structure, which had been destroyed during a Civil War bombardment. Rodger had located the structure so that he was directly across Charleston Harbor from Capers Wharf. Through a telescope mounted in the rooftop cupola, he or one of his men could easily watch closely the comings and goings of all of Southern Shipping's vessels, and maybe get an idea as to what their cargoes were.

The parking lot was empty and Jacob looked to Oliver's second floor windows and his bridge, as Oliver called a deck outside his office. Jacob hadn't spent much time there as he was really still much better friends with Susan than with Oliver. But he wished they were in town.

The building reminded him of the last time he had eaten here. It had been over the Christmas holidays with Oliver and Susan, before their daughters had gotten home from college. Jody had been with him and they were talking about music they both liked while waiting for Oliver and Susan to arrive. Jacob said that of all the musicians he enjoyed listening to, that he especially loved the music of Emmylou Harris. He mentioned that he also really liked the way she looked.

Sort of joking, he had said to Jody "You know, as much as I love you, if I ever get the chance to run off with Emmylou for a few days, I probably will." But Jody had a little too quickly replied "Not if I see her first."

As if realizing what she had just said, Jody blushed for the first time Jacob had known her. Looking quite flustered she added, "Just kidding, you're my type." And she kissed him, but still seemed unsure of herself. Then Oliver and Susan had come in and they all had a wonderful evening together.

But later that evening, back at Jacob's house, Jody had been sitting quietly on the sofa, deep in thought. She looked over at him, and had asked "Do you really love me, Jacob? I mean, no matter what I do? Who I am? Who I have been? What I have done?"

Jacob sat beside her and, taking her hand in his, he had replied, "Of course I do, we each had a life before we met. We haven't really talked too much about this, but since we are, yes Jody, I love you, more than anyone I have ever known, and yes, no matter what. Do you love me?"

And she said she did, resting her head on his shoulder. But then she started crying, first quietly but then the tears came harder and harder. Finally, she stopped crying and left the room for a few minutes.

Returning, Jody had said "Make love to me Jacob, please, right now. Could we go upstairs, please, and will you hold me the way you do, the way I love so much."

The following morning, whatever had come over her was gone.

A tall, thin blonde pony tailed man dressed in black pants and shirt entered the dining room and walked directly over to Jacob's table. His approach brought Jacob back to the moment.

"You must be Jacob O'Leary. I'm Sean and I work for Mr. Goldstein. He wonders if you would care to join him aboard his yacht. If you will, tell me what you would like for dinner and we will have it brought out shortly, so you may dine aboard."

Jacob thought this was an interesting way to begin an evening, and now was even more interested in what Nathan Goldstein had to say. Jacob looked over the menu, but already knew that he was going to order the grouper and shrimp salad. So, he stood, thanked Sean for coming up to get him, told him what he'd like to eat and followed him downstairs. They walked through the restaurant and out to the dock. The yacht Jacob had been admiring was apparently Nathan Goldstein's, because that was where Sean led him.

"Please go on aboard, Mr. O'Leary. I will attend to dinner for you and Mr. Goldstein. He is waiting for you in the salon. Welcome aboard the *Bronx Cheer.*

Jacob stepped aboard, admiring the freshly oiled teak decks and highly varnished woodwork, the comfortably padded stern bench, the gleaming brass fittings.

The cabin door opened and a short, balding man with a brown beard and pale skin walked towards Jacob, smiling with one hand extended in greeting, the other holding a glass mug of beer.

"Welcome aboard, Jacob. I'm Nathan Goldstein, and please do refer to me as Nathan. Thank you for joining me for dinner this evening, especially on such short notice. I am very glad you could come. Do you mind me calling you Jacob?" he asked as they shook hands. "May I get you something to drink? "

Jacob acknowledged the mug and said that a beer would be great.

"Please, come inside."

Following the man, Jacob wondered if Nathan happened to have shopped at a Tommy Bahama shop that very day. He was wearing what seemed to be a brand new dark blue patterned tropical shirt, new pleated cotton trousers, what looked like brand new deck shoes, and had a gold Rolex watch on his very pale wrist. Jacob was glad he had also dressed casually in chinos and a pale blue short sleeved seersucker shirt. He had actually debated whether or not to wear a blazer.

Entering the cabin, Jacob saw it was well appointed. There were several comfortable tan leather chairs, a small library, a dining table set for two; it seemed more a small apartment in the city than an ocean going yacht. Curiously, there were drawn curtains covering the cabins large windows.

"What a fabulous boat, Nathan. How long have you had her?"

"Just for a year or so. I have been a city boy all my life and decided it was time to see the rest of the world. Would you care to take a brief tour?"

Nathan spoke slowly in a clipped manner as if he carefully considered each word before he said it. His accent seeming to be a bit British, if anything, but certainly not a distinct New York accent, at least to Jacob. But then Jacob still noticed a southern accent every time he heard one, which was usually all day long. He was often told that he still had a New Jersey accent. He replied that you can get the guy out of New Jersey, but you can never quite get New Jersey out of the guy.

Nathan led Jacob down a wooden staircase and they walked along a short passageway. There were several guest cabins on either side; the door of one was closed but the other was open and Jacob could see it was outfitted with a desk and computer. It was evidently Nathan Goldstein's office when he was aboard. The captain's cabin was below the staircase in the stern with several windows overlooking Shem Creek behind the boat.

"You have a fantastic yacht, Nathan. You must be very comfortable here. How much time do you spend aboard?"

"Not as much time as I will in the future, Jacob. Let's go back upstairs. I believe Sean is preparing to get underway." As he said that, Jacob could hear the diesel engines firing up below him, and shortly after, he could feel the yacht getting underway.

"Why do you call her the *Bronx Cheer*?" asked Jacob, sitting at the dining table with dinner all laid out for both of them.

"It seemed appropriate. I'm a city boy and love the New York Yankees. Again, thanks for agreeing on such short notice to join me this evening. Have you known Mr. Gaillard for long?"

"The pleasure is mine, Nathan. Tadpole and I are very old friends. We met in college. How are you enjoying your stay in Charleston?"

Nathan and Jacob continued to talk over dinner. Jacob had begun to notice that Nathan generally spoke nearly in a slow monotone, as if he was deliberately not revealing much about himself. While they ate, the *Bronx Cheer* was cruising slowly through the harbor. Jacob could see through the cabins portholes that they were headed down river towards the Cooper River Bridge.

As they finished eating, Nathan said "It's such a beautiful evening. Would you mind if we go on deck and enjoy the evening air?" They each rose, carrying with them their beers, which Nathan topped off from the cabins bar.

"Beer, I just love it. Always have. Something else I inherited from my Granddaddy. He was a lawyer, out in Garden City. My Daddy never liked the law, so he worked in an appliance store until he was able to purchase it. Granddaddy put me through school."

Nathan had an unusual way of speaking; it seemed almost affected, Jacob thought. He didn't normally hear men from the north refer to their father as Daddy.

They sat on comfortable deck chairs, enjoying the magnificent view of a beautiful night on Charleston harbor. The sun was setting behind a huge cloud cover; the city skyline was silhouetted by fabulous red and yellow streaked clouds accenting the deepening blue sky to the west

"My friends at Hamilton Brothers in New York tell me you are a very good stockbroker, Jacob. How long have you been in that business?"

'It's been just over 12 years, almost ever since I've been here in Charleston. It's been an interesting time, as you might guess. But, tell me about you Nathan, what kind of legal practice do you have?"

Nathan basically reiterated what Google had said about him He mentioned going to Fordham because it was his grandfather's wish. After Fordham came law school, at NYU and then he began his career in the city, first for a large New York law firm, before starting his own practice. Nathan said that he had specialized in estate and tax law because he wanted to really understand money and how to make it work. Since his office was in the city, he had lived there on the Upper East Side near Central Park. Nathan described himself as a widower, his wife having succumbed to cancer nearly five years before, and they had no children. His work had been his only real interest. Nathan went on to say he had never really been to Charleston before, but had a case there once for a friend of a friend. Not long after getting the *Bronx Cheer*, he had passed through Charleston harbor on his way to Florida via the Intracoastal Waterway and had decided to stop for a few days to make a quick visit. He had been charmed by the city, especially in that Charleston inspired images for him of all the places he hoped to one day visit. Nathan had realized then that he was ready to leave New York City. He had always liked the idea of giving back to the community. He was involved with a number of charities in New York, mostly those aimed at improving the lives of young people. Then Nathan went on to say again that he didn't really know anyone in Charleston.

Bronx Cheer was cruising through the harbor and darkness was falling. Sean had changed direction and they were heading now towards the ocean, with Sullivan's Island coming up to port. Nathan commented on the magnificent home appearing just ahead. He was referring to Oliver and Susan Marshall's house, which Jacob was surprised to see had several lights on upstairs.

"That is a grand home over there. I have been admiring it since I have been here. Do you know anything about it, Jacob?"

"I know the owners well. We have also been friends since college, which seems like a really long time ago."

"Really, that is grand. Do you think you could introduce me to them one day? Do you have any reason to think they may have any interest in perhaps selling it? I would love to own a house like that."

"I am sure that I could arrange an introduction at some point, although I seriously doubt they would ever have any thought about selling. I am sure you would enjoy meeting each other though."

"Splendid," replied Nathan Goldstein.

They cruised closer to the jetties at the mouth of the harbor, but then the *Bronx Cheer* began turning around, headed back to Shem Creek.

"Tell me, Jacob, what do you make of the story I heard today of a local businessman who has disappeared? Did you know the man by any chance?"

Jacob wasn't surprised by the question in that it had been all over the local news.

"Yes, I know Edmund pretty well. This is really disturbing. I cannot imagine what has happened," Jacob replied as casually as he could, reluctant to reveal any confidences with anyone, especially a total stranger.

"I won't ask in what capacity you know each other. You seem to be acquainted with quite a few of the people worth knowing in Charleston. Jacob, let me tell you why I wanted to meet you. I am planning to relocate my business here very shortly. I rely greatly on my instincts and believe in doing things quickly. I need someone here who can introduce me to important people in Charleston. My impression is you are just the man. Your reputation preceded you and you have already impressed me. You seem to have many acquaintances here. In addition to my law practice, I am also an investment adviser, a financier. My clients are all wealthy and have pooled their funds with me. I would like you to be my local broker. I am prepared to open an initial account with you with the sum of $ 5 million, and will gradually increase that to an amount you would undoubtedly find most interesting. In return, I expect some important introductions. How does this proposition sound to you?" Nathan has been staring into Jacob's eyes this entire time, carefully observing his reactions.

Jacob almost can't believe his ears.' *Is this too good to be true? Is this man really going to turn over $5million to someone he has just met? Am I missing something here?*' he wondered

"Would $5 million be an acceptable amount?" Nathan asked. "You would be granted discretion to buy and sell whatever securities you felt appropriate, but I would expect a steady stream of communication from you regarding those transactions."

"That will certainly be satisfactory, Nathan. I am looking forward to doing business with you." The two men stood and shook hands on the agreement.

The *Bronx Cheer* continued on as the conversation turned to Jacob answering a few more of Nathan Goldstein's questions about financial markets and the weather in Charleston.

"What is the history of hurricanes actually coming ashore here?" he asked.

"It happens, but not very often," Jacob had replied.

The *Bronx Cheer* returned to Shem Creek and docked briefly. Nathan explained that he had a berth downtown at the City Marina. Jacob disembarked, thanking Nathan for a wonderful evening. They agreed to meet again the following afternoon, at Nathan's leased home downtown.

~~

As he turned on to his street on Sullivan's Island, Jacob saw Randy riding his bike just ahead of him.

Randy Miller had been a highly recruited quarterback from Ohio when Jacob met him on what was for both of them their first day in the South Carolina Tech locker room. A tall, athletic kid then, Randy had an arm that could easily throw a football 60 yards. But he never started a game for the Tigersharks. Randy had also loved to play the guitar, much more than he ever liked football. Soon after arriving on campus, he had joined a local band, and not long after that Randy had discovered hallucinogenic drugs. Many too many acid trips later, Randy was out of school and pretty much a lost soul. But Susan Marshall had been roommates at Tech with a girlfriend of Randy's and the two became friends. They were part of a larger social circle that also included Jacob and Matthew Marshall; a group of people who really loved the music played by Randy and his college band, The Loverboys. Matthew Marshall had become friends with all of them during his attempts at college. Matthew eventually had also introduced Susan to Oliver. But school and

Matthew had been a bad mix, and after just several really fun years, Matthew had moved further south, eventually ending up in Key West.

After marrying Oliver, Susan and Matthew had been able to persuade him to let Randy move into the caretaker's cottage on their Sullivan's Island property and look after things. She and Matthew wanted their lost soul of a friend to be in a safe environment where someone could keep an eye on him.

20 years later, Randy was still there, in body, at least. He was still lost in the rest of the world. Now, his hair was well below his shoulders, he had a thick beard, and always wore an old straw hat to cover his head. His body was much rounder than when he first came south. Randy spent every night out on his bicycle, riding the streets near the Marshall's house. He thought he was protecting them from the bad guys. A little paranoid, but an otherwise gentle and harmless man, Oliver and Susan's children had adopted him as Uncle Randy.

"Hey Ran, how you doing tonight?" Jacob asked, rolling his car slowly beside Randy and his bike.

"'OK, how are you?" Randy slowly replied, as if unsure of himself, not taking his eyes off the road in front of him.

"I'm good my friend, you take it easy. OK?" Jacob drove on to his house. It was late and he wanted to go to bed. Jacob continued on, watching Randy briefly in his rear view mirror, thinking he looked like he had lost a good bit of weight.

Jacob wondered about a night just a few weeks ago when he had walked outside behind his house to take the trash out, and noticed Randy just standing with his bike at the end of Jacobs driveway. Jacob had hollered hello, which must have been unheard because Randy had gotten on his bike and ridden off.

~~

Later that same evening, the *Bronx Cheer* was anchored in a secluded area of a deep water creek off the Intracoastal Waterway. A skiff carrying two men pulled alongside. A short, stocky man quickly secured his bowline to a rear cleat, and then he and his partner climbed aboard.

A flashlight beam landed on their faces as a voice asked "Are you sure you two didn't screw up again? No one saw you come in here? There were no other boats out tonight that passed you and saw you?"

"Shove it man. We screwed up. It happens. Not like you haven't. What do you want us to do now?"

"Keep looking for that kid. The man thinks he's at that 'All Stars place on the East Side. Keep looking there. He is bound to show up there sooner or later. You know how they like their basketball. Now look, O'Leary went for the pitch. I may want one of you to continue to keep an eye on him. When Oliver Marshall gets back in town, we want him going down and his pal Jacob is how we get to him. Now, tell me again how you lost that body in the harbor?"

"The prop really backed up on me and then freed itself. The damn body just flew away and we really couldn't find it."

"And you didn't dump him in the ocean like we planned because why?"

"Thought it would work. It didn't."

"The next time you guys don't do things exactly as I tell you too, just keep going out of whatever town we are in at the time. But do not think we will not find you. We will. Do you remember those two smart guys down in Belize? Gotten any postcards from them lately? Do you get this? You will not take us down. You will find that kid. You will be ready for the next step. And now you will get the hell out of here. I will contact you tomorrow, same time as every day. You find that kid tomorrow and there is a bonus."

9

After a fitful night of trying to sleep and continually waking up with fragments of dark and dangerous dreams, Jacob finally dragged himself out of his bed. He was feeling exceptionally restless. Although he was excited about his evening and agreement with Nathan Goldstein, he also realized that doing that business meant he would have to continue to be a stockbroker, probably for a good bit longer than he wanted to.

What Jacob really wanted to do at that moment was to load *Pearl* with enough fuel and food so that he could just sail away to wherever the wind took him. But reality often stinks. His reality was that there were tons of bills to be paid, and he was scheduled to exercise his option to buy his house in six weeks. And if he couldn't buy the house, he would probably have to move from what had been his home the past 5 years.

Reluctantly, he got in his car and drove downtown. It was time to go to his office and do whatever he was going to do next. He didn't care about Hamilton Brothers company-wide suit and tie dress code. Jacob was wearing a blue Whistling Dixie golf shirt, khakis and boat shoes.

Driving across the Ben Sawyer Bridge as he was leaving Sullivan's Island, Jacob turned on his car radio. The local news was just coming on, and the lead item was "Charleston Police are still searching for a prominent Charleston Business executive reported missing. J. Edmund Capers, an executive with Southern Shipping of Charleston, was reported missing two days ago by his wife Julia. A small boat believed to belong to Mr. Capers was found yesterday by Charleston Police, washed ashore on James Island. Police are not denying a report that a boating accident might have occurred and are asking anyone with any information as to the whereabouts of J. Edmund Capers to contact them immediately."

The next news piece didn't sound good either. "Tropical Storm Danielle continues to move WNW towards the Leeward Islands, still following the same path Hurricane Hugo did back in 1989."

As he entered the Hamilton Brothers office complex, Jacob had the sense of having been gone quite a lot longer than two days. He had arrived well before anyone else, and walked to his corner office overlooking Meeting Street and the City Market .He stopped at his doorway for a moment before going inside, looking around at the room he had spent so much time in for all those years.

He had the odd sense of seeing it for the first time.

Three tall windows overlooked the City Market. Before them was a huge wooden desk he had found at Page's Thieves Market in Mt Pleasant along with his brown leather desk chair. He walked quickly to feed the fish in the aquarium, which stood atop a wooden bookcase. There was an oriental carpet over the wide planked heart of pine flooring. There were several comfortable chairs for visitors and several others for a closer conversation with his clients. Opposite his desk hung a Winslow Homer painting which held a soft place in Jacob's heart; a memory from long ago summers, it was an ocean scene of an older man sailing with three young boys.

Somehow this morning, it all seemed somehow unremarkable to him. It was as if it belonged somewhere in his distant past, that he no longer belonged in this space. Jacob had long ago stopped considering that it was the nicest individual office in the complex. The brokerage industry was big on incentives, one of which was the biggest producers always had the best offices. It was a status symbol that all the brokers aspired to. Jacob had been the broker with that office for many years.

Although Jacob had arrived well before anyone else, he still closed his office door before turning his computer on and logging in. While waiting for the computer, he tore off the top page of the legal pad on his desk. The words Southern Shipping were all that was written on it, the name circled in various colors and exclamation marks by him as he had prepared to leave for the meeting. The sight stung him. He pictured the sculpted face of Capt. Capers laughing at him.

Jacob got quickly caught up on what he missed in his absence, which turned out wasn't much. In his Inbox were a number of internal emails, many product and research reports from Hamilton Brothers, but no important emails from clients. He looked through his to-do list and saw little on it, other than Southern Shipping related matters. Those didn't mean anything now. Jacob could have just walked out of there right then and it wouldn't really have mattered.

He opened his calendar and entered a 1:30 meeting later that day with Nathan Goldstein.

Through the window that comprised most of a wall of his office, Jacob could see some of the other brokers and assistants in the office were beginning to filter in.

His assistant Carol walked in to Jacob's office, happily surprised to see Jacob sitting there. Noticing his golf shirt, she asked "So you're not working today? How did the Southern Shipping deal go?"

"It didn't, Carol. I can't explain why. I don't know why, it just didn't happen."

"Have you heard the latest about Edmund Capers, Jacob? I saw it again on the news this morning. Didn't you meet with him on Tuesday? This is terrible. What happened to him? "

"I wish I knew. When I went for the meeting, Edmund wasn't there and his cousin said they had no idea where he was. No one seems to know."

Peter Madison then briskly entered Jacob's office. He was dressed in a splendid blue suit, white shirt, red tie and wore a very serious expression on his face.

"Good morning, Jacob. Good to see you. Carol, would you close the door behind you as you leave? I need to speak with Jacob privately."

Standing, Pete calmly said "Jacob, it is good to see you. I am surprised to have not heard at all from you in several days. I saw the story in today's paper about Mr. Capers. I surmise that the deal did not happen, especially because I haven't heard from you. What has been going on? All indications were that we had the deal. He said as much when we all went to New York in May. What is the story?"

"Pete, I wish I could tell you. When I went over there the other morning, I expected to be returning shortly with the executed paperwork. But Edmund was not there. I met with Buddy Capers, and he told me that they were keeping the accounts with Broad Street Bank and Trust. It was a short and definitive meeting. It blew my mind. I have been trying without any luck to contact Edmund. That's what I know. I didn't know what to think about it, let alone what to say. I figured I'd talk to Edmund at some point and something would make sense. I also remember not only what he told our guys when we all flew up to New York, but everything he had continually said to me and to both of us at each of the meetings we have had. He always told us he was glad we would be handling their money. I was way too stunned."

"Ok Jacob, I can follow that. I am sorry for you, for all of us, that this did not happen. That was a very big deal. I know you have put in a lot of time on this and I can only imagine how difficult this is for you right now. However, since it did not occur, and I am sorry for the timing of this, but I have been getting a lot of comments from Jackie Ravenel about your office. We keep no secrets here about how much business each of the brokers is doing. Your business has been way down the last few years and now, unless you have something new and substantial coming in, Jackie wants your office and I don't have a good reason to not give it to him. Let's just agree that, if by Labor Day your business has not dramatically picked up, you will graciously move to one of the other offices. We go way back, Jacob, but I manage the entire office and have to do what is best for everyone. Are we clear about this? Just remember something, Jacob. That was a gigantic deal. There is no one else I know of in the industry that could have gotten as close to it as you did. Absolutely no one! You are a very capable, very credible, very creative person. When you speak, you are understood. What got you so close to Southern Shipping was you. You can do the kind of business most brokers don't have a chance at doing. Just keep doing what you have been doing."

Jacob nodded, "Sure Pete. Thanks for that. I understand what you said. Let's see what happens."

Pete stood, and walked over to shake hands with Jacob. "I am really sorry Jacob, about all this. If I can help, let me know."

"Thanks Pete."

After his door was closed, Jacob sat back down and turned his chair to look out the windows. *'Great, Well this is it, my friend'*, Jacob thought. *'What do you want to do when you grow up? You better figure this out quick. You have 6 weeks to buy the house, 6 weeks to keep Jackie Ravenel out of this office. What do you want to do? Now Jackie Ravenel is an issue. Damn it!'* John Beaufain Rutledge Huger Ravenel was another broker in the office. Coming from a Very old Charleston family, he was cousins with everyone South of Broad, or so it seemed. Jackie never had to work at building a client base. He was born into it, and loved it. He came in late, left early and spent lots of that time at the Yacht Club. Yet, due to the policies of the brokerage industry, Jacob also knew that Jackie Ravenel was more than entitled to this office.

Jacob had plenty to think about that morning in his office while waiting for his meeting with Nathan Goldstein. But instead of dwelling on all this, he picked up his phone and started calling his clients, just to touch base and say hello.

Several hours later, Jacob went for an early lunch by himself, leaving with plenty of time to arrive for his meeting with Nathan Goldstein. As Jacob walked down Meeting Street, he saw the same female tour guide he had seen as he was walking out of Southern Shipping. He recognized her big smile immediately. And there she was again with a group of people, all of whom were listening to her intently as she was describing another of the historic buildings As Jacob was passing by the group, the woman looked at him, making brief eye contact and seemed to give him an extra smile. Jacob stopped briefly to hear what she was saying. What he noticed again was her enthusiasm, how lit up the woman seemed to be as she was describing a particular moment in Charleston's past.

Jacob wondered what it would be like to do what she did. How fun and interesting it would be! How nice it would be to spend the day outdoors, wandering the streets of Charleston talking with crowds of people about something totally real and interesting, not selling anything but instead sharing information and creating curiosity. History had always been an interest of Jacobs, especially in college. He had majored in History before realizing how much he especially liked writing about sports. So, his History major had changed to Journalism.

Jacob decided to skip lunch. He wasn't really hungry anyway and instead, he walked slowly in the shaded areas around the Historic District. The air was broiling hot, the humidity drenching and he guessed the heat index was well into triple digits. He was glad he had thought to buy a bottle of water at one of the Italian Ice stands that seemed to be on every downtown street corner on summer days.

Many of the historic homes in Charleston have a small wooden tablet mounted near the front door on which is written a brief history of that house. As he walked south on Meeting Street through the heavily shaded and well tended residential district, Jacob began reading them. As he walked from one to the next, he was repeatedly struck by how interesting the stories were. He realized that in all his years in Charleston, he had never taken the time to read many of the little histories written there, very short stories of the families who once lived in these homes. These were glimpses into centuries past, and of some of the people who made Charleston's history happen. Jacob looked more closely at some of the architectural details of a few of those buildings. It was easy to see the imagination someone once used to turn a long ago citizen of Charleston's dream of a house into reality, the extra added details reflecting long departed personalities. Some of the houses had raised rectangular stone blocks in front of them, which were stepping stones to carefully use as one emerged from a horse drawn carriage. These very streets had once been dirt roads, probably alternating from being very dusty to extremely muddy and especially funky.

He stood on the sidewalk, imagining the destruction caused to this street and to all of downtown Charleston during the Civil War, when the Union Army had bombarded the city daily for nearly eighteen months. In fact, despite the two wars fought here, the great earthquake of 1886, the frequent hurricanes, malaria and yellow fever epidemics, Charleston continued to always be not just one of the most beautiful cities in the world, but one of the most resilient: the city had always become an even better place after whatever catastrophes had come its way.

It occurred to him suddenly that a crucial part of the cycle of life must always include extraordinary damage from time to time to enable the great rebuilding that must follow, to make a better world than the one that had preceded it.

'Isn't that my world now, damaged and fragmented? Can't I also rise from these ruins into something equally remarkable?'

He knew in his soul that this was true. Like Charleston, he would rise again, better than ever.

As he walked further, reading more of these legends, another aspect of Charleston's history began to reveal itself to Jacob. There had been a continual infusion of new citizens into Charleston from throughout the other colonies and from Western Europe. With them came new thinking, new points of view, new ways of living and doing business. What new ideas could Jacob find and use? And the colorful yards he passed dazzled him. He wondered about the secret gardens behind many of these houses, the ones you could only see if invited by the property owners. What stories must lurk there?

Jacob had never considered how a short walk like this could leave him breathless with excitement about what the future could hold for him. This stroll to an appointment had done just that.

Jacob finally arrived on 0 1/2 Church Street, Nathan's leased carriage house. Jacob walked down an old brick pathway bordered by azaleas. The walls around him were yellow stucco beginning to crumble, revealing centuries old brick beneath it. Large window boxes were overflowing with red and deep blue flowering impatiens.

Sean answered Jacobs knock on the door and greeted him warmly. Jacob followed him to the library where Nathan rose smiling from a desk, evidently happy to see Jacob again. Today, Nathan was dressed in gray slacks and a buttoned down white shirt. Jacob could see more clearly just how pale Jacobs skin was, as if the man spent no time outdoors.

'Why does he own a boat if he doesn't like being outdoors? ' Jacob wondered.

"Jacob, it is so nice to see you again. I enjoyed your company last evening very much. Would you mind if we get straight to business? I must leave for New York within the hour."

"Certainly, Nathan. Last night really was a pleasure. Thanks again. If you would like to, here are the forms we will need to be completed for you to open an account with us, and to set up an incoming wire transfer of funds. Let's go through them. I only need a bit of information on this form and your signature to establish the initial account. The other forms we can receive later."

"Of course, these forms all look familiar. I will take all of them with me today and return them to you upon my return. My attorney will, of course, have to look them over. Can we meet again here Monday at this same time?"

Jacob had the sense he was getting blown off. After a few moments of closing conversation, Jacob wished Nathan a good trip back to New York and looked forward to seeing him next week.

'Perfect,' he thought,' *this isn't going to happen either. Funny he didn't ask again about Edmund, as everyone else seemed to be asking about nothing else. And, no mention at all of the tropical storm headed maybe our way, which was the other main topic of conversation in town.'*

Jacob walked the long way back to his office, being in no hurry to get back. He thought of the female tour guide.

'*What it would be like to take a tour with her? What it would be like to know her?'*

10

Jacob's sweat soaked shirt was already drying as he pushed *Pearl* away from his dock later that afternoon. He turned the wheel, motoring into a small breeze which stirred the still, dense humid air. The thick aroma of low country pluff mud seemed to form an extra layer on Jacob's skin; to him it felt like an ageless sense of belonging to the vast wonder of existence. His body began relaxing, his mind emptying of thoughts, his senses filling with the movement of the air, the scent of the marsh, the visual delight of the lush green marsh grass, and with the harmony of the redwing blackbirds singing nearby. *Pearl* moved slowly downstream, her hull beginning to absorb his feelings. An egret stood amongst the oyster shells on the creek's muddy bank. Passing some crab trap buoys, Jacob wondered about his own trap under the dock. He had forgotten to check it out.

Before him, high in the afternoon sky, Jacob could see some smaller birds chasing an osprey that turned evasively. He watched the smaller birds turning as if in unison with the larger bird. Jacob wondered just how birds communicated so intuitively, so deeply. He knew that he was jealous of this, wishing he could always have that deep a connection with everyone he interacted with.

The breeze quickened and Jacob raised first his jib and then main, set his sails and then cleated his lines as *Pearl* began to heel with the wind.

The creek finally joined the Intracoastal Waterway at the tip of Sullivan's Island.

Jacob looked over at Oliver and Susan's property, which stood on Sullivan's Island at the edge of Charleston Harbor. Known as The Point, it had been home to the Marshall family since not long after the end of the Revolutionary War. Its four acres were shaded by a large number of live oak trees, many of which had been planted soon after the original house and grounds had been destroyed during the Civil War. Amongst the oaks there stood a two-story island style house, with porches on both levels, along with several out buildings.

Seated on a plastic chair, Randy was fishing from The Point's large floating dock as *Pearl* eased by. Randy didn't respond to Jacob's hello. His head was down, apparently just watching his bobber. '*Must be asleep,*' Jacob guessed. The floating dock, which would normally have Oliver's fifty foot ketch *Susan* tied to it, seemed barren as Oliver and Susan were now off to Europe with their two college age girls. The only boat that was at the dock was a cabined Grady White, which sat out of the water on the boat lift. Jacob couldn't recall when he had first noticed that boat, not quite remembering it arriving, but knew that it had been on that lift for a few weeks now. '*Maybe it was a purchase Oliver had made awaiting his return?'* Something about that boat tugged at his memory and then passed as he neared the entrance to Charleston Harbor. His attention was drawn to a large yawl with a number of people on deck that was heading towards the ocean. Frequently, extraordinary boats passed through this harbor. Jacob was fascinated by many of them, wondering occasionally if one day he would have a sailboat substantially larger than *Pearl*.

And then Jacob and *Pearl* were in the harbor, still following the deep water channel. Across the way, huge cumulous clouds crowded over the city, outlining the rooftops and church steeples of Charleston. There was no immediate sign of an imminent thunderstorm, but Jacob knew that could change quickly on any late summer afternoon in South Carolina's lowcountry.

Thinking of the city, he tried to force his mind to not think of Southern Shipping, Edmund Capers and, most all, to not think of Jody Pickens, at least not right then.

Jacob had no particular destination in mind. He just wanted to be out on the water, to go wherever the wind and currents took him.

The tide was flowing hard out to sea. Jacob wished it would take him with it. However, the wind was picking up and seemed to have other ideas for him.

Three pelicans flew in a low line before him, skimming the harbors surface as they looked for dinner. Passing a channel marker, Jacob continued on in the general direction of Castle Pinckney, an ancient mid-harbor island fortress that now was a crumbling, overgrown relic of old times long forgotten. Jacob could see the silhouette of a large wooden ketch he didn't recognize sailing near there. He decided that he wanted to see that boat up close.

Before him, two shrimp boats drifted side by side. Jacob was close enough to see they were named *Never Easy* and *Miss Trish*. The shrimp boat crews were busy cleaning the decks, dumping into the harbor loads of dead fish, crabs and whatever else the nets had gathered but were not useful to the shrimpers. They must have had a big catch because a large crowd of seagulls, pelicans and terns filled the air above the boats, all diving into the water to grab an easy meal.

Jacob needed to watch this from up close. He quickly lowered the mainsail and altered his course to slowly circle the shrimpers.

Jacob easily noticed there were plenty of dolphins as well, more than he had seen gathered together in quite some time. They were also feeding. More and more dolphins appeared to have been called to the commotion. It seemed to Jacob that there were maybe hundreds of them; many were in a feeding frenzy near the shrimp boats, others made magnificent leaps before splashing back into the water. But some were slowly gliding by, circling the shrimpers. Both boat crews continued their work on deck, while they were also watching the fantastic scene before them.

Jacob went forward, lowered his sails and dropped his bow anchor, setting it in the harbor bottom. It grabbed quickly. Entranced by the pandemonium before him, Jacob barely acknowledged a low rumble of thunder far off to the west. Each leap of a dolphin pulled him with it. Jacob had forgotten his day, his week, all of his concerns. *Pearl* drifted closer to the shrimp boats. He had given the anchor line plenty of slack. Now he was close enough to even see some of the dolphin's eyes. He could hear them clearing their blowholes and see their scarred dorsal fins.

Jacob thought of some friends who had recently returned from the Florida Keys where they had swum with the dolphins. They had described it as a transformative experience, almost mystical. They talked about touching and actually holding on to the dolphins.

Jacob ached for that kind of experience. In fact, he suddenly needed it desperately. He had to know he really was still alive and connected to the life surrounding him. Jacob ached in that moment to instantly transcend his entire life experience, to just be at a whole new authentic level of existence. Most of all, he knew he longed to connect with the ancient streams of experience and knowledge that would finally tell him just what he needed to know. Maybe that stream was here now, flowing through the deep waters of Charleston Harbor. The dolphins, so much a part of these waters, so familiar with all of its depths and mysteries, could perhaps teach Jacob what he needed to finally understand.

And so, without any further thought, Jacob quickly took off his glasses. He ripped off his shirt and quickly went forward to re-check the anchor line. It was holding strong. Then he dove off the deck into the water below.

Jacob was going to swim with the dolphins. It was time for that remarkable transformative moment that had eluded him for so long.

The water felt a little too warm to him as he finally surfaced. He could see that the shrimpers seemed further away than he had guessed. *Pearl* was right where she should be. He began dog paddling slowly towards the main group of dolphins. He didn't have to go far. They were all around him. The water swirled with the life and motion surrounding him. His fingers suddenly brushed smooth skin that just had to be a dolphin. The touch seemed almost electric to him, startling him with its intensity. He didn't realize he was already amongst them. Jacob felt his heart beating way too fast. He made an effort to breathe slowly, treading water and drifting as he looked all around.

Jacob was getting really excited. He was actually surrounded by dolphins! The water filled him with a euphoric energy unlike anything he had ever experienced.

'This is beyond really cool, they were so right!' he thought.

As he drifted closer to the shrimp boats, he could see the t-shirted crews on deck were all looking in his direction.

"You stupid asshole, what are you doing?" yelled one of them.

Jacob couldn't quite make out the rest of what the guy had shouted, but it was obvious to him that the shrimpers weren't having the same peak mystical experience that he was.

Jacob could hear thunder and saw the sky darkening beyond the Cooper River Bridge.

Suddenly, a dolphin came almost straight out of the water before him, crashing right next to him. The animal bumped his shoulder and it really hurt. Then he was smacked again, this time on his left thigh, and that hurt even more. It was beginning to dawn on Jacob that maybe this wasn't such a great idea after all.

He looked for *Pearl* and for a frighteningly dizzying moment couldn't see her. He turned again in the water. '*Where is the damn boat?*" Fear rocketed through him from his toes through his ears. He turned again, forgetting the dolphins momentarily. A wave lifted him and he could see *Pearl*. She was not really far away at all. He began to swim towards her when something heavy banged his legs and feet. He was swimming as fast as he could, keeping his head straight up out of the water. The only thing he wanted to see was her hull and his stern ladder. He splashed wildly, hoping to keep as much of his body out of the water as he could.

He suddenly stopped swimming. His stomach felt like ice. He was barely breathing. His hands and feet barely moved. Time stood absolutely still.

He was being watched.

Perfectly framed in a green wave just before him was the eye of a large shark.

Jacob felt the eye staring at him, through him and moving slowly towards him. The shark's dark snout made a small wake before it as it came even closer. Jacob froze in sheer terror. The flat, deadly eye grew larger as the shark got closer. Jacob felt himself being drawn towards its terrible darkness. The world was silent and still all around him. Slowly, the eye vanished, replaced by a glistening dorsal fin as the shark descended into the water just beneath Jacob.

He exploded into panic. He felt his arms and legs plunging through the water with a primeval energy, pulling him to *Pearl*. If he could have, he'd be running. He swam as hard as he possibly could. His heart pounded, his ears burned, his brain was too shocked to think as his feet pounded through the water. His body felt as if it had turned into some form of gelatin. He hoped the boat was where he thought it was, but '*where was it?*' He stopped swimming to look for *Pearl*, but couldn't see her. He had no sense of breathing; he just wanted to zoom out of the water like a flying fish. He would do anything to get away from that terrible eye.

Jacob rose again on a wave, and as he searched for the boat, something bumped his leg. Fearing the shark, he moved even faster, rapidly going to *Pearl*, putting as much distance as he could between him and the shark. Suddenly the boat was within reach. By some miracle, the ladder was just before his fingers as a huge something banged his feet again. He pulled, launching himself through the air and landing hard on the deck just as a gentle rain began to fall.

Jacob rolled on to his back. He was totally consumed by his aching body and throbbing heart. His chest rose and fell rapidly with each breath. He felt dizzy and suddenly very cold. Slowly, he opened his eyes. The clouds above him were moving rapidly, darkening. Thunder boomed again. Slowly Jacob rose. The shrimp boats were moving away from him towards Shem Creek, the crews out of sight. The last of the sea gulls were still hovering over the waters, searching. Several dolphins cruised slowly past. The harbor was quiet.

Jacob felt remarkably energized. He was alive. He hurt all over but that was alright. His body was well used to some part of being injured. He thought of the shark, the frenzied waters and knew he had been one with it. Maybe he hadn't belonged there at all. But he had been there. He had been exactly in the middle of all that chaos. That energy was now and would forever be a part of him.

Jacob could feel tears beginning to stream from his eyes. His body shook with an overwhelming sense of fear and despair. He began to sob. Falling back to the deck, he rolled over and curled up on his side. Memories of his life flooded his every thought. He had never felt so suddenly alone, so totally unsure of who he was and his place in the world.

Jacob stared at the sky as eventually he sat up. Shivering, he surrendered to all he felt. Thunder boomed as the rain began to fall heavily. *Pearl* swayed as the harbor's waves continued to increase in size and strength. Jacob sat still, his arms wrapped around his knees as he wondered what was next; he watched the storm as it swept around him. He stood and quickly stripped his clothes off. The lashing rain quickly cleansed him before he went below.

Pulling the hatch tight behind him, he felt comforted by the familiarity of *Pearl's* cabin. Grabbing a towel, he wiped himself off as well as he could, then quickly slipped on some old cutoffs and a sweatshirt before collapsing onto the cushioned bench in the cabin. The boat was pitching, moving sideways and up and down. Jacob loved the feel of the boats response to weather, which seemed second nature to her hull. Thunder boomed again with great flashes of lightning. He thought of the storm that brought him to this harbor long ago. He had passed right by this spot. It was impossible for him to have realized then that all these years later, he and *Pearl* would still be here.

Jacob wasn't much of a drinking man, but he kept a new bottle of Jameson's Irish Whiskey aboard for his friends that were. He found the bottle and poured an inch or so into a coffee mug. The sensation of it slowly rolling down his throat was perfect. He thought about the dolphins. His friends had been right; the experience had been remarkable. Jacob felt alive and excited. The experience hadn't been what he expected, but that's the thing about expectations. You have to let go of them so you can be amazed and possibly transformed by what actually happens.

As the storm continued to drench the boat, he laid down on his cabin bed, listening to the storm violently passing over. *Pearl* was rocking steadily. He closed his eyes, thankful to be here, safe and dry, out of the storm.

He allowed his thoughts of Jody, always at least at the periphery of his mind, to finally wash through him.

He began remembering their first actual date.

She was living downtown on Tradd Street in a carriage house behind an eighteenth century three-story brick house. When he walked down the driveway to pick her up, Jacob had been nervous. He hadn't felt that way in a long time. He hadn't even been sure what clothing would be the best choice for a first date. He worried he was over dressed, even though he was just wearing what he considered to be a nice shirt and slacks. He was taking her for dinner at Cecile's, a fantastic local Italian place not found on any of the tourist maps. He had thought about bringing her some flowers, and then had to laugh, realizing that was probably a tad way over the top.

As he approached Jody's carriage house, the scent of jasmine filled the air. Her place was in the middle of a garden. Flowering shrubs grew in abundance throughout the yard that included tea olives, crepe myrtles, azaleas, and oleanders. The carriage house was built with old brick, covered in most places with stucco. It sat beneath a massive live oak. The walls of the little house were mostly enveloped beneath a thick tangle of confederate jasmine still in bloom. On the porch were pots of blooming blue petunias and coleus, along with basil and thyme. He knocked on the old, thick wooden door and Jody was right there before him, smiling. Her hair was done up, just a little, and she wore a fantastic purple and red patterned dress.

"Hey" he said. "You look fantastic!"

"So do you," she responded, never taking her eyes from his.

When he started to reach for her he found she was already in his arms, her arms around his shoulders. Jacob could feel her fingers on his neck as Jody sensually dragged her finger nail across it. The sensation was remarkable, unexpected and totally erotic. Jacob felt instantly aroused throughout his body, all his thoughts drawn completely into that moment

Jody took his hand in hers and brought him into her house. His first impression was of lots of paintings and photographs, mostly landscapes, which hung on each of the walls. In the dining area, there were several sketches of nude women, as well as a photo of a very beautiful woman dappled in sunlight as she lay naked across a fallen tree, her exquisite eyes softly looking directly into the camera lens. An easel in the living room held a half finished oil which appeared to be of the garden just outside the door. Above the fireplace was a portrait of a beautiful, older woman with remarkable facial features and piercing eyes.

"That's my Granny Laurie Lynn, I loved her so much" said Jody. "Momma's momma, they lived across the valley and we played at their house all the time. She and Granddaddy Leon had this little farm with peaches and horses and goats. Granny Laurie Lynn could grow anything. Jacob, she always had a fantastic garden and in the fall we always had gigantic pumpkins. There were lots of chickens. Granddaddy Leon was always working in the fields and used to let me drive his tractor with him. He had huge hard-working hands. That's like my first memory of him, not him, but of his hands in front of me on the steering wheel of the tractor. I'd sit in his lap, whenever I could, riding those fields. I'd love to watch his hands as he moved the wheel, or when he was fixing something. I always thought he could do anything. It's probably why I like to really look at people's hands. You learn lots about somebody just by studying their hands. Like yours Jacob, you've got really strong hands for a guy who sits in front of a computer all day!"

Jacob loved her soft southern accent; the way her eyes flashed excitedly as she gestured with her constantly in motion hands creating air-sketches before him. A big orange cat with a funny looking twist in his tail walked by, rubbing his body against Jody's bare, shapely calves.

"Allieo, can you say hi to Jacob?"

Without a glance in his direction, the cat chose instead to saunter over to the front door that he pushed open wider so he could go outside.

"He's a good kitty Jacob, he'll like you."

Jody and Jacob walked the few blocks to Cecile's. Over dinner, they talked and talked, laughing often into each other's eyes. It had felt as if they were the only people in the restaurant that night. Leaving, they slowly walked arm in arm with no destination necessary, just both of them enjoying the energy between them. The restaurant was not far from Market Street. Jacob happened to notice a flyer taped to the back of a sign that said a band called Blues Blasters was playing that night, in fact right then, at Myskins, the long -time home for great music and dancing in Charleston, and just a few blocks away.

"You got your dancing shoes on, Jody?"

"They never leave my feet!"

Entering Myskins, someone was singing, 'If the house is a rockin, don't bother knockin', just come on in.' And the place was rocking. The dance floor was packed with people dancing wildly to the tremendous beat, and the big room was heating up fast. Blues Blasters were hot and Jacob and Jody jumped right into it. They danced together in a natural rhythm as if they had been doing this for a long, long time. One great song followed another. Jody flew around Jacob as they rocked along to a fantastic rhythm. And then, finally, there was a slow song. Jacob and Jody just fell together, holding each other close, moving slowly together.

Jacob was glowing inside, feeling primal. Every sense was opened up wide. He pulled his head back to look at Jody. She was in a state of reverie. She was looking at him, their eyes locked, pulling them together. Their foreheads met together for a wonderful moment. Then they kissed for the first time, a long, slow perfect kiss. When the band started rocking again, so did Jody and Jacob. Finally, after the bands second set, it was time to leave.

As they neared Jody's house, she turned to face him. Holding both of his hands in hers, she shyly looked away and then directly into his eyes.

"This has been such a wonderful night. I am thinking that I don't want you to leave but I know you should, but this isn't really our first date, and, well, I haven't been with anyone in a long time, and, well, would you like to stay for a while, and maybe you could stay over, if you want? Do you want to come in for awhile? But could we please not have sex tonight? Would that be OK? Am I being too fast here? I haven't felt like this Jacob, not for a long time, and I need to catch up to all I am feeling, but I don't want you to go. Am I talking too much? "

Jacob didn't think so. He kissed her gently on the forehead and said that sounded like a perfect idea.

They returned to her garden. Allieo greeted them, again rubbing between Jody's bare legs as she unlocked the front door. Jody brought out a bottle of red wine. They shared a glass as the cat walked around them wondering who this Jacob was. He jumped onto the sofa and settled in next to Jody, arching his back slightly when she rubbed it. Then Allieo got up and walked over Jody and lay down between them, allowing his tail to gently rest on Jacob's thigh. The cat started to purr.

"He likes you! Allieo never does that with anyone, not even with any of my girlfriends when they come over."

They lay together all that night, kissing, talking softly, holding each other, looking at each other in the moonlight. Finally they had drifted into sleep, still embracing.

Jacob shook himself from the memory and sighed. He could hear and feel the storm was beginning to move out to sea. He went up on deck. Despite the light rain still falling, he hoisted *Pearl's'* sails. He wasn't ready to go back to Sullivan's Island. He felt drawn to the deep waters beyond the harbor. They seemed to be calling to him, as if a voice was speaking to him in a tone that he couldn't quite hear.

Pearl's starboard rail skimmed the ocean's surface as the boat drove towards the open sea. Jacob was exhilarated by the huge wind pushing him. Spray flew back at him as the bow plunged through the storm-tossed waves, chasing the lightning striking again and again in the dark clouds before him. Night was beginning to fall and yet he continued on, guided by a compass deep in his soul.

He felt free. He yowled in ecstasy. The cry came from deep within him as he exulted in the sensation of running free, of feeling released. He was unconstrained by any thoughts or concerns. Jacob sensed the wind passing right through him, as if each molecule of his body blended with those of the sea and the sky. He could just keep on this heading for days and days, and never have to change course. He could just go.

A pair of dolphins suddenly broke the surface together in front of *Pearl*. They leaped in unison, with a huge splash reflecting sunset's last glow sparkling in the air before re-entering the stormy waters. The sight thrilled and spoke to him. It said there was something remarkable lurking just below the surface. He just had to put himself in a position to see it.

Jacob realized that he had no further interest in sailing off any further into the night. Not just then. Now he needed to find out what his special work was. Perhaps this was why he had felt so pulled to come out here.

Jacob knew what he had to do.

He put the helm to leeward. It was time to return to Sullivan's Island. He needed to move on.

As Jacob neared the Intracoastal Waterway, he could see that several lights were again shining upstairs at The Point.

'*Hmmm, what is going on up there? No one is home. Maybe Randy was looking for something and forgot to turn the lights off?*' Jacob wondered.

Suddenly the lights went out. The Point was dark except for some outdoor lighting dimly glowing in the light rain that had begun to fall.

11

'*Tell me again why I am doing this?*' wondered Ginny Street as she jogged onto the Sullivan's Island beach through the dunes at Station 18. Far off on the horizon to her left, great streaks of red and orange splashed across the sky as the sun was just beginning to reveal itself. She turned right, towards Charleston, so that the sun wouldn't do too much damage to her eyes and especially to her brain. Last evening had turned into yet another extra fun, extra late night at Bert's Bar, but Ginny was still determined to fit back into one of her old bathing suits by summer's end, which wasn't far away now.

'*Just 3 more pounds to go, that's why.*'

She had lived on Sullivan's Island most of her life. Being on the beach at this time of day had once meant that Ginny hadn't gone to bed yet. Now, her legs were beginning to ache and she was jealous of her husband Fred, still sleeping. She laughed. Ginny and Fred had a bet as to who would lose the most weight over the summer and she was way ahead. '*He's gonna pay,*' she laughed to herself. Ginny had come to appreciate just how beautiful it was here on the island early in the day. She was glad she had started exercising again because her early morning runs had turned into a wonderful habit that she now didn't think she'd give up anytime soon. Running also made her feel easier about going to Bert's, which she considered a reward for all her hard work.

The beach was becoming more visible. Lights from shrimp boats bounced across the horizon from Folly Beach. A container ship was coming up the channel from Charleston, quietly heading to sea. In the near distance, Ft. Sumter was still in darkness. The rushing waves were mingling with the morning light like a watercolor painting with colors running together in shades of yellow, orange and red.

A bunch of Laughing Gulls were making a ruckus as she rounded the curve on the beach leading to the harbor. Ginny started looking more closely at the gulls. Some were hovering over something large lying at the edge of the waves, others flying about. Ginny feared it might be a dead dolphin or a sea turtle. The gulls were noisily surrounding it. Curious as to what it could be, Ginny trotted over.

And then she was wondering if she'd had 2 or 3 beers too many.

It looked more like a person. As she got closer, Ginny started feeling sick. An awful smell filled the air. Something was dead and rotting.

It was a person laying there, a badly mangled body wrapped in seaweed. A rope of some sort was wrapped around the legs.

'His head shouldn't be like that, and his arm, where's his arm and ..Oh my god, no!'

Ginny fell to the sand, vomiting. Crabs covered the corpse before her, crawling over what little remained above the bodies neck.

~~

Jacob slept late that morning. His dreams had been awful. Dolphins with giant teeth chased him down his street while a group of turkey buzzards sat on top of his car which was parked next to the road but without any tires. People were watching him running without any pants on as he searched for trees to climb in the middle of the beach.

As he had been hosing off and squaring away *Pearl* back at the dock the night before that there was no way he was going to the office today. He would take the day off, have a long weekend and start to figure out just what he was going to do with his life.

With his morning coffee in hand, he stepped out on to his porch. Immediately, he saw a Sullivan's Island Police SUV driving along the beach before him with blue lights flashing.

'*What in the world?*' Jacob quickly walked down the path to the beach. Standing on a dune, he saw a large crowd gathered together further up the beach, surrounded by police and emergency vehicles. When he started walking in that direction, he could see something being lifted from the sand and placed in the back of one of the trucks. As it drove off with red lights slowly turning, the other vehicles began driving off as well. The crowd began to disperse.

Seeing no one headed his way, Jacob returned to his house, knowing if there was something he should know about, he would hear about it sooner or later. He was anxious to get out of town, eager to get away from the craziness of the past week. He yet again thought about all of the details of last few days; the missing Edmund, the no deal with Southern Shipping, Nathan Goldstein, and then, the shark. He could still see the shark's flat dark eye staring at him with that dead on arrival look.

'What was I thinking?'

Jacob thought about Capt. Anson Caper's statue, the look in those eyes. They reminded him of the sharks. Come to think of it, so did the look in Buddy Capers eyes when he told Jacob there was no deal. And what about his brief and to the point meeting with Pete? The bottom line on what Peter Madison had told him was clear. If Jacob was going to continue being a stockbroker, he had better get a move on with his business.

Jacob knew that it wasn't at all about having to give up the premier office. For him, now, it was about whether or not he wanted to continue being a stockbroker. Nathan Goldstein maybe offered a way to do that, but Jacob wasn't sure being in the securities industry for even another day was what he really wanted to do. However, his option to buy his house was due at the end of August, in just five weeks. He really wanted to never move from this house and had counted on the Southern Shipping deal to make that happen. There was no back- up plan. What investments he had left wouldn't be nearly enough unless he succeeded at something incredibly risky and stupid to even try. His most recent personal investment choices had been more than dumb, it seemed.

Jacob was overwhelmed. He needed to get settled down somewhere else to be able to digest it all. Maybe then he would be able to figure it out and be able to move forward.

Then in his mind he could again see the deadly eye of that shark; it still seemed so close, so intense. He could still feel the sensation of the shark disappearing beneath him. It had been frightening and yet exciting, the energy surge unforgettable. It was a sensation he had been missing. He knew he was lucky he had been able to get back to *Pearl* alive, without any damage to his body.

'*Why is all this happening?*' Jacob wondered.

Then he remembered the awesome beauty of the storm moving away; the twin dolphins leaping, creating a rainbow with their spray.

'*That was why!*'

There was something out there for him. He needed to find it.

'*Where was Edmund Capers? What had happened at Southern Shipping?*' Maybe he was over thinking it, but not landing the business didn't completely make sense because of Edmund's repeated comments at all of those meetings that it was a done deal. Yet, it hadn't happened.

'*And what about with the sudden appearance of Nathan Goldstein? What about the encounter with the shark last night? What had he been thinking?*' It had definitely been exciting. He was grateful he had survived. Maybe the opportunity

Nathan presented was just what he had needed, but that also didn't completely make sense either.

'Why would a guy just show up like that and be so quick to offer $5 million to a total stranger? Is something else going on here that I am clueless about? It makes no sense. Maybe life isn't supposed to make sense, maybe what it is, is all it ever is."

Jacob called the office, leaving a message for Carol that he wouldn't be in until Monday, but to call him if something urgent came up. He hoped he wouldn't hear from her.

Jacob knew exactly where he was going. For him it was a no-brainer.

He was going to Whistling Dixie.

Whistling Dixie was an island, a golf course, a great place to fish, a forest and black water swamp. For Jacob, it was a state-of-mind.

It was a place where pirates had once camped and, very likely, had buried some treasure. Since well before the Revolutionary War, blockade runners and other smugglers had known this island well.

Every Saturday night there was world class barbeque as well as great music. Whistling Dixie was owned by his friends Oliver and Matthew Marshall.

Its actual name is Conch Island. Several miles long and equally wide, the northern end of the island is bounded by Conch Creek, which runs from its deep water entry on the Intracoastal Waterway through the marshes before flowing into the Great Wambaw Swamp. Miles into the swamp, Conch Creek eventually joins up with Chicken Creek, which in turn runs all the way through the Francis Marion Forest before finally emptying into the upper Wando River, which forms part of Charleston Harbor.

The island had been owned by the Marshall family for centuries. Family legend had it that William Marshall, the son of Maxwell, had purchased it on advice from his mother, who at one time had been known as Anne Bonny, the infamous female pirate. William initially used it as a base for smuggling goods into Charleston during the days when it was still a British Colony. The British tariffs then on any imported goods had made it impossible for any merchant to survive unless they turned to the black market, which the Marshalls had made every effort to dominate.

The Marshall's ancestral wealth began in those days. The business that had come to be known as Coastal Traders had been started by the Scotsman, Captain Maxwell Marshall, back in the early 1700s. Captain Marshall brought trade goods to the Caribbean and returned to the American colonies with cargoes of sugar cane and rum. Eventually, William had successfully expanded the business into smuggling. Conch Island, as it was then known, had remained in the Marshall family ever since.

It was Conch Island where the Marshall-Capers family feud had found a home base. The legend was that Matthew and Oliver's ancestral grandfather, Maxwell Marshall, had met Anne Bonny in Cuba while he was delivering goods on his ship *Raven*. Anne had been in hiding in Havana, on the run because of her piracy. She was pregnant as well. Maxwell had quickly fallen in love with her and married Anne there. He had assumed the role of the child's father.

The real father was believed to have been another pirate known as Calico Jack Rackham. Maxwell brought Anne back to her hometown of Charleston in disguise and with the new name of Sarah. Upon returning to Charleston with Anne, Maxwell had been proud to proclaim the child to be his first born son. William.

Anne was soon pregnant again, and many more Marshall's were to follow.

Inevitably, the Capers had at some point recognized her as being the cursed Anne Bonny. Immediately, they began plotting to avenge what she had done to Capt. Capers. None of those plans had succeeded. And then, some years later when Capt. Andrew Capers was fleeing some British patrol ships, he had attempted to sneak through Conch Creek with his smuggled goods to hide in the swamp. He was stopped by the Marshalls, who kept a well manned barge with a deck mounted cannon at anchor across Conch Creek. They wanted to be sure no one slipped by, anticipating that the Capers or other smugglers at some point would need to use the creek, and then would have to pay the Marshall's for the privilege. When they demanded payment for access, Capers had refused to pay. The delay allowed the British the opportunity to capture and execute Andrew Capers, as well as seize his cargo.

When word of this reached downtown Charleston, the Capers family began planning their own form of revenge. They began sabotaging the Marshall's ships wherever and whenever they were found. The Marshalls retaliated. The feud grew from there. It has been completely no holds barred ever since, ruthless cutthroat competition being the operative agenda for both families.

Around the turn of the century, Oliver's grandfather Willie, a direct descendant of William, had built a golf course on Conch Island. Willie had been to Scotland on business and, while there, played golf at St Andrews. He had never played the game until then and he had instantly loved it. Recognizing the physical similarity of Scotland with parts of Conch Island, he brought back with him a young Scottish golf architect named Alistair MacBryde to design a golf course that blended perfectly amongst the dunes and forest along the South Carolina coast.

MacBryde created a masterpiece of a golf course on Conch Island. Willie Marshall intended the course to be just a private place for him and his friends to play, and so it remained until the Great Depression of the 1930's. Some decades later, Oliver's father William had slowly brought the course back into shape and now it was still a very private course. Matthew Marshall referred to himself the Touring Pro of Whistling Dixie because he traveled so much and hoped this self-designation might help him play on other more exclusive private golf courses around the world.

These days, the only grounds keeper for the course was Old Noah, a man who had simply showed up at Whistling Dixie one day during a storm. He had been on a crab boat out of McClellanville, and Old Noah had decided to stay and look after the place, which was fine with Oliver Marshall. Noah had a real gift for fixing machinery, as well as an instinct about how a golf course should be maintained, especially when to mow the fairways and greens. He let the rough along the fairways grow as much as they wanted to, just as he had once noticed while watching the British Open on television.

Jacob was anxious to arrive at Whistling Dixie It was a special place and he loved being there to do whatever he wanted to. It was the one place beyond the cockpit of *Pearl* or his home where life seemed to rearrange itself perfectly. It was a place where he felt a sense of peace and comfort.

He acknowledged he was just running away. He didn't care. Running from the life he had been living, towards what, he didn't know. He felt maybe he was a fake. He had a strong sense of no longer knowing who he was, what he wanted. He was afraid. He recognized that he was filled with self doubt. And Jacob knew this wasn't really the first time he had sensed this. It had been there for a long time, since well before he first met Edmund Capers and started chasing the great Southern Shipping deal. Maybe the truth was that deal was just an excuse for him, a form of denial that sounded good and looked real.

He wished he could sail *Pearl* right back into the middle of that tropical storm and find a way through it, go back to New Jersey for awhile, and then continue on with the life he thought he was living up until that moment when sailing into Charleston Harbor was the only possible thing he could have done.

He had stopped traveling. The trip to New Jersey was really when he had started running.

From what or to what he didn't know.

Now, he needed to get to Whistling Dixie. Quickly!

He was eager to get started out of town. He needed to be as far away from the past week as possible. He visited *Pearl*, making sure all her lines were secure and everything was ship-shape .Jacob returned to his house, packed a few items in an overnight bag, threw his golf clubs and shoes into the Honda and left.

12

Just the idea of leaving town was allowing his sense of anxiety to drop. Jacob was suddenly quite hungry as he drove north on Hwy 17 towards Whistling Dixie and he began to wonder where he might get a quick bite to eat. Luckily, Jacks Cosmic Dogs, arguably the home of the South's best hot dogs and french fries, was just opening as he entered the parking lot. He was always hungry for one of Jacks meatloaf and chili sandwiches and thought maybe he should get two, at least.

Walking into Jack's low slung single story building was always fun even before you went through the door. It was just like walking into any of Jacob's favorite eating places when he was a teenager in New Jersey. Hanging from the ceilings were some old flying rocket ships, plenty of 1960 period pieces were everywhere you looked and the walls were covered with old posters of great rock n rollers. Jack had crates of Nehi and Cheerwine sodas as part of the décor and draft root beer on tap.

Even though Jacob didn't especially care for hot dogs, lots of other people did, especially Charlie. It occurred to him that the last time he had been to Jack's was earlier that spring, during a weekend Charlie had spent at Jacob's place. He brought Charlie to Jack's for dinner and apparently the food agreed with him because after eating four chili cheese dogs and a pile of French fries, all of which was washed down with two bottles of Cheerwine, Charlie had claimed to still be hungry.

Jacob thought about the boy, remembering that Tadpole had said Charlie wanted to speak with him. It had seemed urgent. '*About what?*' Jacob wondered, having not heard from him.

In the line at Jack's counter, there was a man with an Ohio State hat on backwards just in front of him. The guy was dressed in plaid shorts and a t-shirt which read on its back 'Follow me to the Magic Kingdom.' Jacob had a feeling this guy might just be passing through town. When the out-of-towner got to the head of the line, the young man working the counter asked:

'What can we get for you?'

'I'll have a Swiss cheeseburger all the way, with fries and a draft Root beer.'

'We don't have cheeseburgers. How about a Cosmic Dog? Most people love them."

"Then make it a cheddar cheeseburger with all the rest."

"We don't serve cheeseburgers. How about an Atomic Dog? They are really good. "

"Then make it an American cheeseburger, all the way."

"Mister, let me ask you something. Can you spell cat, as in catbird?"

"Sure. C-A-T."

"Can you spell dog, as in hotdog?"

"Sure D-O-G."

"Can you spell freak, as in cheeseburgers?"

"'There's no freak in cheeseburgers."

"That's what I've been trying to tell you. We don't have any freak'n cheeseburgers .How about a chili cheese dog?"

When Jacob ordered, he started by saying "I guess I shouldn't order a chili cheeseburger."

Jacob ordered his meatloaf sandwiches to go. While waiting for his food, Jacob sat at one of the tall round tables, savoring a Nehi grape soda. He called Tadpole, inviting him to come up to Whistling Dixie the following day for some golf, barbeque and some serious dancing. Jacob then asked about Charlie. Tadpole still hadn't seen or heard from him, but would ask Smalls to find Charlie and have him call Jacob.

Hanging up, Jacob listened to some local radio station music being played throughout the restaurant. Tom Petty finished performing 'Refuge' and then a news bulletin came on. 'Sullivan's Island Police are confirming that the body of a man did wash ashore this morning in the vicinity of Ft. Moultrie. No further details are available. In other news, Tropical Storm Danielle continues to gain strength and could be a Category One hurricane by the end of the day. The current track has Danielle passing through the Leeward Islands by night fall and headed towards the Bahamas.

"*Oh my god,*' Jacob thought, immediately thinking of Edmund Capers. '*No way!*'

His order was ready and he headed on to his car, fishing several of Jack's outstanding french fries out of the bag to eat as he walked to the Honda. It was scorching hot outside with almost no breeze.

Just for the heck of it, Jacob called Edmunds cell phone again, but the voice mail box was full. Driving north, he thought again about Nathan Goldstein, wanting to make sense of that meeting. He wondered about the tropical storm that was now a hurricane that was maybe headed to Charleston.

'That would fit perfectly with this week, wouldn't it?'

Jacob continued driving north. Relaxing even more, he was glad to be headed out of town, making an effort at not looking in the rear view mirror at the days and years behind him.

Finally, as he neared the turn off Hwy 17North to Whistling Dixie, Jacob passed a group of sweet grass basket roadside stands clustered around a restaurant called Crab Cakes n' Such. Although these basket stands were simply constructed with 2x4's and plywood, they couldn't have been more important to the locals who worked them. The baskets were created by the original slaves to arrive in the Charleston area. Working in the rice paddies of the original plantations on the Ashley River, those slaves had needed a means of sifting the rice. Utilizing the only materials available to them, they fashioned the various marsh grasses, pine straw and palmetto leaves into crude baskets. As the decades had passed, their basket making techniques improved Centuries later, these baskets had evolved into an art form. They came to be made in many different shapes and sizes and have various purposes. Many thousands of these baskets were sold every year for hundreds of dollars each. They could be found not only in the City Market or along Meeting Street downtown, but also in road side stands going out of town. For many of the people in this part of Charleston County, making and selling sweet grass baskets was their principal form of income .Jacob owned several of them, primarily because he liked looking at them. He was always impressed by how hard the woman who made these worked. The basket making techniques were a priceless heritage. The ingenuity of the slaves had resulted in a cultural identity and an economic basis for the future generations of their offspring that was a perfect form of continuity.

Just past the basket stands, Jacob turned onto the long pine tree and oak lined dirt road from Hwy 17 that led to Whistling Dixie. As he drove along, he passed through the little community known as Destiny.

Destiny had been founded just after the Civil War by a group of newly freed slaves who had all lived in the area. It was what you would call a small town. The business district consisted of an old faded clapboard convenience store that didn't seem to have ever needed a name. The building next door to it was one of the tiniest post offices in the United States. Scattered nearby under the pines and scrub oaks on either side of the dirt road were a number of small houses, all of which were painted a variety of vivid colors. The little homes were well maintained and each had small vegetable and flower gardens. Many of the ladies who made the sweet grass baskets lived in Destiny. Making and selling sweet grass baskets was the community's primary business. They kept their children constantly busy either making baskets or gathering the materials, which were found on the edge of the marshes that wove through the surrounding forest. Some boys were playing basketball in one of the yards Jacob passed. Others were walking down another dirt road from the forest, each carrying long bundles of marsh grass.

As he finished driving through Destiny, Jacob thought of the contrast between the little community and Charleston's East Side neighborhood. Many of the residents from the two communities were related, one way or another, but the inner city neighborhood was a shambles and this little place in the forest was orderly and thriving. He always wondered why that was.

Driving through Destiny always gave Jacob a good dose of optimism and happiness. It calmed his mind and helped him to be more aware of just where he was and where he was going, that the past never equaled the future.

The familiar entrance to Whistling Dixie finally appeared on his left. The white wooden gates stood open between ancient, lichen covered brick walls that trailed off in both directions deep between the old oaks and pines. The sign above the gate simply read Whistling Dixie Fishing and Golf Club, the words wrapped around a crossed golf club and fishing rod. Spanish moss dripped from a huge live oak limb above the gate.

Driving in, he immediately crossed over the little wooden bridge that covered Sammy's Creek, which ran from the swamp down to the Intracoastal Waterway. Jacob could see Old Noah's wooden shack well off to his right amidst the pines down near the waterway, but no one seemed to be around. Jacob continued down the dirt road dappled in sunlight under a thick canopy of huge live oaks so thick that the limbs whose limbs twisted and dipped in all directions. The forest stretched on either side of the entry road. The Great Wambaw Swamp was near, off to the left at the edge of the golf course. Several wild turkeys crossed before him and he stopped to let them pass. As he waited, Jacob lowered his windows to let the air circulate in his car. A breeze filled the car with fragrances of the forest, swamp and great marshes; the lush smell of ancient trees and pluff mud blended together. The rich aroma of pluff mud is the defining scent of the Lowcountry of South Carolina, an aroma that once it is in you, it never quite leaves you. It is a fragrance you either love or dislike intensely, and despite his generally poor sense of smell, it was one Jacob found thoroughly irresistible.

Despite the great heat, it felt mighty good to be in nature again, far from the world. Susan Marshall had once said that perhaps a better name for the island was The Land of the Lost Boys because here you were ageless in a place where time did seem to stand still. Jacob looked about him. A slight breeze was coming up. He could see white and yellow flowers, thick wisteria vines running up some of the pines as well as many of the oaks with an abundance of low plant undergrowth.

Jacob came finally to the beginning of the golf course to his left. He could see Old Noah was on his tractor mowing the elevated 7th green. Recognizing the car, Noah raised his hat in greeting while never slowing his mowing.

Jacob passed a giant magnolia on his right. The old mansion at the end of the road came immediately into view, with most of the golf course to his left. Looking across the fairways as he continued on, he could see the small church as well as the high stone walls surrounding the Marshall family graveyard that Andrew Marshall had built there primarily using ballast from their ships. Family legend had it that pirate treasure believed to have been Blackbeard's had been found in the very spot where the grave of William Marshall had been dug. Marshall family history also said that many other pirates had frequented Conch Island. It was positioned close to Bulls Bay and had several creeks and nearby rivers that would have been useful for a quick getaway. Long ago the island had many tall sand dunes near the creek, which had served as lookout posts with a good view of ocean vessels headed towards Charleston. Legend went on to say that Blackbeard had often put ashore there. The pirate was said to have once come on the island with a small crew to carry and bury some of his treasure, after which he murdered them so that only he would know the exact location of the loot.

Jacob stopped the Honda in front of the mansion, which was now a combination pro shop, dining room, business office and sometime home for the usually traveling somewhere Matthew Marshall. Jacob was glad to be there and got out of his car and stretched. He looked over the waterway to the marsh and the scrub oak and wax myrtle covered islands to the southwest, knowing Bulls Bay and the Atlantic Ocean were just beyond them. Continuing his stretch, Jacob could see the four little cabins beneath the ancient cedars near the boat and fishing dock on Conch Creek and looked forward to getting settled into his place.

A massive, centuries old oak which had withstood countless storms was over on the edge of the waterway. Amongst the limbs of that tree was a small dock which had somehow lodged there after the great hurricane of 1964. The dock had been fashioned into what was now The Treehouse Bar, accessible by a circular wooden stairwell Oliver had constructed to provide a safe way for over-imbibers to safely leave. Near the old oak, Jacob could see smoke rising above the old shed that Noah and his brother Hiram used to make their barbeque, which many connoisseurs considered the best on the coast of either of the Carolinas.

Jacob felt almost as at home at Whistling Dixie as he did at his own house. There was such a familiarity to the place. The golf course was one he especially loved because it was beautiful and extremely difficult. Winding back through the swamp and forest, and then coming back into the dunes near the clubhouse, the course had big wide fairways and the most difficult putting surfaces to be found anywhere. The grass on those greens was never perfectly cut, and had so many tremendous slopes that there were few level spots on any of them. The only good news about Whistling Dixie as a golf course was that it had no sand traps. The bad news was MacBryde had created, instead, many deep earthen bunkers which were always so overgrown with grass that they were not only really hard to find your ball in, they were all the more challenging to hit your ball out of. The greens were placed in every single spot a diabolical golf architect would put them to make the course as difficult as possible. Par was 72 for Whistling Dixie, and 6 of the greens served as double holes, meaning there were 2 pins on them and you better know which one you were aiming for.

Matthew Marshall had once said that any golfer who thought this course was easy might as well start Whistling Dixie. That seemed an apt name and it stuck. Each of the holes had only one tee, so no matter who you were and how good your game was, at Whistling Dixie, each of the holes were the same length for every player. Only the really good and competitive female golfers enjoyed playing there for that reason. It was a private course with no more than 50 members. The Marshalls did not operate it as a business, but just as a place they enjoyed going to and bringing along some friends. Since during the summer most of the members rarely played due to the heat, Old Noah generally only mowed each fairway once a week and the greens twice, so the summer putts were always difficult. The pin locations rarely changed. The course was never watered. Oliver and Matthew felt it rained enough in the Lowcountry to make the course manageable, and if there was a drought, it wouldn't kill the Bermuda grass, it would just keep it a bit shorter.

The other thing people did at Whistling Dixie was fish. There was an abundance of opportunity in the marshes, as well as in Bulls Bay which was close by. Jacob fished off the dock sometimes, but really enjoyed drifting with the tide down the many little creeks in one of the small Jon boats always on hand. He didn't consider himself much of a fisherman, but he nearly always caught something he could share with others to eat. The mansion had a great kitchen and Dickey, the full time caretaker, was a really good cook.

Oliver Marshall had long ago given Jacob exclusive use of one of the cabins. Since there were so few people there, Oliver liked the idea of someone keeping an occasional extra eye on the place. The cabins were built from heart of pine, each just one big room with a bathroom, a stone fireplace, a little kitchen area, a sofa, chairs and a big old iron-framed bed. Jacob's cottage usually doubled as a store room filled with golf and fishing gear, so he really didn't need to bring anything with him except some clothes. Old wooden rockers sat on the covered porch in front and were the perfect place to watch before you the ever changing view of Conch Creek and the marsh all around it. Sitting there, one could easily see faraway to the forest and the edge of the Great Wambaw Swamp. Huge azaleas and camellias filled the open space between the cabins amidst the cedar trees whose trunks were thick with age. There were no other vehicles visible other than the old Land Cruiser Oliver kept on the property.

As he stood stretching before the mansion, a younger dark haired man with a ponytail came walking down the steps to greet him.

"Jacob, what a great surprise !"

"Hey, Dickey, how goes it?' smiled Jacob. Other than Noah, Dickey Macoun was the only full time resident at Whistling Dixie. He was not only a caretaker as well as the cook, but he also took care of any golfing or fishing needs that any of the members might have. In the absence of both Oliver and Matthew, Dickey was additionally the organizer and occasional emcee for the Saturday night music at Whistling Dixie.

"Dickey, I am going to be here for the weekend. Which band do you have playing tomorrow night?"

"We have a great one, Jacob. Do you remember Doc Rock and the Disorderlies? They played a few months ago. Some guys from around here somewhere, I think they are mostly computer geeks. They really cook!"

Every Saturday night for many, many years, a band of some sort, usually rock n roll, blues or electrified bluegrass, played in the barn at Whistling Dixie. It had originally been an idea of Matthew Marshalls to help Randy, hoping if he could get settled back into the music he loved, that maybe he could get his life more on some sort of track. It hadn't helped create much in the way of good music though, because Randy tended to do extended solos that veered far away from wherever they had started and never seemed to come back. But other bands were eager to play at Whistling Dixie. The bands were ever paid except in barbeque, beer and oysters because the music was all for free. The combination of Noah's barbeque and great music brought a whole lot of people out most Saturdays. It was good practice and exposure for the bands, who were mainly groups of different guys playing for fun anyway, and the old barn had great atmosphere, with its roomy dance floor and the hay loft upstairs

"Oh yeah, I do remember those guys. You're right, they are a great band. Anybody else coming out today, Dickey?"

"No, I'd guess you've got the place to yourself. Are you playing golf today, Jacob?"

"Yes and Tadpole Gaillard will be out tomorrow for our annual Duel in the Sun, so I'm going to cheat and go practice. Do you have any bait, by the way? I'd like to fish later."

"Plenty of minnows down in the well and I can get you some mullet if you want."

"Whatever is easiest for you, Dickey. I'm taking a few days off so don't go to any trouble."

"You hungry, Jacob? I've got a fish stew that is amazing, if I do say so myself. Homemade corn bread too. Interested?
"

"Sold" said Jacob. "Let me put some things away and I'll be right with you."

Jacob got back in his car and drove down near the dock. He went to his cabin with his things, throwing his bag on the bed after pulling the big cover off of it, checking under the sheets to be sure there weren't any critters lurking. He put his sandwiches in the little refrigerator and stepped out on the porch, glad he was there. Conch Creek was before him, a tidal creek flowing from the Intracoastal Waterway well into the black waters of The Great Wambaw Swamp. The deep water creek was fifty or so yards wide at this point. Banks of brown pluff mud on either side held many oysters. A pair of Ibis flew down the creek. A number of redwinged blackbirds flitted about. The view was like a postcard; a perfectly blue sky, a few clouds over the expansive green marsh, Conch Creek just in front of him, the whole scene bounded by the Great Wambaw Swamp and forest to his left, the Intracoastal Waterway off to the right. Jacob was glad the breeze was building, hoping it would continue to pick up as he played golf. It might help keep the bugs away.

He didn't love the heat, but could tolerate it and not let it interfere with doing things he loved, and golf was absolutely one of those things. Jacob had been playing since childhood. Golf was something his whole family really enjoyed, and the O'Leary's were a competitive family. Jacob had gotten good enough in a hurry that he could hold his own. He was a good enough golfer that he could play on any course in the world and have a great time. He especially liked this course at Whistling Dixie and was looking forward to being out on it. The last time he had played was a month or so prior up in New Jersey with his brothers, the annual family competition in which there had been yet again not a clear winner. Jacob hadn't been able to play since returning. He felt he really did need to get in some practice, to see what swing problems had been developing while he hadn't been playing. No matter how often you play golf, you never know what your game is going to be like the next time out. Actually, you never knew from one swing to the next.

Lunch with Dickey was fabulous. The fish stew was especially perfect. In addition to his talents in the kitchen, Dickey Macoun was also a nature photographer and showed Jacob his new photos. This series were all black and white views of the marshes and the swamp. Dickey felt the brilliance of the summer created a really lush feel to the pictures. There was one in particular that Jacob found amazing. Taken from under the branches of a huge live oak, it was the crisp image of a tremendous reach of fern encrusted limbs extended out over a lily pad covered pond in the midst of a marsh, the black water reflecting scattered images of a magnificent cloud filled sky.

13

The breeze was still building as Jacob stepped on to Whistling Dixie's first tee. Looking down the fairway, he loved what he saw. A wide, undulating landing area legged slightly to the right along the marsh. Old growth oaks, cedars and pines lined the edge of the left fairway. He knew that none of the fairways on the course were flat. MacBryde had the ground rolling in every direction he could think of. Noah's mower blades didn't usually get into all of those spots. Even if your golf ball was in the middle of the fairway, you probably still did not have a great lie.

He took a practice swing, and then teed up his ball. Relaxing into his stance, Jacob exhaled slowly as he started taking his club back, and then slowly swinging through the ball. The golf ball blasted through the summer heat, rising and rising before settling down right where Jacob had been aiming, which he unfortunately didn't realize was way left of the fairway until it was a little too late. Luckily, the ball hit a tree and dropped back into the left hand rough. Jacob looked down at his club. *'My driver disguised as a tree-wood again,'* he thought. He picked up his golf bag and headed off down the fairway. Some egrets flew overhead. He could see some mockingbirds and bluejays chasing around the cedars. It was very quiet; the only sound was the occasional rustle of some tree branches. Being here, alone on the golf course, felt really good to Jacob.

His only work now was to relax and play well. Jacob searched through the thick grass and was glad he found his ball. He guessed he was 180 yards from the flag, so he pulled out his 5 iron. One of the things he liked about Whistling Dixie was that there were no yardage markers of any sort, just as courses had been when he was growing up. Swinging his club, he hit the ball well, but not long enough, and wasn't happy to see the ball disappear in the tall grass close to the right front of the green. As he reached that area, he finally found the ball deep in the grass of another depression below the green. '*Great, thanks MacBryde, nice to see you again too.*' Jacob grabbed his sand wedge and swung way too hard and not very accurately .The ball moved forward about a foot. *'This is fun, right?*" But his next swing was perfect, the ball landing just a few feet from the pin. The grass on the green was about an inch high, but Jacob hit the putt perfectly for a bogey 5.

Golf! He loved every part of it and was so glad to be here. Jacob played the next several holes about the same, just enjoying being alone, with no cell phone and no bad news except his wayward shots. He watched a Red-Tailed hawk up high in a dead pine tree, hopefully not waiting for Jacob to get run over by Old Noah's wayward tractor and mistaking him for road kill.

As he was teeing his ball on the 6th hole, he suddenly thought of a moment with Jody back in the spring. They were at Morgan's Point for the Capers spring party. They had been having lots of fun. Jacob danced the Shag with Jody, even though he didn't particularly care for what was called Shag Music. After dancing for quite awhile, they were both thirsty and went to get something to drink. As they had stood near the bar, Jacob saw Jody's face suddenly flush, her eyes widening for just a moment. Jacob turned in the direction of her glance and saw a tall, masculine looking woman with her gray hair cut more like a man's would be. Wearing a long sleeved blue shirt and black pants that didn't exactly seem like a spring party dress, she stood with a shorter, long blond haired woman wearing a soft red dress.

The tall woman said "Jody, what a surprise!'" and walked over to her, ignoring Jacob although he stood next to Jody.

Jody said nothing for a moment and then looked to Jacob and said "Dee, I'd like to introduce you to my boyfriend, Jacob"

Dee had turned, looking at Jacob in a way that seemed particularly more curious than friendly, before turning and sticking her hand out.

"A pleasure," she said shaking hands with a strong grip and put on sincerity. Dee said "See ya," as she walked off, putting her arm possessively around the other woman's shoulder.

"Who was that?" Jacob asked.

"I'm not sure" Jody replied uncomfortably. "Come on Jakie, let's dance."

The rest of the party had been fun, but there was something about this interaction with Dee that really bothered Jacob. It had a bit to do with the look Jody had briefly in her eyes when she first saw the woman, but had more to do with the way Dee had looked at Jacob. It was just the way another guy would look at you if he was attracted to your woman, and thought he had a chance.

When they returned to Jacob's car and got in, he had turned to Jody.

"Is there something you need to tell me?" he asked, watching her eyes closely.

"About what?" she answered.

"About anything I think I should know about, but don't."

"I don't know what you're talking about."

"This feels like an Abbott & Costello routine, Jody."

"Who are Abbott & Costello?"

"Don't get cute."

"But you always said I was cute."

"Screw you Jody, just answer the damn question."

"You're asking about Dee. She's just somebody who walked into the studio the other day. She said she's a homeopathic healer who also does body work, and she was wondering about taking some classes. Are you jealous about something?"

"Have you ever been with a woman, Jody?"

"Do you think I have something going on with her, Jakie? I'm with you and only you. What's going on?"

"I don't know."

"Well forget it. You don't have anything to worry about."

Jody kissed and hugged him and then looked him in the eye.

"Really, whatever is bothering you, forget about it, OK? You know you are pretty cute when you get all jealous."

As he teed up his ball, Jacob had to gather himself.

'Why am I thinking about all of this? Why can't I just enjoy being here at one of my favorite places in the world, alone , with my only work being to focus on a golf ball just lying there in the grass? All I have to do is make an easy swing and hit as good a golf shot as I can. Why was a painful thought better than the wonderful feeling of hitting a perfect golf shot? What was there about the past that was so much more important than being where I am right now?'

He took his stance, let out his breath, took an easy swing, and topped the ball. It stopped rolling maybe twenty feet in front of him. Perfect. He barely had to move to hit his next shot, which landed short of the green to the right.

Jacob thought he had a hole-in-one on the short par three 8th hole, except he couldn't find his ball. It wasn't in the cup. It wasn't anywhere he could see on the green, so he began pacing around, searching until he finally found where it had rolled completely off the back of the green, deep into another of Alistair MacBryde's bunkers, just winking at him through the thick grass. It took three swings just to get the ball onto the green. With any luck, Tadpole might have the same problem when they played the following day. They were friends but this was golf, after all.

Thinking of Tadpole made Jacob again think of Charlie, and Jacob wondered what was going on with that kid.

Jacob had really gotten to know Charlie earlier that spring. Tadpole, Rosie and their kids were coming out one day for a late afternoon sail and dinner out on the harbor, and probably they would also go swimming. When they had arrived at Jacob's house, another boy was with them.

"Jacob, I'd like you to meet Small's new friend, Charlie Mack. He's just moved here from Baltimore" introduced Rosie.

Charlie was tall and athletic. He had an Afro, which was somewhat unusual these days, and he resembled a teenage Michael Jackson. Charlie seemed shy, but he had looked Jacob in the eye. They shook hands, although somewhat awkwardly, as if it wasn't natural to him.

"Charlie, I'm glad to meet you. Have you ever been out sailing before?" Jacob asked.

Charlie said he hadn't, so Jacob announced "Great, then you are our captain today Charlie. I'll just help out."

Charlie smiled quickly, and then looked nervous. But they had a wonderful time. Jacob gave Charlie the helm when they were out on the water. Jacob sat close by in the cockpit, prepared to grab the wheel if needed, but Charlie got the hang of it pretty quickly. It had been a fun day for everyone, especially for all the kids, who had a great time swimming when they anchored off of the beach at Fort Johnson.

Later, back at Jacob's, while Rosie and the kids fixed dinner, Tadpole told Jacob what he had learned about Charlie.

"He's a good kid who needs somebody to look out for him Jake," Tadpole had concluded.

Jacob realized then the reason Charlie had been brought with them. Tadpole was hoping that Jacob would mentor and otherwise help Charlie, now that his Mom was gone. There wasn't anyone else reliable in Charlie's world to do this.

"Let me get to know him Tadpole, I'll do what I can."

So it came to pass that Charlie had often spent the night at Jacobs without too much coaxing, enjoying listening to the sound of the ocean through the open doors and windows. He had really enjoyed being on the beach and island life.

One morning, after Jody had fixed breakfast for the three of them, she did a sketch of Charlie which had especially thrilled him. He asked her how she did it. Digging through her shoulder bag, she had found a sketch pad and drawing pencils and gave him some pointers on how to use them. He sat next to her and began to draw a picture of Jacob's porch. They had worked together on other sketches for the rest of that afternoon

"You ask really good questions and you pay attention to the answers. You're a fast learner, Charlie. If you keep drawing you could become a great artist!" she said to him.

Charlie looked up at her, his eyes smiling at Jody."I've been drawing all my life. Mom is the only one I ever showed my pictures to. Never had any lessons though."

On other visits to the island, Jacob had taught him what he could about sailing and fishing, while Jody helped him learn more about drawing. Charlie steadily seemed to relax around Jacob, and especially Jody. He had not spent this much time with white folks before. He was not sure why they were so interested in him, but he relaxed into it.

One night, over dinner, Jacob looked at Charlie. "I want to ask you something. Please answer however you best can. Jody and I are in some ways different than you. We are older, and we are white. Does being with us make you uncomfortable in any way?"

Charlie nervously looked down and then sideways before looking up at Jacob apprehensively. "Yeah, sometimes. But everybody I meet is different. I likes both of you and you been so nice to me, so it's good."

Jacob smiled, "It's good for us too Charlie. We like you a lot and that's why I ask. If anything comes up and you feel uncomfortable about just –well anything, please just talk to me or to Tadpole about it OK? I know this isn't so easy for you, being here in this new town and not back in Baltimore. But this is a good place to live. I'm not from here either. Charleston is the kind of place you can really make a life for yourself, Charlie. You've got friends here now. We are all glad you are here. Except maybe Smalls, sometimes. He say's you're getting pretty good on those video games you guys play."

Charlie laughed at that. "Thas' cuz I beat him last time."

Jacob remembered all this fondly, but it wasn't helping him get out of this hazard. He took one more swing and the ball popped on to the green. He was able to sink the putt, for a five on a par three.

On the 12th hole, the afternoon breeze came up and blew into Jacobs face. This was a long par four, basically straight with forest to the left and the old church and grave-yard midway down the fairway to the right. He took his swing .The ball rose high into the afternoon sky before the wind caught it and the ball started heading off to the right, and then a little further in that direction before disappear-ing over the graveyards stone wall. It fell deep into the shad-ows between the magnolia trees.

Jacob had been in there once before on a day he was playing with Matthew Marshall. Because Matthew was the much better golfer, Jacob tended to take a much harder swing with his club than he needed to. There is a line be-tween being friends and playing golf. Somebody has to win and Jacob liked winning. That day, Jacob again was swing-ing his club way too fast and his tee shot had sliced through that same row of trees and over that same wall .It wasn't technically out of bounds, as there was no out of bounds at Whistling Dixie, but he recalled having some difficulty getting out of the graveyard the last time. He had to hit a wedge to a spot well behind the spot he had initially hit from. *'Great, maybe when I die I can be buried there and have eternity to figure out how to get out.'* He picked up his golf bag, and headed towards the stone wall.

Jacob hoped there weren't any snakes in there. It was fairly dark and shaded most of the time. The grass was espe-cially high and thick this far into the summer, which would make it difficult to see a snake until after it had struck. Jacob didn't mind snakes as long as they were 100 or so yards away from him. He pulled out his sand wedge for protection.

As he approached the graveyard, he saw something on the ground that seemed unusual. It was an odd looking turd. Long, thin and curved up at one end, it was not like any piece of scat Jacob had ever encountered. He looked about him, investigating. Nearby, he could see several paw prints in the mud under the thinning grass here in the shade near the trees. They were large paw prints, not especially wide, but still big. They didn't quite look like that of a dogs, but more like something he didn't recognize. Jacob began to notice a peculiar odor. It seemed like strong, acrid urine.

An old iron gate rusted open was the only entrance through the high moss covered stone walls that towered above him. In a number of places, the old rocks had just tumbled to the ground. It was darker inside the graveyard, and Jacob had to take a moment so his eyes could adjust. The late afternoon light was settling into the stones walls, glowing amidst the moss and ferns that covered them. Some tall and thick grass grew in spots, but mostly the ground was muddy, strewn with magnolia leaves. A very old marble crypt was in the center of the graveyard, surrounded by several prominent grave-markers along with a number of more modest stones, many illegible, the markings long obscured. Jacob couldn't immediately see his ball, so he began hunting, working his way to the corner where his ball had gone over the wall. Carefully he started looking. He could see the same large paw prints in the muddy ground, some larger than others.

Something moved off to his right. As he looked, Jacob felt a chill coming over him, not feeling the hairs rising on his arms and the back of his hands. It looked like a good sized dog, maybe a German Shepherd. But, this animal was thin and stood taller at the shoulder than any dog Jacob was familiar with. After looking at it a moment, Jacob realized he had seen a photograph of an animal in the newspaper not long ago that looked just like this.

He was looking at a coyote, apparently as surprised as Jacob was.

The wind was strong, blowing into Jacob's face. They were not more than ten yards apart. Jacob froze, gripping his wedge firmly. He knew he should not move. He could see the coyotes yellowish green eyes. The animal was thinner than Jacob might have imagined. On the ground behind the coyote was what looked like a raccoon; perhaps he had been surprised while eating. Jacob felt no noticeable fear. He kept looking at the coyote, not quite making eye contact. He had never seen one in the wild before. Yet somehow there seemed a familiarity about this experience. Although there was a break in the stone wall just behind it that the animal could easily escape through, the coyote stood still. Its legs were splayed a little, ready to move if it had to, but clearly waiting to see what moves Jacob might make. It did not seem to fear him. The coyote just remained wary of him, watching, waiting.

Jacob finally began to back slowly towards the gate, ready to move on from this. Although he didn't take his eyes completely off the animal, he still scanned the ground, hoping to find his lost golf ball. Jacob really hated losing golf balls, even to a coyote. He didn't see it, which was probably a good thing.

When he finally was able to clear the gate, Jacob moved rapidly to the middle of the fairway, back into the sunlight. He dropped a ball in the middle of the fairway, invoking the brand new Coyote Rule; a free drop far from dangerous critters but no closer to the hole. Golf was a strict game of rules, and he didn't like to bend them, even while playing alone. He also felt the rules needed updating as new situations arose, like this one.

The next few holes went by quickly. Jacob was now warmed up and hitting the ball well, and was starting to make some birdies. If he could make par on the next and final hole, he would be just nine over for the round, a stroke below his ten handicap .

As he stepped on to the eighteenth tee, Jacob felt he was being watched. He wondered if the coyote was following him. He stood and looked around. A finger of the swamp was to his left, a bit of the forest ran all the way down the fairway on his right. The Mansion was beyond the hole. Jacob slowly turned completely around, scanning the trees and adjacent fairways. He saw nothing looking back at him. But the feeling was real and wouldn't go away. He accepted it. Knowing there was nothing more to do, he inhaled very slowly and hit his best tee shot of the day. It was long and turned slowly to the left before bouncing nicely along the curve of the fairway. The breeze continued to pick up. The sun behind him was slowly starting to descend. The colors surrounding him were becoming more golden. Shadows were just beginning to deepen. As he walked down the middle of the fairway, he realized he hadn't seen or spoken to another person for hours. It felt good to him. He had put his watch in his golf bag before teeing off on the first hole. He had wanted to just free himself from any concerns. He had no idea what time it might be, and that felt good too.

Jacob stopped walking. He stood still for a moment as he began taking a deep breath with his eyes closed, and then did so again. He focused only on his breath, aware of a thought he couldn't quite get to. He took another deep breath, and slower, another.

The words *'Don't worry, keep your mind on your work. Just don't worry'* slowly came into his thoughts and then, went through him.

Jacob opened his eyes and walked on. Approaching his ball, he could see it was sitting up on the thick Bermuda grass. He guessed he was about two hundred fifty yards from the green. He also knew there was a bit of marsh down there that ended about fifty yards from the front of the green. He had a choice-he could either try his driver and go for an eagle on the par five, or he should be smart and lay-up, hitting a ball that would land short of the trouble. His tendency was to go for it, pull out the driver and make a big swing. He paused as he thought of the words that had just come to him from somewhere-*'Don't worry-keep your mind on your work. So, what was his work, at least right now? It was to be smart.'* Jacob pulled out his seven-iron, made an easy swing and the ball landed perfectly, no more than 100 yards from the green, sitting up again. He walked to the ball, used his wedge and nearly holed the shot. He made his putt for a nice birdie on the last hole, and that was all any golfer could ever ask for. *'Don't worry; put your mind on your work. What was his work?'* he wondered. *'Sure as heck it's not being a stockbroker.'* That much he knew for sure.

Jacob went to his cabin and removed his clothes. They were soaked from the muggy, hot afternoon weather. He took a very quick shower, selected a fishing pole from the bunch in his cabin, and then walked down to the dock. Dickey had stocked the live well built into the floating docks floorboards with mud minnows, and Jacob opened the lid, and scooped out a bunch of the little baitfish, picked one for his hook and fished for a while. He realized he still hadn't eaten his meatloaf sandwiches from Jack's, so he knew he would eat something.

Sitting on the dock, the marsh before him glowed dimly as night was beginning to fall. Birds called around the marsh as tree frogs began their special music. Jacob felt relaxed, serene and not anxious to move. Looking across the marsh to the forest, he thought about the coyote, wondering if it traveled alone or if there was a mate nearby. The yellow green eyes especially captured Jacob's imagination. He wondered what the world looked like through those coyote eyes. What would a person seem like to the animal? Did the coyote spend a lot of time worrying where his next meal was coming from or where it would sleep? He thought about the shark, those eyes, so dead, but that was just an illusion. The shark probably never thought of anything other than what it was doing at that precise moment, just like the coyote. That was a good thing for Jacob to keep in mind.

He half expected Jody to be sitting right next to him so that he could turn and talk with her about all of this. He thought of her eyes, of a rainy afternoon when they sat on her sofa downtown, legs overlapping as they faced one another, Jacob reading, Jody sketching. It was the first time Jacob really noticed how amazing her eyes were, how lively they were. Their focus could quickly change as if she was alternately imagining what she wanted to see on the paper and then closely inspecting the details. Jacob could watch and see lots of little lines seemingly opening and quickly closing around her eyes. She showed him the drawing she had completed, a sketch of Jacob reading. It was an amazing likeness. He noticed how detailed the visible bits of his fingers were as he held the book in the sketch. "You have amazing hands, have you ever noticed, Jacob? They seem so strong, but they are really gentle and sensitive, even if they are bent a little bit. I'd like to do a sketch of just your hands holding Allieo. I'd really like both my guys in just one piece, you know, do you think you could hold him for a long time or should I take a photo? I really don't mind working from photos but real life is so much better. Think you could hold onto him?" Jody leaned closer to him, looking softly into his eyes. "You know what I like the best about you, Jake? You really listen to me when I talk to you. You try. Not many people I've known do that, mostly they just get ready to speak. You want to come for Thanksgiving with me, up to meet all the Pickens?' Jacob sat up, taking her sketch pad and carefully laying it on the floor. He gently placed his hands on her wrists as he lowered his body gently on top of Jody. He could feel her hips rising to greet his as her legs slowly encircled his."I would love to," he had said, as he lowered his face to kiss her.

Jacob's fishing rod suddenly pulled strongly, nearly ripped out of his hands. Line peeled off for a moment and then Jacob set the hook. It was heavy, whatever it was. For the next few minutes, Jacob played the fish, finally getting it to the dock. As he pulled it in with his net, Jacob could see it was a good size spot tail, a beautiful fish. Jacob removed the hook as carefully as he could, and then released the fish back into Conch Creek. There was a little swoosh of its tail in the water, and then the fish was gone. Jacob wished he could be released as easily.

He watched the last of the daylight ripple away on the darkening waters. An owl hooted in the swamp. Another called back from across the marsh.

For as long as he could remember, he had always felt a tinge of loneliness at the approach of dusk, a feeling he never quite understood. Maybe it was a sense of some unfinished business as night time nears with whatever may be lurking in its ever spreading shadows. Jacob put the fishing pole down after securing the line. He sat quietly, feeling the tide rush below him, feeling its pull. He took another deep breath, breathing slowly. As he quieted his mind, a distant thought beginning to form. It disappeared as quickly as most of his dreams did when he woke in the morning. There was a little splash in the creek, something swirling in the water. He watched the moon rising before him, a half moon neither full nor empty, just there like a question maybe someone knew the answer to. A chorus of tree frogs suddenly erupted from the swamp, their song murmuring across the tips of the marsh grass, rippling in the moonlight spilling over the marsh.

Jacob turned to search the night time sky. The Big Dipper was there, with Jody's star leading to the North Star. He remembered again falling back into *Pearl* just the night before. He had survived his adventure in the harbor. It was a lesson to show that things happen for reasons and are to be learned from. Maybe his lesson was to just keep moving no matter what, like sharks do. Today he had encountered a coyote, and it seemed the same. *'Maybe it was as simple as that. Just keep moving, do your best and move on.'* Jacob listened to the sounds of the marsh for awhile longer and went to his cabin, looking forward to his meatloaf sandwiches from Jack's.

14

Jacob had trouble falling asleep again. He could not find a way to keep his thoughts from going back to all of the strange events of the past few days; the emptiness he had felt leaving Southern Shipping, his very unusual meetings with Nathan Goldstein, and the intensity of the encounters with the shark and then the coyote.

Mostly he thought about Jody, wishing she was with him. Not only did he achingly miss her, but at that moment, he would have really liked to just be able to talk with her about what had gone on since he last saw her. Jacob had learned much about the world as he heard it reflected back to him from Jody's perspective.

His mind drifted back to the day in the spring after they had left the Capers big party and the brief encounter with Dee. He easily remembered how awkward he had felt. Even afterward, in the car with Jody, he had felt a bit of distance between them, despite what she had said to him. Instead of going to his house on Sullivan's Island, which was where they spent most of their time together, he had driven her to the little carriage house downtown.

Quietly, they had walked to her front door, and he had no idea what would happen when they got there.

Jody had simply walked directly to her door. Opening it, she had turned and looked inquisitively at Jacob, apparently wondering, as he was, what was next.

She stepped inside, and turned to him.

"Please come in, Jacob."

Not sure what was going to happen, he followed her to her sofa, and sat down.

Jody sat next to him, taking his hand, looking at him.

"I don't know what happened with you in the car a little while ago. I love you, you know."

"I love you too."

"Then sit here for a minute and relax. I'll be right back."

As Jody disappeared into the back of her little house, Jacob removed his jacket and necktie. Allieo jumped on the sofa and lay next to him. As he gently stroked the cat between its eyes, he wondered what the strange feelings were that he had been having in the car. He hoped he wasn't just being an asshole, but something was bothering him and he couldn't figure out what it was.

The cat was beginning to purr loudly as Jody returned several moments later. She had changed from her party dress into a faded indigo nightgown. A long, thick, silken cord holding a number of large pearls hung below a pale blue scarf tied loosely around her neck.

She sat beside him again, taking his hand in hers, turning him towards her.

"Jakie, look at me. Do you trust me?"

"I'm not sure. What do you mean?"

"Will you completely trust me, for a little while?" she asked, looking deeply into his eyes.

Smiling, he replied, "If you insist."

'Oh, I do. Come with me."

Her fingers intertwined with his. She rose, pulling him upward.

Walking backward, smiling into his eyes, Jody led him down the hallway. She stopped before a closed door that he had always thought was just a closet.

Jody kissed him gently, opening the door behind her with her free hand.

"Come on in, said the spider to the fly."

Jacob was immediately enveloped in warm, moist air as he followed her in. The room glowed from the light of a dozen candles.

Two large paintings hung on the deeply red painted walls.

One was of the back of a nude woman, her arms outstretched, beneath a wild array of dark hair. She stood before a roaring fire, her head looking upward to a vast sea of stars. The other was of perhaps the same woman, emerging from a foaming, deep blue sea, her dark hair streaming down over her breasts, her eyes shining above her mouth, open as if she were in ecstasy.

"Jacob, please sit right here," she said, indicating the white comforter covering a bed which filled most of the floor space. There was no other furniture.

"Jody, I..."

"Shhh. Trust me Jakie. Please take your shirt off. "

As he got comfortable, Jody knelt before him, removing his shoes, socks, and then reached for his belt.

"Lay down."

Jacob could feel sweat forming on his scalp as Jody let her nightgown drop to the floor. While her eyes never left his, she removed the pearl necklace and placed it next to him. She climbed on to the bed, her legs straddling Jacob's hips. Leaning forward, her breasts glistened with a sweaty sheen, her eyes locked on his.

She whispered "I love you, Jacob O'Leary. You and only you! I want you to relax and let me show you how much you mean to me. Now, trust me."

"Jody,."

'Shhh..."

Jody kissed him again and Jacob sat up, wrapping his moist arms around her back already beginning to drip with sweat, their lips passionately joining.

The intensity of their embrace turned to rapture. Their sweat mingled, lubricating their rhythm.

Jody broke the kiss long enough to reach into a bowl she'd placed next to the bed. She traced an ice cube across the back of Jacob's neck, sending an ecstatic spasm down his spine.

Jacob opened his eyes to look at her

Jody glistened with sweat. Her eyes were lost in a primal surge. Her burning eyes locked into his. Her lips were in a snarl as she locked them onto his. Jody pushed Jacob back onto his back.

"Trust me now, Jakie." She said, removing the scarf from her neck, wrapping it around his head into a blindfold.

She raked the fingernails of her left hand through the sweat covering his skin as her mouth started going lower on his body. With her right hand, she had reached for the pearl necklace.

15

For the first time in days, Jacob was feeling good and relaxed. After having slept for a very long time, he had leisurely wandered up to the mansion to enjoy the blueberry pancake breakfast Dickey had offered the night before. Jacob spent the rest of the morning drinking coffee on the big screened which ran the length of the mansion house and overlooked the water. Jacob was determined to take the day off from any heavy thinking. All of the questions the week had left him with were unanswerable at the moment. He needed to let his mind go somewhere else for a while and hope that solutions would appear when they were ready too.

He was in the right place for a wandering mind. There was so much to look at right in front of him. Pelicans were circling a particular spot in Conch Creek, occasionally plunging for fish. There were an endless variety of boats traveling up and down the Intracoastal Waterway.

The marsh was golden under a bright blue, nearly cloudless, South Carolina summer sky. The air was achingly hot with almost no wind. Jacob hoped that changed before he and Tadpole played golf. The big man might like it extra hot, but Jacob preferred at least a breeze. But right then, he didn't care. It would be a good afternoon whatever happened.

Jacob hadn't realized that he had dozed off until a huge hand was on his shoulder. A familiar voice whispered in his ear, "Wake up, you sorry ass. It is time for you to lose a bunch of money."

Jacob looked up to see Tadpole all decked out for golf, Whistling Dixie style. He was wearing an old South Carolina Tech football t-shirt sized XXXL, worn out exercise shorts, basketball shoes and a floppy straw hat.

Jacob and Tadpole got some bottles of water and Gatorade from the cooler in Whistling Dixie's pro shop, as they called it. You could buy golf balls there, as well as Whistling Dixie Golf Shirts, in either large or Extra Large, all pale blue with the Red and Green logo. You could also purchase live bait and there was a good assortment of fishing gear. Delicious sandwiches were generally available, either made by Dickey or Old Noah after the Saturday night barbeque, the big event every week at Whistling Dixie.

Jacob and Tadpole walked out to the first tee, carrying their golf clubs. There were no golf carts at Whistling Dixie.

"Didn't want to say this in front of Dickey, but did you know the police believe they have found Edmund Capers?"

Jacob's day of not thinking about anything important came to an end.

"What? Where? When?"

"The paper this morning said a body washed up on the beach yesterday near your house. They guessed it was him, and then on the way here the radio news guy said that Edmunds wife and his cousin have both positively identified it as Edmund. But he didn't say much else."

"Yesterday-like in yesterday morning! That was the police finding Edmund Capers on the beach yesterday morning? I was watching some of that and never walked over! That was Edmund? Are you sure? Or are you just trying to get me distracted before we tee off?"

"Me, would I do somethin' like that?"

"Shit! Edmund's dead? I don't believe it. How could he be actually dead? Did the paper say what happened?"

"Nah, just that he was found was all. Didn't say much else. You still want to play? I could understand you not wanting to."

"No, I'm good, but now you've got to give me some strokes."

"Me give you strokes? You been smoking something this morning, Jacob? Havin' some sort of college revisited moment? You been out in the sun too long. You giving me strokes. And I still will end up havin' to pay you."

"Alright, let's do it."

As they arrived on the first tee box, Tadpole asked "You been hitting balls out here, Jacob?"

"Me? Would I do something like that? Man, I can't believe Edmund is actually dead."

They tossed a tee to see who had honors and Tadpole won, so he hit first.

The big man stood over his ball, and stood over it, looking at it, and stood over it some more before making a huge swing that had his driver moving in every conceivable direction it could possibly move before actually making contact. The ball streaked far off to the left before zooming back to the right and finally landed almost on the fairway and then bounced left again, into the fairway.

"T, we have to get that swing of yours on tape. We could sell it on The Golf Channel. 'World's Worst Golf swing that almost Works." We'll get rich. No one would believe me if I tried to describe it. How about we post in on YouTube? I can see it now-New York Giant creates the world's most bizarre golf swing-what do you think?"

"Very funny, Gordon Gekko, Jr. Let's see your smooth swing.'"

Jacob's ball started straight down the middle of the fairway, before hooking left into the rough. Fortunately, he hit a great next shot and was able to win the hole. Tadpole won the next, and that was the way it typically went when they played. Tadpole was a great athlete, and it came out in everything he did.

After teeing off on the 4th hole, Jacob turned to Tadpole.

"I have to ask you for a straight answer to this question. Do you think I've changed much from when we first knew each other?"

Tadpole looked at him and could see Jacob meant it, so he paused for a moment.

"Yeah, sometimes I think you are a lot different. Not the gettin' older and life being more serious something different. It's more like you holdin' back or something. Like, do you remember that 'Bama game way back? You had kicked the hell out of the ball and that 'Bama runnin'back who was so famous, what's his name, anyway he comin' hard up the sideline, blockers every which way, our guys are like nowhere to be found, and then you came runnin' right thru those three big guys in front of him and just jacked that guy. You hit him so hard you both landed on the ole Bear hisself. Whooee, that was a hit! That took some balls too, going thru those big men like that. Stopped him, stopped a score for sure, and we won. You did stuff like that a bunch. Those stories you kept writin' for the big paper up there, man those sure were good readin'. I got the paper in New York, showed some of them writers there what you wrote, they thought you wrote some world class stuff. I knows there were some trouble about your story about that coach, he was an asshole and everyone knowed it, but it took balls to write it and you did. But when they canned your ass I didn't understand why you didn't just go to Atlanta or somewhere and keep writing. We didn't talk much for a good while back then, me being in New York and all. That happen a lot after college, you know, guys movin' around, getting into their lives and such. So, yeah, you ain't that Jake, I don't sees you takin' on the 'Tide maybe this week, but you could, Jake, you could. You are one smart, tough, good guy underneath all those Wall Street clothes."

"But then when I see you at the 'Stars with the kids, or when I see you with Jody, or we're just talking, that's all you Jake. But sometimes I see you in that suit and I wonder, but you seem like you're doin alright. Life ain't never gonna be perfect you know. Always got to be givin' something up. I guess you just doin what most got to do, whatever work you got to do. I guess it's like you are trying too hard sometimes, and if you do that enough, then you gets the habit. So, that's they ways I sees it.

"You think I'm the same? Nah, too much life been happenin', we can't never be the same. It's like that river over yonder, the water ain't the same comin' by here as it was way back over there before it got here. Stuff's happened, fish copulatin', fish eatin each other, people going by in the boats peeing in the water, so I guess life's about keepin' up. Just doin' your best this minute, you know? Just keep on going, finding out what's just round the next bend in the waterway. So that's what I'm thinking about all that. Why you asking, now that I told ya what I'm thinking?"

"I looked at myself in a mirror the other day and didn't recognize myself. Seriously. This guy was standing there wearing my clothes, my glasses, and I was trying to figure out who he was. I hate my job. I'm wondering what I'm doing and don't have a clue. I'm just trying to figure out the next step and I need to know it soon. Sorry to be a downer on top of a downer, but it just seems like a lot of stuff is happening all of a sudden and since I'm in the middle of it, I wonder what it's all about. You wouldn't believe half the stuff that's happened this week, Tad, you really wouldn't. Somehow I'm in the midst of some deep shit and I don't know how I got here. That big deal didn't happen, Edmund was missing and now you tell me he's washed up dead on the beach. I was literally face to face with a damn shark in the harbor a couple of days ago and then, yesterday, I was playing golf here and on number twelve, I came face to face with a coyote. I don't quite get what's going on, and most of all, I'm missing the daylights out of Jody. I'm thinking somehow, I made all this happen. I was reading some spiritual stuff this morning, something I found down in the cabin, and this guy asked his friend a question. He asked 'In what way is God trying to get your attention right now?' I know, heavy stuff. Probably I'm thinking way too much about everything when I ought to be just thinking about how I'm going to hit a perfect golf shot right now and kick your butt.

"Thanks for telling me what you think, T. You're the only guy I can speak about stuff like this to. I don't know really know how to talk about myself, it's just that I know I've been a lot happier than I am now and that I just want to feel good , you know. I don't think you just decide to feel good and that's it. It's about what you're doing first, then you feel something about it. I'm making some decisions here. By the way, what do you think about this tropical storm?"

"You mean Hurricane Danielle that's gonna drop a bucket of crap on Charleston next week if she don't head out to Bermuda first?"

"Hurricane Danielle! Tadpole, did you bring any good news with you?"

"Yeah, Rosie and Smalls and the girls are comin out tonight to do some fancy dancing. You talked so much about this place they want to see it for themselves. Plus, we'll be eatin' some good ole barbeque. That Noah, he sure knows how to do it right. Now, are we gonna finish playin some golf? Cause today's the day I gets some of that big money you always got. Let's see that perfect golf shot, cause if you don't hit one, I am gonna, you can count on it."

They walked down the fairway and played their own shots, Tadpoles was perfect, which Jacob thought remarkable considering how he swang a golf club They ended the match tied.Tadpole and Jacob walked directly from the eighteenth green down to the floating dock and dove fully clothed into Conch Creek, fulfilling another Whistling Dixie tradition.

16

Saturday night at Whistling Dixie meant Old Noah's barbeque and great rock and roll.

After showering and putting on some dry clothes, Jacob and Tadpole wandered over to The Treehouse for a beer. They found a space in the gathering crowd to lean against the railing, enjoying the end of a day in the South Carolina Lowcountry. Rosie and the kids were due at any moment for some fishing, dinner and dancing.

A short distance away and below them was an old shed that had been converted for Noah and his brother Hiram to smoke their barbeque. The special magic they exquisitely added to the pork had twice won the World's Barbeque Championship held annually in North Carolina. Noah and Hiram smoked the meat over carefully selected hickory logs found only in a hidden Appalachian valley somewhere in eastern Tennessee. The hogs always came from the same farm in Lexington County. Old Noah and Hiram mixed a special blend of ketchup, vinegar and secret spices to produce a tasty barbeque sauce unmatched by anyone anywhere. No one had ever known the brothers last name. What people did know was for $10 they got all they could eat of the best BBQ pork, ribs, chicken, coleslaw and baked beans to be found anywhere.

Across the property at the edge of the forest was an old barn. It had been transformed into a wonderful venue to enjoy live music, primarily because Oliver and Matthew loved rock and roll, the blues, country western and anything in between. They also liked the idea of having it every weekend at Whistling Dixie. They had a stage built, brought in plenty of amplification equipment to be sure the music would be appropriately loud, added a dance floor and some lighting equipment, plus an extra generator to supply all the power any band needed. It was a fantastic place to listen to music and to dance.

Whistling Dixie had music almost every Saturday night, and it was for free. The bands were local, either new groups trying to develop a following, or they were musicians playing together because they loved to share the groove they got into with each other inside the chords.

Jacob leaned back into the railing that ran around the bars perimeter. The view was spectacular. Because they were high in the sky, they could see well beyond the islands dotting the marsh between the waterway and the bay. To the west, a warm glow was filling behind the clouds, casting rays of orange and red sunlight in all directions. A flight of pelicans soared by headed up the waterway. Running lights from a boat out on Bulls Bay could be seen hurrying somewhere before the advancing indigo sky to the east. A very large yacht was heading south on the waterway below them. The breeze brought with it the smell of barbeque.

From the barn came the opening strains of "Foxy Lady' as the Disorderlies were tuning up.

"You know something, T? I never get tired of looking at this. I love it here."

"I hear ya. We couldn't wait to get out of New York and get back here, even though I didn't like the way it happened. See those dolphin down there, them ospreys up there. It's what it's all about."

They clinked their beer bottles together.

A familiar looking Lexus SUV appeared from the forest, headed rapidly towards them as it left a cloud of dust behind as it swerved down the dirt road into Whistling Dixie.

'Smalls is driving. You can tell. He just got his learners permit and now he's ready for NASCAR."

Jacob followed Tadpole down the winding wooden stairwell back to the ground to greet Rosie and the kids. Smalls and his two younger sisters, 9 year old Jasmine and her 7 year old sister Malia, jumped out of the car first and immediately surrounded Tadpole in a way that seemed like they hadn't seen each other in months. Jacob and all the Gaillard's went down to the dock as other cars continued arriving. Rosie walked arm in arm with Jacob, as Tadpole and the kids followed them. The girls were showing off some new dance moves they were working on for tonight's music.

The fishing was just kid fishing-throw a line in the water, reel it in right away and then do it again, hopefully with the bait still on the hook. The kids were having a big time. Rosie and Jacob sat together on a bench by the sink and cleaning table. They hadn't seen each other in weeks and were catching up. They had been the best of buddies since those long ago days in college. Jacob was part of their family. Rosie wanted to hear all about what had been going on with him, but carefully avoided bringing up Jody. It was starting to get dark and the kids were getting tired of reeling in their lines without any fish. It was time to eat.

With paper plates loaded down with food, they sat at one of the picnic tables in front of the barbeque shed. Jacob sat between Malia and Jasmine and told them about his adventure with the shark.

"So there I was, swimming in the harbor the other day. I saw all these big dolphins swimming around so I jumped right in the middle of them. I was surrounded by hundreds of dolphins. They all thought I was a dolphin too because I would swim really fast and jump right out of the water, spin in the air and dive back in. It was way too much fun. But then this big old ugly looking shark showed up. He was angry that he couldn't spin in the air and dive back in like I could. So, do you know what he did?"

"No!" the girls said in unison.

"He jumped at me with his mouth wide open. Swallowed me without taking a bite. And then he swam down to the bottom of the harbor. Well, it was pretty boring, being in the middle of this shark. It was really dark and it smelled terrible with all those dead fish and stuff in there. Plus, I was all covered in extra yucky fish guts. So, do you know what I did?"

"No!" the girls squealed.

"Being inside him, I grabbed that big fin he has from underneath, you know that pointy thing on his back? And then I put my feet back there where those flippers of his are and I started kicking and kicking, and the shark started going faster and faster and he didn't like that very much. Then I started moving his fin all over the place, just jerking it this way and that way, and the ugly old shark was jumping all over the place. He was just completely out of control and getting all dizzy. He had never swum like this before and he didn't like it. So, do you know what the shark did?'

"No!" the wide-eyed girls shrieked.

"He tried biting me with those big old teeth of his. Just pointed them backwards inside that big mouth of his. He even tried poking me with that ugly nose of his. His mouth was all funny looking as he kept trying to get me. He was so funny looking all the dolphins started laughing and laughing and they laughed so much they all started swallowing sea water. Then all the dolphins were burping and making an awful racket out there in the harbor. There was a whole lot of burping going on. So, do you know what happened next?"

"No!" the girls laughed together.

"Now that mean old ugly shark, he's getting pretty upset right now. Embarrassed at being laughed at. Swimming all over the place, out of control. Mad because he can't bite me with those big old ugly teeth. All the dolphins were laughing and burping. But then I aimed the shark right at my boat and kicked faster and faster. At just the right moment we went flying in the air right over my boat. So, do you know what I did?"

"No," the girls said curiously.

"I jumped and landed on my boat. So, do you know what the shark said before landing in the water?"

"No," the girls suspiciously replied.

"Bu-u-u-rp."

Rosie was the only one to laugh. Tadpole groaned, covering his eyes.

Smalls made a point of looking bored.

Malia leaned closer to Jacob, sniffing the air. "Unky Jacob, you still smell like fish guts." Laughing as she leaped to avoid Jacob trying to grab her, Malia burped. Jasmine said " Ee-uuu," holding her nose and also running away.

More and more cars were arriving, parking along the dirt road. The crowd was building. Whistling Dixie on a Saturday night just couldn't be beat. They never advertised. People had to just know about the music, the barbeque, and the oyster roasts all through the cool months, all of it. It was known strictly by word of mouth, and the word seemed to go out in lots of directions, judging from some of the license plates.

The band was just blasting into their version of 'One Way Out' when Jacob and all the Gaillard's entered the barn. There was a dance floor in front of the stage, and there was definitely some dancing going on tonight. After several songs, Doc Rock announced a semi-original song done to the tune of 'Freight Train:'

"Hurricanes a blowin'. Gonna blow us right out of town:

Hurricanes a comin', better get your shutters down:

'Cause when this hurricane starts a blowin, I'm getting the hell out of town."

'Sorry to announce this, but if you haven't heard, Hurricane Danielle is headed our way'

Then Doc Rock counted of 1-2-1-2-3 and The Disorderlies started rocking with 'Who Do You Love?' and the crowded barn was alive with people dancing all over the place. The song had barely ended when the band started right in on 'Rave On', the great Buddy Holly song, followed by 'Midnight Rambler.'

Jacob was digging the music, dancing with each of Tadpoles daughters. He tried his best to follow their moves, which were amazing, considering this was probably not their kind of music.

Suddenly, he realized that there was a musician who looked remarkably familiar on stage playing harmonica. He was a tall, thin guy with long, dark hair and a full beard. Jacob hadn't noticed him earlier. He tried to figure out why he seemed so familiar. The more he looked at him, the more he was sure that he definitely knew the guy.

'Who is that dude and where do I know him from?'

But at that same moment, Jacob was distracted by the sight across the dance floor of the female tour guide from downtown. She was there in the crowd, rocking along to the music, and she seemed to be alone.

'Oh boy, I don't need this,' thought Jacob, as part of his brain was simultaneously trying to decide how he would introduce himself to her.

Tadpole came walking up and didn't look very happy. He gestured that Jacob should follow him outside.

"*Something's* weird here, J- I didn't tell you about this before because I wasn't too sure if there was anything to tell. But some guy has been hanging around #1 all week. I saw him outside, sort of across the street, a couple of times, just sitting in this old truck, like he was waiting for something. He came walking in one day. Just walked in and looked around, asked if he could use the bathroom, and then left. But it more looked like he was casin' the place. I even saw him parked behind the courts a couple of nights. Watchin' some little kids play ball? Kinda strange, I thought. Then Huck came in. He never does that, but he wanted to tell me something. He said this guy seemed to be watching the place. Same dude. Described him and the truck exactly. Been parked up the street every day. The thing is, he's here. I just saw him, standin' behind the crowd. This is kind of strange. Let's go back in. Look over to your left, real casual like. He's a short guy with big ass arms, got an old ball cap on, leaning against the wall."

They went back into the barn. Jacob tried to be casual about it, but he looked and then froze, recognizing the guy instantly. It all came right back.

The guy leaning against the back wall was named Hank. He was always seen with a guy named Smithy down in Key West. Hank was powerfully built, short but definitely not small. Jacob's quick impression was of a ball cap pulled low over a large nose that looked slightly bent. He wore a white t-shirt worn over very powerful shoulders and huge arms.

His thumbs were casually hooked into the front pockets of some very tight jeans.

Jacob had never actually met Smithy, but at the time the guy was legendary in a town full of pirate wanna be's. Jacob instantly remembered that one night while Smithy was in the bar that Jacob worked pretty often, he had noticed Hank back in the shadows, keeping an eye on things.

Smithy had quite a reputation back then, but not just as a drug smuggler. Running pot was really common and lots of Jacob's friends were into it. No big deal, at least not in the Key West of those days.

The stories were that Smithy had supposedly actually killed several different people somewhere out in the Caribbean. The murders were said to have had something to do with drug deals gone bad.

One night especially came back to Jacob. He had been tending bar at The White Room in Key West .His friend, Captain Stan, came over to get a couple of beers. Noticing Smithy sitting at the bar, Stan had quietly asked Jacob if he knew the guy. Jacob replied that he didn't. Stan said "Good-don't. He is really bad news. Couple a nights ago, my pal Vernon, you know Verne, he's got that boat next to mine he calls *Sheba*. Anyways, one of his crew was hittin' on some gal over at The Sundowner and Smithy over there comes walkin' up and tells him to take a hike. Verne's guy didn't dig that, thinkin' he's soon to be headin' out with that lady there, and tells Smithy to fuck off. Next thing anyone knows, Smithy's buddy Hank had laid that dude out, and then they walked him outside, and Verne ain't seen his mate since. Bad pair of dudes, man, bad dudes." Stan had then taken his beers and headed off.

Smithy was definitely the guy on stage playing the harmonica, something else he had also been well known in Key West. Being considered a seriously good musician covered up all kinds of other personal flaws someone might have. Jacob also remembered that awhile back, he had heard a bit of a rumor about Smithy having some sort of compound up some creek near McClellanville. This was the first Jacob had even really thought of him since leaving the Keys.

'Smithy and Hank. Why are they here? And so, why would Hank be hanging around the east side of Charleston? Why would he care about Charleston's #1 All Stars? Why were these two showing up right now? Is this just a coincidence? Tadpole was right, this doesn't add up. This is weird.'

Jacob got closer to the stage to take a closer look at Smithy. Now that he recognized him, Jacob could see he hadn't changed much. Still tall and thin, with a nose like a hawk's under a huge set of black dreadlocks, his full black beard made him look an old-time pirate. While he played, Smithy's dark eyes were in constant motion; alertly scanning the crowd no matter how deeply felt his music might have seemed to be.

The band took a break. Smithy happened to head in Jacob's direction. As he got close, they made eye contact. Smithy walked past him, then stopped and stepped back so that he was suddenly standing next to Jacob.

"Hey man, where do I know you from? You were one of them hippies down in the Keys, weren't ya? Or are ya still?

What's your name man? They call me Smithy, but don't believe it."

Jacob was at a loss so he quickly said "Yeah man, I know you too. Used to see you play down at The White Room down in Key West, I worked the bar there. My name's Jay. Good to see you too."

"Jay, huh?" Smithy's dark eyes bore into Jacobs, one eye almost squinting, the other widened above his hooked nose. "That one of those hippie names from way back when? Why am I thinkin' you are full of shit man? Zero's probably a damn better name for you. Later Dude, whoever you are. I got an eye out for you."

Smithy then semi-saluted at Jacob, never breaking eye contact until he turned to walk away.

'*Well done, asshole,*' Jacob commented to himself. '*In thirty seconds flat you managed to piss off probably the most dangerous guy you're ever likely to meet. Way to go. Now, how do I quickly grow eyes out of each side of my stupid head?*'

Jacob had not wanted that guy to have a clue as to who he was. There was no taking that one back now.

He found Tadpole and the girls. Jacob danced some more with Rosie. He could see the tourist lady was also dancing, and looked like she was really into it. Jacob discreetly watched her to see if she kept dancing with the same guy. Smithy came back on the stage. Jacob looked as subtly as possible for Hank, and finally saw him up in the loft area above the barn floor, talking with a woman. Jacob danced for a few more moments, but his heart wasn't in it. He was glad that Tadpole was coming over to him.

"We're headed home Jake. The girls are going out with some friends and so is Smalls. What a night, huh?   That short guy is right above us, right now. He's watchin everything. That's what I bet he does. He's a lookout. Very bad news. We got to figure this out. I don't need him round the Stars. You OK?"

"T, you won't believe what just happened. This just keeps getting more out there. That guy on stage playing harmonica, his name is Smithy. He was with Hank down in Key West. They were inseparable. Smithy had a reputation down there of being the worst of the worst, truly evil. A few minutes ago, he just happens to see me, walks over to say he knows me and asks what my name is. Damned if I wanted him to know, so I said it was Jay. The guys BS detector is wired so high he knew instantly that I was lying. He called me on it. He said he's gonna keep an eye out for me. I am glad you are taking all your pretty women home, Tadpole. This just keeps getting slightly more insane."

'Jake, you want me to send one of my cousins over here to hang out with you? They all pretty big guys, no one messes with 'em."

"I'll be alright. No need to drag anybody else into what is probably some whole other deal that's got nothing to do with the All-Stars and you and with me. Right now it's all just funny coincidences with some guys who talk a lot and act all mean, and then you never ever hear or see of them again. You just get back downtown and think about battening down your hatches."

"I hear ya. Don' you go doin' somethin' nuts out here on me, alright? You hear me? You promise callin' if any other unusual stuff just happens to happen? This is one week of the unusual. No need for there to be anymore."

Jacob walked with Rosie, Tadpole and Smalls to the Lexus. Jasmine and Malia followed behind, dancing matching steps in time with the music pouring out of the barn doors. Jacob gave Rosie a big hug.

"When are you going to show up with an identical twin sister, Rosie? I think Tadpole is probably the world's luckiest guy."

"Oh, he is Jakie Boy, He is. Lucky for me he doesn't need any reminding. You're gonna find that right gal Jacob, don't you be worrying about it. There is some special, special gal out looking to meet you right now, you watch. It is definitely time for you to settle down and get some little girls of your own, so I can come spoil them like you do with these two."

"How 'bout me, Ma, when do I get spoiled?" asked Smalls.

"Ain't happenin," answered Tadpole."You ridin' home with me. "

Once the family was gone, Jacob didn't return to the barn. Instead, he went back to his cabin. Arriving, he could see that in addition to the Jon boats Oliver kept at the floating dock, that there was now a skiff tied up there. Jacob wondered if that was Smithy and Hanks.

'Great, those guys are hanging around here. Why does this pile keep getting deeper?'

Jacob had never really been afraid of anyone in his life and had never backed down from anyone. He had quick enough feet and could usually think himself out of a tight spot, and luckily he had also never actually been in much of a fight. He wasn't a fool either. He knew that Smithy and Hank were undoubtedly two very dangerous guys. He was not very anxious to cross their paths again. And yet, here they were. It sounded like, for some reason, Hank was spending a lot of time watching the goings on at Charleston's #1 All Stars.

Jacob would do whatever he needed to for Tadpole.

Jacob sat on his porch and, while looking off to the marsh and the forest beyond, found himself starting to think about Jody. He caught himself.

'No man, you are just making yourself crazy. Go meet that tourist lady.'

Jacob returned to the barn just in time to hear the beginning of 'Heat Wave' played in a way he'd never heard it before. The crowd was thinner but that tourist gal was still there, alone. Jacob walked right over to her. She smiled in recognition. He reached out both hands, and she took them and they started dancing. The next song was 'Devil in the Blue Dress.' They kept dancing, looking at one another curiously, like are we going to introduce ourselves sometime soon?

Finally, the music stopped and he was able to say "Hey, I'm Jacob."

"I'm glad to finally meet you, Jacob. I'm Patti. I remember you from the other day." Before they could say another word another song started and they kept on dancing.

Dickey came on the stage and thanked everyone for coming out and hoped to see everyone next week.

Jacob realized Smithy was gone. He was no longer on stage with the band. Jacob walked Patti to her car, where they talked for a while. She gave him her cell phone number, but told him she was probably headed out of town in the morning,

"I'm going to the mountains until Hurricane Danielle is long gone. I've been through one hurricane, and I'm not doing it again," she said.

Jacob returned to his cabin for the night with a lighter step. He was glad to have met Patti, but felt like he was cheating on Jody. For quite a while, he sat on the porch, looking out over the marsh. He could see the skiff that had been tied to the dock earlier was gone, and he figured it had to belong to Smithy and Hank.

'How odd, those guys being here.'

Actually, it almost seemed to fit into everything else that he had experienced these last few days. He thought of Smithy's eyes, so intense, looking right through him it seemed.

'How could Smithy possibly remember me from Key West, where we had never met, let alone recognize me so quickly and unexpectedly on a crowded dance floor years later in South Carolina? It made as much sense as being eyeball to eyeball with a shark and a coyote within 24 hours'.

Jacob thought about the coyote, wondering where it might be right then, if it was still in or near the graveyard or out hunting in the forest, maybe finding food for a little coyote family somewhere. His mind wandered for a moment, thinking about the week, to what had happened to Edmund.

Most all, he wondered where Jody was. This was a moment just holding her would have been really perfect. What would she say was his work?

Jacob could see a large sailboat of some sort passing in the waterway, its running lights the only hint of it quietly gliding by. It was probably headed north, probably getting as far as possible from the storm that was coming soon.

Jacob knew he needed to get *Pearl* ready for such a journey. He knew where he was taking her to get away from this oncoming storm, and for that he was glad. Jacob couldn't imagine what it would mean to him if something terrible happened to that boat. It had been the one very constant thing in his life all these years. It would take him wherever he wanted to go, if only he knew where that was.

An owl hooted from somewhere, just once. He sat quietly, listening to all the night time sounds of the swamp and forest. It told Jacob how close he was to a force more primal than any he had known. He wondered why he was drawing to him all these over the top moments, especially the shark and the coyote, and now a pirate. *'Why were they in his world, so in his face?'* The breeze that had been working across the marsh now picked up, blowing more strongly towards him. Jacob could hear the marsh grass rippling, and thought of those words that had come to him not long before on another breeze. Not so much the words themselves, more how they had touched him in a place deep inside. It was a place he hadn't felt before, a place he didn't know. And yet how instantly he had recognized that feeling, how so close he had been to that place so well hidden in his soul.

'So what is my work now? Was it simply to find the totally wild place growing in my heart?'

But then, he had a different memory, the one he had been avoiding, the one he did not want to accept as being real.

Jody had called a few weeks before Jacob's disastrous visit to Southern Shipping, wanting to come see him. She had arrived looking very sad, and asked if they could sit and talk. Nervously, she began, looking through tears into Jacob's eyes, a searching look, worried at what she would see there as she spoke with him.

"Jacob, I have to tell you something. I don't know how to say this. Do you remember Dee, who you met at Edmunds party on the Wando? Well, she has asked me to take a trip with her to San Francisco. I am going. I am so sorry. I –I- I can't hide this anymore, Jacob. I do love you. I love being with you. But the thing is, women excite me in a way I can't describe. They always have. It isn't something I ever really wanted to happen and I kept resisting it every which way I could. It's one of the reasons I went to France to study. I didn't know what it was about, going somewhere far away, but it sure wasn't about art history. I had been with some women before I met you. Jacob, you were so perfect to me and brought me so many kinds of joy and satisfaction, I felt fulfilled in every possible way. I thought maybe that was all behind me and over and done with. I so wanted you to be able to trust me. I wanted to trust myself--I just need you to know that this isn't at all about you, and who you are as a man, as a person. I had really hoped this was all just the past and that you were the future. I don't want to be this way, but I am. When I met Dee, I fought it, I really did. But, I can't say no to who I am, any more than anyone else can. I'm so sorry, Jakie-I do love you, more than you can possibly understand, especially right now. I know you love me and that this is going to hurt you for a long time. I would do anything to not hurt you. I hope you will find someone special, very soon."

Jody had then walked over to Jacob. Standing before him, she took both of his hands in hers, and looked into his eyes for the last time.

"Good bye Jacob," she had said before breaking into tears again as she turned and hurried out his back door and driving off.

He had not heard from Jody since that moment.

He was deeply hurt then. His soul had fallen deeply into an abyss. It was still there, buried in a landslide of crap.

He just couldn't relate to what had happened. He had tried, was trying, but still couldn't. Maybe one day he would be able to. She has asked him to trust her. And he had. Would he ever be able to trust anyone again?

Jacob stared off into the marsh. *"Is this going to be your life from here on, thinking only about Jody or the deal that didn't happen or whatever the hell else comes along that doesn't work out? Why are you thinking so much about what you don't have? About what is in the past? You have a future. Look at what you do have, at what's right in front of you right now. Let's get moving. It is time to roll back through the gates of Whistling Dixie, to whatever is next.'*

"It is time to move on with your life, buddy. It is exactly what it is and the sooner you can accept what it is, the sooner you will start feeling happy again. Let's roll," he said out loud to himself.

17

When he arrived home on Sullivan's Island the following morning, Jacob gathered up his newspapers and went straight to the porch, hoping he would find some stories about Edmund Capers. He didn't have to look far. There had been a front page story every day. Saturday's paper reiterated what Tadpole had told him, that the body washed ashore on Sullivan's Island had been tentatively identified as Edmund Capers. His boat had been found earlier in the week: the engine had been up, out of the water but the ignition was still turned on and the gas tank was empty. All indications were that it had been a boating accident of some sort. The Sunday headline said the body had been positively identified as Edmunds by both his wife Julie and his cousin Buddy. Police wouldn't directly comment further, but the article hinted at an unfortunate boating accident. The article had gone on to provide a lengthy biography of Edmund and a very brief history of Southern Shipping. Jacob turned to the obituary page and found Edmund's. A local company specializing in cremations was handling the arrangements. The obituary concluded by stating that a memorial service was planned for the following Friday afternoon, at the Yacht Club.

'Edmund must have been mutilated beyond recognition,' concluded Jacob as he dropped the papers in his recycling bin.

He walked down to the beach to the approximate spot he had seen the police and crowd gathered. He stood still for a moment, offering a prayer for Edmund and his family. Jacob then continued walking slowly down the beach towards Charleston.

A low, dark cloud cover hung above the city.

18

Jacob woke suddenly.

He had been dreaming that he was much older, sitting on a large, comfortable chair in the middle of a room with very high ceilings and no wall coverings of any sort. He had been reading a book when there was a sudden knocking on the wooden door before him. He rose and walked to the door. Opening it, he could see it was night and it was raining heavily. Lightning flashed in the distance as thunder boomed all around him. The surf crashed not very far away. Before him stood a young, dark haired boy who was soaked and wearing only a red bathing suit. Without speaking, the boy walked past him to another door on a side wall. He opened the door, and then the boy walked down a stairway to a basement. In the dream, Jacob had walked to the doorway and looked down the steps. He could see the shadow of the boy on a rocking horse, moving energetically back and forth, a squeaking sound rising up the stairway.

It was at that moment in the dream when Jacob had suddenly awakened.

His phone was ringing.

"Is this Jacob?" a young, nervous voice asked. "It's Charlie, is it OK I call you?"

"Charlie-Hi,-" Jacob replied, noticing through his windows that it was not quite dawn. "You all right, Charlie?"

"I hopes you don' mind me calling. Mr. Gaillard said it be alright. I'se hoping maybe I could come back out to your house again. Would that be OK?" Charlie asked quickly. Jacob was still waking up, thinking of his dream.

"Sure Charlie, that would be fine. You sound nervous Charlie. Is something going on?"

"Yeah, I'se pretty afraid about something. Would it be OK for me to come out there to your house?"

"Where are you? Are you downtown? I'll be down there in a little while. I could get you. Have you eaten yet today, Charlie? Would you like some breakfast?"

"I'se down in the City Market. You know where it is? Could you come gets me Jacob? I…I'se in trouble."

Jacob was there a short while later.

Another hot summer morning was already pouring down over Charleston's steeples and rooftops, covering the streets with a hot, thick air. Palmetto tree fronds were moving softly in an unusual morning breeze. The brick buildings and old city sidewalks were quiet, waiting patiently for the new stories the day would create upon them.

Jacob drove slowly alongside the old brick walls and block long metal roofs of the old City Market. It was deserted. Row after row of wooden tables sat empty. Jacob stopped quickly as Charlie suddenly bolted towards him, running out from a hidden, shadowy corner and he quickly got into Jacob's car.

Charlie was tall for a sixteen year old. His usual quiet smile was gone as he nervously glanced around the streets and shadows as they drove off. Jacob tried to make small talk as they headed across town to Freddy's Chateaux de Grits.

Freddy's had been an uptown Charleston breakfast and lunch institution for generations. Located next door to the Francis Marion hotel on Upper King Street, it was an old time café. Dozens of round stools lined the well worn counter on one side of the room, while a number of small booths ran along the side and back brick walls that were covered with photos and posters of College of Charleston basketball players and coaches. A few diners were enjoying breakfast as the two entered and made their way to booth in the back. Jacob sat facing the doorway while Charlie gratefully slid down into his seat, hidden from view.

Maggie the waitress came to the table with menus and a smile. Jacob said good morning and asked for coffee, as well as orange juice for both of them.

Jacob looked at Charlie. The boy was wearing his worn and dirty Charleston's #1 All Stars shirt. Jacob had noticed he was wearing white basketball shoes and long navy blue basketball shorts when he had dashed into Jacob's Honda. Jacob wondered if Charlie owned any other clothes, because these seemed to be all Jacob had ever seen him wearing. Jacob looked at the scar below Charlie's eye and wondered how it had gotten there.

"Charlie, you look like you should order everything on the menu. What do you feel like eating?"

Charlie didn't respond. Instead he looked nervously at the menu, and then back at Jacob.

"You like pancakes, Charlie? I like mine with blueberries. Have you ever eaten blueberry pancakes?"

Charlie hadn't, so when Maggie returned Jacob ordered blueberry pancakes for both of them, plus some scrambled eggs, grits with gravy and biscuits, plus a glass of milk.

"You gonna eat all that?" asked Charlie, amazed.

"No, just some of the pancakes are for me. The rest is for you. Charlie, what is going on? You sure seem pretty worried about something."

Charlie's eyes began to fill with tears. He lowered his head.

"I see something I wished I didn'. I think somebody is trying to find me. I'se really scared. My Momma's dead and I'se got nobody to help me. Can...can you help me, Jacob?' whispered Charlie nervously, his head still faced downward, shoulders pressed up to his ears, his body completely tensed.

"What did you see, Charlie? Look at me Charlie. I'm your friend and I will help you anyway I can. But, come on, look at me. Tell me what happened. What did you see, Charlie?"

A tear ran down Charlie's cheek. He sat up straight, looking directly at Jacob.

"Speak to me, Charlie. It's Ok, whatever you saw."

"One night last week, Aunt Berthie and her new man Cootie Boy were drinking and startin to talk all kinds of trash. Berthie, she gets crazy drinkin and Cootie Boy, he is a bad dude. I don' like him. I just didn' need that and so's I went out. You know that maritime center place on the harbor? I went there and I'se walking around and no one else was there. It was nice. There was this good breeze coming off the water, you know. And I sees this kayaky thing there on the dock, paddles and stuff. So I just puts it back in the water and climbs in –almost fell in the water- and I took it out on the harbor. I know's it wrong but I had to get away and I was comin back soon anyway. So I'se on the water and it real dark and quiet and cool and it feels so nice. The current was pullin me along and I didn't really need to try and paddle. But then there's this island and I figured out how the paddles work, and so I'se went over to the island and tried to get out but fell in the water. That made me laugh. I ain't laughed in a while so this is all pretty cool. There's this fort kind of thing there so I walk over to it. You know about this place, Jacob?"

"It's called Castle Pinckney, Charlie. Used to be a fort before the Civil War and Ft. Sumter was built. Did you see something there, Charlie?"

"Yes sir I did. I was walkin along when I hears a boat headed my way. I'm thinkin it's the police out lookin for the kayaky boat I took. So I hides behind this wall trying to figure out what to do. Then these three guys get out the boat. I can see them cause of the lights on the shore and then this big light keeps comin across the water. I sees the big guy and the little one good. The other guy, he was a shadow. I din't see his face. He jus' standin' there the whole time. They got this other guy, they was just draggin him across the beach there. And then they kinda held him up and were putting this thing in his mouth and pouring something into something in that man's mouth. I sees them real good when the light came back, two of them anyway. I still couldn't see the third man at all but he was there just watchin. I tries to gets a better look but this rock thing I was standin on broke and made lots of noise. Then this light shines on me and those men started hollerin. I took off and was in the water before they find me. So I swim. Momma taught me how to swim real good and I found this buoy thing and just held on. I could still hear them hollerin at each other. After a while I could hear them leaving. Saw them too in the light. I was getting real cold, you know, so I'se goes back over to the island. Couldn't find anything. That light kept coming by and so I went back to the kayaky boat and started paddling real hard but didn't need to cause the current was OK. After a while I back at that maritime place and puts the kayaky and paddles right back just like I found them. I was still kind of cold but walkin around I was alright. Didn't know where to go so I'se go back to Berthies. It was real quiet so I went in. Cootie Boy is passed out on the floor, Bertie in a chair kind of on the floor so I go to bed."

Jacob had to take a moment to absorb this. "What happened next, Charlie? "

"Then I'se at de 'Stars one night .One of those two guys I seen on the island- one o' dem guys was sitting in this ole truck, you know a pickup, and he was watching the ball game going on. But he wasn't watchin the ball game, he was lookin around. I hides behind a tree, you know watching him. Then he gets out the truck and he walked right by me. He kept on walking round the block and come back and gets in the truck. I sees him he don't sees me. So yesterday I'se walking on America Street goin' to the All Stars and I see that man again! He on the street walking by the ball courts lookin' in. He don' see me but I sees him. He look like he lookin' for somebody and I'se 'afraid it be me. So's I go back to Berthies. Cootie gone but Berthie was there so I spent the day in my little room readin .When it be dark I go over to Jimmy J's house and then out walkin'. I don' know what to do so's then I call you."

Jacob tried to absorb this.

'The guy was probably Hank because this is just what Tadpole told him. But what did Charlie see on the Castle Pinckney? Is this also connected to Edmund's disappearance? I believe Charlie. I am sure that Charlie is a really good kid who is mighty frightened. There is no doubt he saw something happen. But what?'

"Charlie, the man who was lying on the beach, Did you see his face?"

"Too dark. The guy holding him between me and him, I just know he was there."

"You want to talk with the police about this, Charlie?"

"No, I take that boat. I'se wrong. I'm not talkin' to the police. What was those men doin', Jacob?"

"I don't know, Charlie. Tell you what. Let's call Tadpole. Maybe you can spend today over at his house while we think about this. You can come home with me later if you want. I have business today that can't wait. Plus this hurricane is coming so I have lots to do. Let me call Tadpole and we will figure this out, OK? Don't be afraid, Charlie. You are not alone here, OK? Will that be alright with you?"

Jacob called Tadpole to ask if he could bring Charlie over for a while. Fortunately, Tadpole was still home, having breakfast with Rosie, Smalls and the girls and said that would be fine.

After arriving at Tadpoles, Smalls took Charlie to go play some video games. Jacob quickly told Tadpole what Charlie had told him.

"Oh man, I told you something was getting weird, Jake. Why am I thinking this is about that guy Hank we saw out at Whistling Dixie? What's his friend's name, Smithy? But I don't know what we could tell the police. They for sure have their hands full of Hurricane Danielle stuff this morning. He can stay here for now. We'll be over at the 'Stars a little later .We'll see what's going on. Call me when you get done with your business.'

Jacob got back into his Honda and drove off, heading to his office. He needed to talk with Pete Madison, after which he had his meeting with Nathan Goldstein.

19

Jacob arrived at Hamilton Brothers later than usual. He went straight to his office and, as he sat at his desk, waiting for his computer to log on, and his eyes roamed over this room he had spent so many years in. Did he care to spend another minute here, let alone several more years? He didn't think so. He looked at all the different stock symbols on his computer screen. He could see his clients accounts were doing well, but his own stocks were still in the doldrums.

Jacob immediately put in orders to sell all that remained of his personal investments. Whatever they were currently worth would have to do.

His phone rang and he could see it was Carol, his assistant, calling.

"Jacob, glad you are in. There are two men here to see you, a Lieutenant Johnson and a Detective Condon with the Charleston Police."

'What? What in the hell?' "I'll be right there Carol, thanks."

Jacob walked to the lobby and found two serious looking men wearing dark suits and very short haircuts standing there, watching him as he walked over to them.

"I'm Jacob O'Leary. Are you gentlemen here to see me?"

The two men quietly introduced themselves as Detective Jimmy Condon and Lt. Marion Johnson of the Charleston Police Department.

"We would like to ask you a few questions, Mr. O'Leary."

'OK, sure, let's go talk in my office." Jacob led the way.

'"Please, have a seat," indicated Jacob to the men as he sat down. "Can I get you fellows some coffee or anything?"

The police officers shook their heads no as they both showed Jacob their identification. Lt. Johnson sat on the other side of Jacob's desk, but Detective Condon preferred standing. He leaned against Jacob's office door, his arms folded across his chest, observing Jacob very closely.

"How can I help you?" Jacob was aware that a number of his co-workers were candidly watching whatever was going on through his office window, including Jackie Ravenel.

"Mr. O'Leary, we have some routine questions to ask you. Sorry to disrupt your morning like this but we shouldn't be here long. You do have the right to have an attorney present for these or any other questions we may have for you. Do you request the presence of an attorney?"

"An attorney? Why do I need an attorney?

"Do you want to phone someone now, Mr. O'Leary?"

"No, I don't need anyone. Would you mind telling me what this is about?"

"When was the last contact you had with Mr. Edmund Capers?'

"Edmund? It was last Monday morning."

"Did you see Mr. Capers then?"

"No, it was just a phone call. I called him at his office."

"When was the last time you saw Mr. Capers?"

"I guess it was a few weeks ago. Why are you asking me this?" Jacob was beginning to feel anxious.

"When, specifically, was the last time you saw Mr. Capers?"

Jacob looked over at his calendar on the computer.

"It was Thursday the 22nd. We had lunch at Pompeii, over on Society St."

"And you haven't seen him since?"

"No, why are you asking?"

"Mr. O'Leary, what was the nature of your relationship with Edmund Capers.? "

Jacob gave as brief a version as possible, adding, "So I was expecting to see him last Tuesday at our meeting, but he wasn't there. No one knew where he was."

"And at that meeting, you were expecting to complete a substantial business deal with Mr. Capers?"

"Well, yes. He had assured me that was the case."

"And you say you never knew that deal was not going to happen until you met with Mr. Buddy Capers last Tuesday morning?"

"That's right."

"Where were you last Monday evening at 6PM?"

"No idea, off hand."

"Please think about this question, Mr. O'Leary. Where were you last Monday at 6 PM?"

Jacob was quiet for a moment. He was starting to freak out a little. The whole time Lt Johnson was asking, Jacob could feel Detective Condon watching him very carefully.

"I was out on my boat. I left early and went out on the water."

"You are sure about that? Was anyone with you?"

"No."

"Can anyone say they saw you out on the water?"

"Not that I know of."

"When was the last time you met with Julia Capers?"

"What? Julia Capers? What do you mean?"

"Mrs. Capers, Edmund Capers wife. What is the nature of your relationship with her? When is the last time you saw her?"

"Wh-I barely know her at all. I don't understand your…"

"When did you last visit the Cayman Islands, Mr. O'Leary?"

"The—Cayman Islands? I've never been there."

"You are stating you have never been to the Cayman Islands?"

'I don't understand why you are asking these questions. I have never been to the Cayman Islands."

"One last question-when you last met with or spoke with Mr. Edmund Capers, did he indicate to you the deal was off?"

"No, not at all. He said everything was fine."

"How did it make you feel to find out that deal was not going to be completed? What did that mean to you financially, Mr. O'Leary?"

"I wasn't happy about it. I had spent a great deal of time on that deal. It was big."

"How did that make you feel?'

"Like I just said-not very happy. Would you tell me why you are asking me these questions?"

"Thank you, Mr. O'Leary. That will do for today. Again, our notes indicate you waived your right to have an attorney present for this meeting. Do you agree with that, Mr. O'Leary?"

"Like I said, I don't need an attorney. Why do you think I do?"

"Mr. O'Leary, we appreciate your time. Do you live at the I'On Ave address on Sullivan's Island?"

"Well, yes, I have lived there for a number of years. Why?"

"Do you have a card with your cell phone number on it that we can have?"

Jacob gave Lieutenant Johnson a business card, which was promptly handed to Detective Condon. The police officer then dialed a number into his cell and the phone in Jacob's pocket rang immediately.

"Are you planning on leaving town because of the hurricane, Mr. O'Leary?"

"Of course."

"Do you have a destination in mind?"

"Yes, I am taking my sailboat to a hurricane hole I know of up the Wando River. This storm will probably not come near here but you never know."

"You never know. Here is my card, Mr. O'Leary. You can reach me 24/7 at this number should any thoughts about this matter occur to you. We will probably want to speak with you again at another time. Thank you for your time today, Mr. O'Leary. We can show ourselves out."

And the two policemen were gone.

"What in the hell? Am I a suspect?" Jacob spent a few minutes staring out his window, deep in puzzlement.

'What is going on with my karma? How can all this even be happening, and how did I get in the middle of this?'

After the officers left, Jacob sat back into his chair, breathing deeply as he did so. He then called Pete Madison, arranging to go meet with him in a few minutes.

"Morning, Jake. Thanks for coming by, please, have a seat .Hope your weekend went well. Monday sure got here fast. So, why were the police here to see you this morning? "

"They were asking about Edmund Capers. They wanted to know about how I know Edmund and where I was on Monday night."

"Why on Monday night?"

"I have no idea. I guess they are trying to figure out what happened to him, I don't know. It was a pretty strange experience. Anyway, that's what it was about. I was going to talk to you anyway this morning. I am sorry I bailed on you last week. The whole thing, the deal not happening, it really caught me by surprise. I really thought it was a done deal. I never even considered that anything could go wrong. And then I wasn't able to contact Edmund. I figured I would at least speak to him and get a clue as to what happened. But I could never get him on the phone. So I took some time to get grounded. But I should have called. I apologize,

Pete, you've been a friend for quite a long time and I should have called you. Sorry."

"Apology accepted. I get what you said. I understand it was quite a blow. I hope you realize I am your friend, but I'm also the branch manager here. My responsibility is to the entire office. I had, of course, hoped this business with Southern Shipping was going to happen, for all of us. But I have to do what is best for the branch. Let's get back to your visit from the Charleston Police. Why you, Jacob? Why did they specifically want to speak with you?"

"They said it was because they had reviewed Edmunds calendar and saw our appointments. Apparently there was one that said we were supposed to have met late last Monday. I don't know anything about that meeting. We hadn't scheduled getting together then, and we didn't."

"But why, again, did the police think you did?"

"They said it was on his calendar."

"But, you say it wasn't. What do you make of that?"

"I don't know what to make of it. Why are you asking about this, Pete? I don't know anything about it."

"Look Jacob, I'm not suggesting anything. I'm just curious. You must have been devastated when you found out that we were not getting that business. That was going to be a huge commission, definitely the largest I have ever heard of, and suddenly it wasn't there. You never seem to show much in the way of emotions and so, I just can't tell how you are reacting to it. That's why I am asking.'

"I'm still numb, Pete. How else could I be? Except I can't do anything about the fact that the police were here! I am sure they are talking to anybody that might know some-thing and I 'm on the list. It isn't any more than that."

"Just seems peculiar. Anyway, I am sure it will all be-come clear. It must be a mistake of some sort. So, let's talk about your business. You are a legend here, everyone looks up to you. You have been an inspiration to lots of these guys, Jacob. You were the guy that got into this business and had great success without any connections. Doing what you did is still inspiring. And you are still that guy, Jake, still that guy. But your business production has drifted down and you know how that is. I've got a boss and he has a boss. And my boss in Atlanta knows Jackie Ravenel, and I have to deal with that reality. If we had Southern Shipping's business, great, but we don't. Something has to change. Do you have anything in the pipeline? Any new business that might be coming in soon?

Jacob started to tell Pete Madison about Nathan Goldstein. But Jacob wasn't sure what he wanted to say about that. At least, not until he had decided what he wanted to do regarding his future, especially if he was going to contin-ue working as a stockbroker. Until Nathan actually signed the new account documents and the funds were deposited in his account, he couldn't say that was a done deal. Jacob had learned his lesson. He had been there and done that with Southern Shipping and didn't need to go there again.

So, he simply replied "I'm not sure. We'll see. Anyway, unless Danielle changes course in the next hour or so, I'm going to be out of here in just a little while. I've got to get my boat someplace safe and need a head start. So, I may not be here for a few days."

"Yeah, this damn storm. Hurricanes are one thing I never had to deal with in New York. They are really a pain. Alright, let's do this. After this storm clears out of here, why don't you and I put our heads together and get your business back to where it ought to be. It might mean you have to change offices, but if you do what you are capable of, that shouldn't be a big deal. You are a winner, Jake; don't doubt it for a minute. But if you hear from the police again, I need to be informed immediately, understood? Immediately, and I mean that."

"I appreciate your support, Pete, see you later."

Jacob called Nathan Goldstein when he got back to his office, but wasn't surprised to get Nathan's voicemail. Jacob left a message asking him to call.

At 1:30, the time of his appointment with Nathan, Jacob knocked on the man's door on Church St.

There was no answer to his knock.

20

Jacob called Tadpole as soon as he returned to his car. This had been an especially unusual day so far, becoming par for the course his life seemed to be on. Jacob hoped it would get no stranger. He was tempted to drive by Jody's house, just a few blocks away, but knew that was not going to make anything better.

"Hey, Mr T-what are you up to?"

"Hey yo'self. Just sittin' here at #1 and wonderin' about this storm. Thinkin' I need to get up to Awendaw and be sure my folks are all set up there. Smalls and Charlie are here playin some ball indoors. Haven't seen that dude from the other night. I told Jaybird to ask Mr. Hucklebuck to be on the lookout too. He's been wandering around The Center lookin and he hasn't seen anything. Least as of yet. What do you want to do about Charlie? He was glad to get in here. Not sure how he feels about leavin. If Miss Danielle comes through here, we need to be with my folks over at Jaybirds house."

"I'll come and get Charlie. I was planning on taking him out to the island. I'll be there in a little while. He'll be fine. Did he tell you any more than what I told you he told me? "

"No, he hasn't said anything to me. I don't think he said anything to Smalls either, 'cause Smalls hasn't said anything to me. And he would have, even if he promised Charlie and swore on a stack of Nike's that he wouldn't. That boy keeps no secrets from me and his momma. But you know what I figured out? I bet Charlie was wearing his #1 shirt that night. He only has a little bit of clothes and wears that shirt all the time. That and his 'fro make him kinda stand out, you know. Makes sense, that guys suddenly are lookin' for somebody round here. You think those guys Smithy and Hank from the barn are those guys Charlie saw on Castle Pinckney?"

"Your guess has always been better than mine. I'll be there in a few minutes, Tadpole."

Jacob was thinking about everything that seemed to never stop happening as he drove over to pick up Charlie.

'Holy crap. Oh man. Smithy, Hank, Charlie's story! Do the police really believe I had something to do with this? Can this be real? Who was the third man?'

Jacob was intermittently looking at the sky as he drove. The clouds were moving quickly under the blue afternoon sky. There was definitely plenty of dark gray in them. Jacob needed to get out to the Island, crank up the computer and see the latest storm update. He'd make a plan to get some portable food and water, get the house ready and take *Pearl* somewhere safe.

'Maybe it would be good to take Charlie with me. Getting away from town would be good for him. Probably the storm is going to

miss us completely. Charlie seems to trust me. He's a smart, compe-
tent guy who will do what I tell him to.'

Before stopping in front of Charleston's # 1 All Stars, Jacob put on his Red Sox hat. He wished he had a big pair of sunglasses and a fake mustache or something with him as he slowly drove around the block, looking for an old Dodge pickup without a tailgate. Fortunately, he didn't see the truck or anyone just sitting in a car who might have been watching.

He stopped out front. Hucklebuck was nowhere to be seen. Jacob found Tadpole in the gym, refereeing a 3-on-3 game with Charlie, Smalls and some other guys. One kid was exceptionally tall and talented. He was easily going up and down the court, blocking shots and making some easy dunks. Jacob sat in the bleachers, watching. Finally, the game ended and Charlie walked over to him.

"Hey, Charlie, you were looking pretty good out there handling the ball. I liked that behind your back dribble. How many points did you get?"

"Jus' eight. Dat KD is something else man, you see how he get off the floor? Eight is a lot of points against dat guy."

"Charlie, I was thinking about something. There's a hurricane coming, probably, and I have to move my boat somewhere safe. I need somebody to help me .You did a really good job of handling her the last time you were out on Pearl. How would you like to come with me for a few days? Think that would be OK with your Aunt Bertie?"

'She don' care what I do, but yeah, I sure would likes to do dat. When you want to go?"

"Actually, now. We'd need to get some clothes for you, and some food, water and stuff for a few days. What about we stop at your place so can grab some of your clothes and then you come out to Sullivan's Island with me? We can take the boat in the morning. If the storm comes, it won't be until late tomorrow or the following day. Then we'll be coming right back. That OK with you?"

Charlie's eyes were lit up with excitement. "Dat sounds good to me."

"Look Charlie, we have to be clear about one thing. The storm is more likely to miss us, but if it does show up, then the weather will get really nasty. Whatever happens, I need you to do exactly what I tell you to right when I tell you to. I have been in some pretty bad weather and *Pearl* is a very good boat to be on during a storm, so we will probably have a pretty bumpy time. I wouldn't bring you if I thought there was going to be a good chance something ad could happen to you. But, if I start yelling and sound really unfriendly, it will be because things have to happen really fast right then. Can you promise me that whatever I tell you to do, you will do it, just like I tell you to?"

"Sure, I can do that."

"Good enough. I hope the weather is going to miss us completely but I doubt it. Well then, go take your shower and then let's get going. By the way, I brought you a new shirt. Here," he said, tossing Charlie a red South Carolina Tech Athletics t-shirt with the Tigersharks logo.

Charlie looked at the shirt for a moment, and then at Jacob, with an expression that said I don't know the words to thank you with. "Thanks Jacob" was all he could quietly say, before he hurried off.

The young guy Jacob had been watching play against Charlie and Smalls was still out on the floor, practicing his free throws. The kid was something else with a basketball. Jacob walked over to Tadpole.

"That kid is great. Where did he come from?

"Oh, he's been here all along, he just grew about a foot in the last 6 months and then he got really coordinated. The kids just started calling him KD, his name is really Kendrick. It is amazing to just watch these kids grow up before your eyes here, you know. Probably the best thing about having The Center is seeing these kids changing. Glad we don't have many windows so it will all be like this after the storm passes. Is Charlie going with you?"

Jacob told Tadpole what his plan was. He wanted to be sure somebody knew where he was going, and that Charlie was coming along. Tadpole thought that was a good idea.

"So you takin' *Pearl* to Osprey Creek again, Jacob? Told you that was a good place for ridin' out bad ass storms".

Years before, Tadpole and his brother Jaybird had first taken Jacob there while they were out fishing one day up the Wando River. They told him then it was the best hurricane hole around. Their Granddaddy Abraham had used it a lot, and he had learned about it from his Granddaddy Hiram who had worked on a plantation near there after gaining his freedom.

It was a perfect place to keep a boat safe in a storm; Osprey Creek was wide with good, deep water, and enough bends and lots of trees, mostly pine trees but also plenty of huge old oaks all along the banks. The trees should cut the wind some and he could secure *Pearl* to a few of oaks to keep the wind down.

"Going to go up first thing tomorrow so we should be there way before the weather picks up here. Are you going up to Awendaw tonight?"

"Leaving in just a bit. Glad you goin' someplace you can get away from all the crazy stuff you been dealin' with.'

"Yeah, lucky us. Nice little break from the action. We only have to deal with a hurricane in a small boat. Piece of cake."

"You da man, Jacob, remember that."

"You too, T. Keep those women safe.

Jacob and Charlie left shortly thereafter. Jacob still didn't see any old Dodge pickups lurking around.

Several minutes later, they stopped in front of the grungy apartment building Bertie lived in. "I be right back" said Charlie. It took only a few minutes for him to return, carrying a small bag.

Sometime later they arrived at Jacob's house. Along the way, they had picked up groceries and extra fuel for *Pearl*. They were also able to pick up a pizza from Andolini's while workmen were covering the glass windows with plywood to protect the restaurant from the coming weather.

Jacob and Charlie spent the next few hours at the house putting loose objects away. They closed the old storm shutters on most of the windows, and did whatever else the needed to do to keep the house as safe as possible. Jacob went out to the garden and cut back some of his plants. Realizing the tomatoes were probably doomed by the storm, he picked all of them and tossed them into the overgrown area under the trees. He preferred losing them to the raccoons rather than to the storm.

They loaded the Honda with everything they could think of and drove down to *Pearl*. After topping off her fuel tanks, unloading and storing their provisions, Jacob was ready for a quick getaway, if necessary. He parked under the house, and walked up the stairs and into the house with Charlie.

He did not see the old Dodge pickup truck parked further up the street. Its occupants were watching them intently through night vision binoculars.

After finally eating dinner, Charlie fell asleep on the sofa while watching television. Jacob was going to wake him, but the boy seemed so at peace, he just put a blanket over him. Jacob grabbed a rocker they had brought in from the porch and took it back outside to enjoy the night air before the storm. It was a quiet night. A growing breeze was blowing across the water as more dark clouds began to roll steadily in from the south.

The Dodge truck remained parked where it was. One of the men slept while the other kept watch on Jacob's house.

21

Jacob woke early in the morning and quickly checked on the weather through his bedroom window. He could see the sun was just beginning to rise with a warm red glow hanging on the eastern horizon. The trees were bobbing in a breeze coming steadily from the south. Otherwise, it seemed like just another summer lowcountry morning.

He opened his windows wide and closed the storm shutters, being sure they were secure. He found some shorts and a shirt and went down stairs. Charlie was still asleep. Jacob turned the TV to see what the Weather Channel was saying about the storm. They were on to some other news, so Jacob began making coffee. Charlie barely stirred.

Finally, just as his coffee was ready, the weather report turned to the Tropical Storm Update. Hurricane Danielle had been upgraded to a Category Three and was still on a collision course with the mid-South Carolina coastline. Charleston was specifically mentioned. The report went on to say that the area should begin to experience the storm by dark that very day. Landfall was expected before midnight if it maintained current direction, speed and strength.

Jacob brought his rocker back in from the porch. He secured the remaining storm shutters, and started putting his food and ice into coolers to take down to the boat. He awakened Charlie and said it was time to go.

Jacob and Charlie rechecked the fuel, food and gear aboard *Pearl*. They stored the extra heavy line and large spare tires Jacob had brought along the night before to act as fenders. There was no way of knowing what they might run into on the creek. He lashed the tires to the foredeck, did a final inspection and they cast off.

Jacob wanted to get to the harbor as quickly as possible. They made good time down the creek. He could already feel heavier wind, even though that portion of Sullivan's Island was usually pretty well protected from the weather. The marsh grass on either side of the creek was swaying gently. There was not a single bird to be seen.

As they neared the waterway, large dark clouds were moving quickly overhead. Jacob looked over to Oliver and Susan's house. The Point looked peaceful enough, although the wind from the South was blowing even harder. Randy was again sitting in a chair on the floating dock, fishing, seemingly oblivious to the weather. The Grady White was in the boat lift. Jacob hollered to Randy, hoping to get his attention, to be sure he knew he should be getting inside soon. Randy's only reaction was a small wave. That puzzled Jacob; however he knew better than to stop now for Randy. He would have to take care of himself. Jacob had hoped he was far away from here in a safe place where someone could look after him.

Soon, they were in the harbor. A large container ship was in the shipping channel, making its way to the ocean while another ship at the Columbus Street docks downtown was just beginning its departure. Other sailboats and small vessels were in the harbor heading in a variety of directions. Jacob and Charlie continued towards the Cooper River Bridge, and then on to the Wando River beyond it, totally unaware that a skiff was following them at a discreet distance

When they entered the Wando, they headed north. The wind was strengthening. Dark, gray tinged clouds seemed to be massing together from the South. They laughed as some pelicans descended clumsily into the river near them, with none coming up with fish but still looking for food despite the oncoming storm.

Charlie was proudly wearing his new South Carolina Tech athletic shirt. He asked Jacob if he would introduce him to some of the coaches at the school. "The guys I knew then are all long gone, Charlie, but Tadpole is the guy to talk to. They all still love him up there. He was an All American, you know."

Charlie asked, "What is an All American?"

Jacob suddenly stiffened. He had finally noticed the skiff headed up the river behind them. As that boat drew nearer, he could see a familiar looking and much larger vessel not far behind it. It took him a few minutes to realize that larger vessel resembled Nathan Goldstein's *Bronx Cheer*.

'Couldn't be', he thought, 'Nathan has left town. I guess he's back in New York. But that isn't the same thing as his boat being gone.'

Jacob looked quickly back at the skiff and realized the two men in the skiff look uncomfortably familiar as well.

Focusing his binoculars, he could see it was Smithy and Hank.

'What in the hell?" Jacob watched as the skiff passed them well to starboard, and could see that both men were looking in their direction. Hank was on a radio of some sort. There were none of the usual friendly waves going back and forth that almost always accompanied two boats passing one another. The Bronx Cheer was several hundred yards to the stern of the skiff, and Jacob assured himself that just maybe this was all just a too weird coincidence.

Nonetheless, he told Charlie to go below, and to stay there until he told him otherwise. Jacob looked back through his binoculars at the Bronx Cheer's wheelhouse. Sean was at the helm, but there was also another man whose back was turned and walking away before Jacob could see his face. Sean was looking through binoculars as well, looking back at Jacob. Jacob put down his binoculars and waved his hand in the direction of the Bronx Cheer, which began moving in his direction. It never got any closer than a football field away, continuing upriver as it also passed Pearl while still following the skiff.

'Too weird, but how could they know each other? This has got to be a coincidence. '

After both the *Bronx Cheer* and the boat carrying Hank and Smithy were well up the river and out of sight, Jacob went below to make lunch. He sent Charlie up top to man the helm. They sat in the cockpit, enjoying the feel of *Pearl* moving through the waves that were beginning to form whitecaps on the Wando while they enjoyed some turkey sandwiches and chips.

Finally, Jacob left the Wando River, turning into Osprey Creek. He took down his sails, and motored to the spot Tadpole and Jaybird had showed him. No other boats were there and Jacob anchored as close to the creek bank as he felt comfortable. His depth finder showed that even with the tide going out there was plenty of water beneath *Pearl's* big keel. He felt that they are reasonably well protected from the winds because of the old oak and pine forest lying between his boat and the direction the storm should be coming from. The creek was wide enough so that the storm surge shouldn't do much damage, if any. There were plenty of oaks on the either bank that he would easily be able to tie up to. This was an excellent place to ride out this hurricane, he assured himself.

The wind continued to pick up and Jacob went below to listen to the latest radio reports. The National Weather Service was issuing small craft warnings for the Charleston area. Jacob came back on deck with the thick ropes and inflated a small life raft. He secured one end of a rope to a forward cleat and then put the life raft over the side. Climbing aboard, he gathered the balance of the rope and paddled ashore to wrap heavy line around a huge oak near the bank to secure *Pearl's* bow. He had spotted another oak directly across the creek that he planned to attach to her stern later on in the afternoon. He hesitated to do so right then in case another boat came along.

Jacob and Charlie took a swim in the black water. Jacob could feel that the current running through the creek was much stronger than he would have guessed. After they dried off, the two put out some fishing lines, wondering what they might catch back here on the edge of the swamp.

The wind continued to build. Tree limbs on either side of the creek were swaying. The air was thick with an energy that Jacob did not like very much, because it instantly reminded him of that storm that blew him into Charleston.

That day he was way out on the ocean, far from shore, hoping to completely avoid the Outer Banks of North Carolina. He knew they were called The Graveyard of the Atlantic for good reason. The wind kept rising as was the sea, and he was alone. The day got darker and he started following his GPS, getting closer to the coast line just to be careful.

He knew he was south of Charleston when his electronics had suddenly failed. The only working radio was his hand-held radio. His radar and GPS were gone, as was his depth finder. The sea kept building. *Pearl* was running through bigger and more dangerous waves veined with foam and spray. Some had great valleys between them, others with waves crossing in every direction. The wind continued to intensify .Even though he was only sailing with a reefed jib, Jacob fought the weather in a way he never had. *Pearl* heeled sharply to starboard and then to port. Water crashed onto the deck. The wind screamed at him. It seemed he would be torn from his safety belt at any moment. Although he was on the verge of terror, Jacob had felt oddly euphoric as well.

Then it started to rain. Great sheets of horizontal rain made visibility extremely difficult for him, especially with his glasses. He feared a huge rogue wave would suddenly crash through the clouds covering him; the wave suddenly looming above him before smashing *Pearl* into tiny bits of fiberglass. Jacob was soaked under his storm gear. As *Pearl* rose to the crest of a huge wave, Jacob saw a flicker of white far before him amidst the heaviest seas he had ever experienced. At the top of the next wave, he saw it again.

He realized it was a fishing boat headed rapidly to his port, with another not far behind it. Jacob had fired up his engine and followed the two boats, whose captains seemed to know exactly where they were headed. A huge rock jetty suddenly loomed before him. He was able to round a green buoy to port and continued forward through the huge swells until another jetty appeared before him out of the gloom. Jacob knew from his charts that this had to be Charleston. These jetties would lead to the harbor, and hopefully to some shelter from the storm. A large fishing boat passed him on his port side and Jacob adjusted his course to follow directly behind it, wanting to be sure he was as far from those jetties as he could be. Finally, he could see the fishermen way in front of him as they passed through the edge of the storm. He entered the harbor and anchored on the lee side of an island, thankful to be somewhere safe.

Sometimes, it seemed to Jacob that he was still sailing in the middle of that storm of twelve years ago.

Now he was on Osprey Creek, far from the sea, but again he felt a great wind building. The pine trees in the forest around him were beginning to noticeably sway. The marsh grass across the creek swayed. A great blue heron flew low down the creek .Many birds silhouetted against the gray clouds moved quickly above him.

Charlie's fishing pole was suddenly bending sharply downward. He definitely had something on his line. Jacob talked him through setting the hook, letting the fish run a little, and then slowly bringing it in. Jacob grabbed his net and got the fish, finding a good sized sea trout there. Jacob got it off the hook and showed Charlie how to hold it. Charlie had never caught a fish before and was very excited. When he asked what it was, Jacob replied it was a "Charlie Fish, related to the Charlie Horse, of course." Charlie was thrilled, and very proud of himself.

"Charlie, that is a sea trout. Keep it in the net while I get my camera." Jacob jumped below and was back quickly to photograph Charlie holding his fish. "Now we have to do something very important, Charlie. We are going to put that trout back into the creek." Charlie was surprised and disappointed, but as Jacob helped him, they both leaned over the gunwale with the fish and released it. Jacob then reached over to shake hands with Charlie, as if to congratulate him on his great catch, but instead grabbed his wrist and tossed him back into the creek. Jacob cannon balled in right next to him.

22

The wind continued to intensify.

By late afternoon the skies were covered with huge, thick gray clouds. The air was still quite hot, almost alive with an unusual, volatile energy. Jacob paddled the little life raft to the far bank to begin securing *Pearl's* stern to the great oak he had decided on earlier. He noticed several dark snakes gliding by in the creek and was glad he and Charlie were no longer swimming. He turned his body, looking for gators, but was especially glad to see none. An otter swam across Osprey Creek. Charlie called out to Jacob, wondering what it was. The creeks and marshes were all new terrain for the boy; he was captivated to be amongst all of the wild things living there.

Back on the boat, Jacob set two anchors in the creek. He felt like at that point that he had done all he could to be ready should the storm hit them. He was sure it would. The National Weather Service had just updated landfall for Hurricane Danielle to be before midnight, somewhere between Kiawah Island and Charleston Harbor. Jacob hoped it would swing out to sea before then. Jacob had several sets of foul weather gear below and retrieved them. They each put the yellow jackets on. Jacob didn't mind his legs getting wet, but worried a lot about hypothermia. Fortunately, Charlie's jacket fit him reasonably well.

Sitting together on a little bench seat in *Pearl's* cockpit, they watched the darkening clouds. Jacob was suddenly chilled. He was glad they had put the jackets on because the drop in temperature was so sudden. It began to rain, a swirling cold rain. The cloud cover kept thickening. Through the tress across the creek, Jacob could see a huge dark cloud suddenly drop lower in the sky over the river in the distance. A funnel suddenly appeared, then pulled back up into the cloud before funneling downward again as the huge dark system continued moving up the Wando. Jacob suddenly wondered why he had brought Charlie with him and potentially endangered the boy's life.' *Nothing to do about that now, though.'* They were there, and Jacob knew he would do everything he could to keep them both safe.

As the storm approached, it was time to have some dinner. This would be their last chance to eat before the storm hit. Jacob knew they would need every ounce of energy they could consume. They went below and started to prepare some food. Jacob put Charlie to work slicing tomatoes while Jacob pulled out the already cooked ham he had purchased at the grocery store, sliced it, and then ladled out some potato salad. Finally, he cut up some big chunks of French bread to complete dinner.

Jacob pulled out two cans of soda. They sat at the little fold-down table to feast.

"Here's to you, Charlie-the best fisherman on Osprey Creek."

Charlie was embarrassed but loved the moment as they touched their soda cans together in a toast. They ate quietly, feeling the wind outside building. They began hearing a weird whistling sound as the gale driven air passed through *Pearl's* rigging. The light fading through the little cabin windows changed colors from red to black and then to a strange, glowing green color. *Pearl* rocked back and forth beneath their feet.

"My Momma's name was Bessie," Charlie suddenly said, shyly looking first at his feet and then directly at Jacob. "Momma was a police officer in Baltimore, where I lived before coming here. She said she always wanted to be a cop. Her Uncle Ezra Mack was one and so was her grandfather. Her father was named Earl. I never met him 'cause he died in Vietnam when Momma was still little. But she remembered him, she remembered this great big man who would sweep her up and hold her over his smiling face as he twirled around on the floor. But he died and one day he wasn't ever coming back. So Momma and her sister Berthie, they went to live with my grandma Belle and her sister Auntie Joyce. Momma just wanted to be like her uncle. So she went to Police School. She learned how to be a really good police officer. Sometime she met some man and was really happy. Then I got created and the man left. She never told me his name .We quit talking about it. We had lots of good times together. She always took me to school except when she was on duty; then Auntie Joyce did. Momma used to read to me all the time. Me just sittin' in her lap and she would tell me all kinds of stories. And Momma really loved Michael Jackson and could dance just like him. You should a seen her do the moon walk, Jacob, she was something else. She always thought I looked just like him so she made sure I had a 'fro just like Michael's. You know, when he was younger before he got all weird.

Well, one night Momma was on duty. She just stuck her head in the door of a liquor store on her beat to say hello, but the place was being robbed. Momma didn't know it till too late and she got shot a couple times before she could do anything .The next thing I know we are standing next to her coffin in the church and everybody is crying except me cause I couldn't look at Momma there in that casket. I just kept imagining her doing the moonwalk and I haven't cut my hair since cause the last time I saw Momma, she was saying good bye with her fingers in my hair and tellin me she loved me and I should mind Aunt Joyce that night. But then Aunt Joyce got real sick and then she died too. So I had to come here to live with Aunt Berthie. She come here a long time ago 'cause she always in trouble with drinkin' and men and I don't know what else. Momma said if Berthie was in Baltimore she'd probably have to arrest her so it was good she was down here. But now I'm here and I miss Momma a lot. Berthie, she gets this check that's supposed to be for me every month from the police in Baltimore, so she don't even work at McDonalds any more. She just not feedin me much with it, or buying clothes. All the clothes I got are in that bag over there. So I'm not missin Berthie one bit. I like this storm a whole lot more. But I miss Momma. Every night when I'm in bed, I keep thinking she's gonna walk right through the door and lay down next to me, hold me in her arms and tell me everything about her day and ask about my day and then tell me a little story." Charlie finished, still looking right at Jacob.

"You're a good boy, Charlie. Bessie sounds like a remarkable person. I am sure there is a lot of her in you. Thank you for sharing all that. I know she's mighty proud of you right now, Charlie."

Jacob put on his rain slicker and went up on deck to check the lines and the weather. It was raining hard. The wind was over powering. The sky was dark with huge clouds moving rapidly just above them. Lightning was flashing constantly off in the distance back towards Charleston. The pines he could see were beginning to whip back and forth. He thought he saw a light moving through the trees down the creek and hoped another boat wasn't going to come in through the storm and the growing darkness. He could hear the wind screaming through the pines. *Pearl's* rigging was vibrating wildly.

Jacob checked everything to be sure he was ready for whatever might happen. He had to be cautious as he walked carefully on the pitching deck, watching for flying debris. The sail covers were tight. The spare tires hanging on each side of the boat were in place. Both anchors were still secure. Even so, *Pearl* was moving from side to side and up and down like she was dancing the Charleston. Using his flashlight, he could see the tide was now full in the creek with waves of at least a foot and a half. The rain was falling steadily. Going below, he did his hourly check on the weather news, and it wasn't good.

Earlier, it appeared Danielle had started to turn more to the north, but she was now back heading northwest, straight towards Charleston at 20 mph, with winds of 110mph. This was not good news; this was Category Three bad news. Jacob thought about how he had wished to be back in that storm of 12 years ago. Maybe he needed to be careful about what he wished for.

"You scared, Charlie?" Jacob asked. Charlie said he was. "That's OK. The truth is, I'm a little scared too. It keeps us on our toes, being scared. I've been in some really bad weather before and we are far away from the ocean up here. There are lots of big trees to keep that wind down. We have an entire forest out there to protect us. We'll be fine as long as we do what we are supposed to do. We are pretty far from the path of the storm, but it's going to be pretty bumpy for a while .Some waves will start building even back here. But we'll be OK, that's why we are here. I'm glad you came with me, Charlie. I appreciate you telling me about your Mom, she sounds like such a fine woman. I'll bet her spirit is with you. Maybe she is even here with you now Charlie. Don't get too into worrying, it won't help you. Keep your mind on your work and everything will be OK. Just know what's coming. It will probably get really loud and we'll be hearing strange sounds. Probably there will be lots of air pressure changes too. Just keep your mouth slightly open and keep clearing your ears like you would if we were flying. You ever been on an airplane Charlie?" Charlie hadn't. "Well, you will one of these days, so you'll know what to do. Yawn and hold your nose a little bit and blow out of your ears. Just do what I tell you to Charlie, and we'll be fine. You are quite a guy. We're going to be just fine."

And then the storm really hit. It sounded like hail was blowing against the deck with lots of pinging sounds over and over. The wind was enormous. A huge roaring sound like that of a freight train filled the air.

"Jacob, look at your arms," Charlie hollered. The hairs were standing straight up on his arms and hands. Charlie was scared. Jacob grabbed his hand. "Look at me Charlie, you take a deep breath right now and blow it out. You get nervous, you take a deep breath. You might never have an experience like this in your life again. Don't let the fear overwhelm you, just let it keep you alert."

Pearl was listing to starboard, but straightened right up. Jacob was thankful that her keel was very heavy,

The storm continued to bash them for another hour or so with tremendous winds. The port cabin windows were constantly blazing with a strange green phosphorescent light. The boat was in constant motion. They could hear trees breaking amidst the tremendous wall of sounds. Jacob silently prayed that the oaks they had tied up to were big enough that their root systems would keep them in place. Charlie sat on the cabins bench in a tight ball, his eyes closed. Jacob sat next to him, remaining as calm on the outside as he could in case Charlie looked at him for comfort.

Inside Jacob was as frightened as Charlie appeared to be. His body was extraordinarily tense as he waited to hear or feel a serious problem. He mainly feared that one of the pine trees might fall directly on the boat, or that something large might be propelled by the wind or the water directly through the hull. The tension built as the storm continued gathering force. *Pearl* was rocketing from side to front to side again. The wind screamed violent sounds through the rigging. The mast shuddered so strongly it could be felt throughout the boat. Jacob could only hang on, be prepared and most of all, keep an eye on Charlie, to protect him if something went terribly wrong.

23

And then the wind just stopped.

"What is happening?' shouted Charlie. 'Is it over? Omigod! It's over! We did it, we through it!' Charlie was jumping up and down in sheer happiness.

'It's just the eye of the storm, Charlie. The worst part is coming. But let's go up on deck and enjoy it while we can.'

They opened the hatch. The cockpit was covered in branches, which they quickly threw over the side, clearing their way to the bow. Jacob quickly checked all the lines, using his flashlight to look around them. Ahead of the bow, they could see a huge pine tree lying across the creek. Jacob was relieved that it didn't have them trapped in the creek. He could see the dark water rushing by. A small tree passed by with lots of what looked like red eyes everywhere. When he shined the flashlights beam on it, he could see the tree was full of snakes just drifting towards the Wando River. Jacob shuddered. He hated snakes, which was probably why he preferred sailing and fishing in the ocean and the harbor and not up around these black water creeks.

The sky was clear. Osprey Creek was very choppy. *Pearl* was bobbing significantly. They could see stars everywhere.

The air temperature rose quickly. It was very quiet; a breeze rattled through the rigging. They could hear the swaying sound of distant trees and the occasional thump of limbs smashing to the ground. In the distance, they heard a loud creaking sound followed by a big splash, which was probably a pine falling into the creek somewhere.

Jacob sat on the cockpit's bench. Charlie was next to him, his eyes closed, exhausted after this very full day on the water. Jacob felt tired as well, but he knew a long night still lay ahead for them. He watched the stars, marveling at the clearness of the night. He felt a great stiffness in his neck and shoulders and stood to stretch; bracing his legs against the swaying of the deck, he began swinging his arms slowly back and forth in an arc trying to loosen them up. He was also rotating his head as much as he could, hoping to lessen the ache in his neck from the stress of the last few hours, all the while watching the trees, hoping none were poised to collapse on *Pearl*.

He looked about, wondering if any boats were in trouble nearby. There had been so much confusion on his radio earlier as he had scanned from channel to channel, he had turned it off. He had left just one overhead light on in the cabin during the lull. He would turn that off when the storm returned to save as much battery power as possible. Looking about him, he was glad *Pearl* was in such good shape with no apparent damage. He hoped for the best when the storm returned, wishing it was peeling away from the coast as had been forecast earlier.

Something was catching his eye in the darkness. He suddenly realized something very big and dark was moving very rapidly directly at them. It took Jacob a moment to realize that it was a huge boat, seemingly on a course to ram them.

Instinctively he turned and shoved Charlie back into the main cabin, hollering "Charlie, brace yourself." Charlie looked puzzled but jumped back on to the bench seat, grabbing a hand hold.

There was a huge banging sound. *Pearl* lurched sideways, but there no accompanying tearing sounds of damage to the hull. '*The spare tires must have really helped, and maybe the wave action.*' The wind started in again. A wave picked *Pearl* up and then quickly put her back down. Jacob slid down the deck, nearly going over the side. The other ship loomed above him, silhouetted by the green fluorescent skies flashing around them. The wind was suddenly tremendous. Jacob was stunned by how suddenly the tempest had reappeared. He disbelieved what he was seeing. Another wave brought *Pearl* even higher, and Jacob slid back towards the cockpit as the other boat bashed *Pearl's* starboard hull before it fell into a trough just at impact, hitting with a glancing blow that knocked Jacob tumbling through the hatch into the cabin. He landed hard on the deck below, his funny bone not in a comical mood.

Another brilliant flash of lightning illuminated the cabin. Jacob jumped to his feet. He turned towards the hatch when suddenly he saw first one boat shoe and then another with a leg following through the opening. They started down the ladder.

Ignoring the pain in his arm, Jacob reacted instinctively. A huge powerful surge thundered through him, carrying him forward. In a rising motion, powered by a primal energy that roared through him, he smashed his face and shoulder into the stranger's chest, driving him into the wall of the stairwell. Images flashed before Jacob's inner mind: he saw the coyote's eye, the sharks, and then his own from long ago. It was like hitting that Alabama running back, driving him upward into the sky.

Jacob realized it was Smithy's body that had crashed backwards, whose head smacked hard against the wooden hatch. Jacob's momentum brought Smithy's head forward; it smashed into the wooden frame of the other side of the stairwell before he began falling to the cabin floor below, dropping a pistol from his hand Jacob lost what balance he had and fell backwards, landed on top of Smithy just as the pistol hit the cabin floor.

Jacob began twisting his body around, wanting to get off Smithy, who was unconscious beneath him.

Just as Jacob began to rise, there was a huge explosion from a gunshot, just behind him. He looked up to see Charlie crouched before him, holding the pistol with both hands, the barrel aimed back up through the hatch above Jacob. Gun smoke filled the cabin. There was a tremendous ringing sound in Jacob's right ear.

"It's him!" Charlie shouted franticly. "It dat little guy from de island."

'Hank!' realized Jacob. He started up the ladder and then stopped.

"Charlie, you must not let this man get up," Jacob commanded, handing Charlie a small baseball bat he kept near the hatch way, just in case. "I have to go find that guy. Did you hit him? "

"I'se hopes so," Charlie replied, taking the bat as Jacob grabbed the pistol from Charlie's hand. Turning, he bounded up to the hatch.

The wind knocked Jacob momentarily backwards. It was beginning to flatten everything it smashed into. Jacob was in as low a crouch as possible, holding desperately on to the firmly cleated mainsail's line as he scanned the deck. Huge flashes of lightning illuminated everywhere Jacob looked .There was no sign at all of Hank.

Jacob pulled his flashlight out of his pocket, thankful it still worked. He crawled his way carefully on the pitching deck to the other boat, which he saw was attached to one of *Pearl's* cleats with a line. Jacob wasn't surprised to see it was the *Bronx Cheer*. He crept on her deck, staying low as he searched for Hank. He could see no sign of him. Jacob quickly returned to *Pearl*, knowing Smithy was alone in the cabin with Charlie. He released the rope connecting the two boats before leaping down the steps back into the cabin.

Charlie was standing over the motionless Smithy in the gun smoke filled cabin, the bat in his hand poised to do business. Jacob reached back and pulled the hatch door securely shut, and then knelt, feeling for a pulse. It was strong. He examined Smithy, glad he heard him breathing heavily. His eyes were shut, his prominent hook-nose was bleeding heavily. More blood streamed from a gash on his forehead. The blood gathered into his full beard. Jacob used a rag to clean the nosebleed, then removed the bandana from his own neck and carefully wrapped it around Smithy's head wound, hoping to at least stop the blood from flowing.

In addition to Hank being outside somewhere, Hurricane Danielle was definitely back. Cascades of rain smashed *Pearl*. The boat was again very much in motion. Jacob needed to be prepared to act on whatever came next. He had some line and bungee cords in a locker. Pulling them out, he bound Smithy's hands and feet before dragging him by the shoulders down the cabin floor to a small storage locker. He hoped the unconscious man would fit. Fortunately, he was able to push Smithy into it without hurting him any further. He closed the locker before double bungee cording it to secure the door from being pushed open from within.

Jacob turned to Charlie. "What the hell happened, Charlie? Where did you get the gun?"

"It fell off that guy you smashed into the stairwell. Wow! Jacob that was .. Mom, she showed me, she said maybe I might..if I shot at somebody. Dat short guy. Jacob, those were the guys I saw on de island, the tall guy, short guy.. what...why they here? Dat tall one.. he locked in back there ?'

Charlie checked the small cabin door and could feel it was secure.

"Jacob.. de udder guy.. did I hit him?"

"I don't know Charlie, I didn't see him. I better look for him again."

Pearl was bouncing wildly up, down and sideways. Thunder was booming. The cabin windows lit up with a weird pulsing green and red light from outside. There was again the sound like that of a freight train in the distance.

"Keep your eye on that locker door, Charlie. Hold this." He handed the gun back to Charlie. Jacob looked directly into his eyes very briefly. He was certain Charlie got the message that Smithy was very dangerous and Jacob was trusting Charlie to be sure Smithy stayed in that sail locker.

Jacob headed quickly up the ladder, pulling the wooden door closed behind him as he sprang back to the deck.

24

The wind was vicious. Jacob knew he was in constant danger of all kinds of nasty things happening. But he had to know where Hank was. The *Bronx Cheer* was silhouetted by the peculiar pulsing green light in the sky towards Charleston. Pine straw smacked his face. Non-stop blasts of tremendous lightning pulsed through dense clouds in every direction. An intense roaring sound surrounded him. He whipped the flashlight around him, doing his best to remain out of harms way while the deck pitched and rolled beneath him.

And then something big was coming right at him. Jacob managed to duck just in time. He heard a horrible scream. Someone was down, just in front of him.

'Crap, its Hank!' he thought, just as *Pearl's* mast crashed next to him, barely missing his shoulder. With his flashlight, he could just make out the form of someone under the fallen mast.

Jacob thought he was hallucinating. Edmund Capers was before him pinned to the deck by *Pearl's* mast. The man was in agony. A revolver lay next to his hand. Jacob grabbed the gun and put it into his pocket after being sure the safety was on.

"Help me!" screamed Edmund. Jacob pulled on the mast. It wouldn't budge. He grabbed Edmunds arm, which produced another scream. But he was able to start freeing Edmund as he began dragging him from under the mast.

"Easy man, easy," moaned Edmund.

"Fuck you," said Jacob.

He pulled the screaming man from under the mast and then into the cockpit. The weather was awful. The hurricane driven rain hurt as it kept hitting Jacob anywhere he wasn't protected by his foul weather gear. He grabbed Edmund again and started inching him towards the hatch. There was a huge lurch and splash as *Pearl* rolled off of *Bronx Cheer's* deck.

Jacob was operating totally on instinct. He opened the hatch and stepped onto the top rail, grabbing Edmund under both of his arms, pulling him. Jacob wasn't sure how he was getting him down the steps and to safety. The power of the storm was tremendous. *Pearl* was rocking and rolling. Jacob just kept moving down the steps as well as he could. Edmund screamed with each step but there wasn't anything else to do. Finally, Jacob had Edmund on the cabins floor. Jacob went back up to close the hatch, securing it.

"You OK, Charlie?' Jacob was glad the cabin light was still on. He realized that it would have to stay on now, and hopefully wouldn't pull much of the charge from the battery.

Charlie's eyes were wide but fearless. He was holding onto a handhold with one hand and the other held the gun, which was pointed at the sail locker holding Smithy.

"You OK?" Jacob asked again. Charlie just nodded, his eyes not leaving the little door.

"Ever seen this guy before?" Charlie looked quickly, and then shook his head no as he kept his feet braced against sliding on the cabin floor.

Jacob dragged the passed out Edmund through the boat, depositing him in the stern sleeping cabin. He kept the door open so a faint light from the cabin lantern could come in to the little room. With his flashlight, Jacob examined Edmund as well as he could. The boat was fully in motion, rocking up and down while also moving back and forth, doing lot's of fancy dancing in the stormy creek. Jacob hoped the heavy lines had plenty of elasticity to them and prayed they would keep *Pearl* approximately positioned in the center of the creeks deep water. Jacob could see that Edmund's leg was at a bit of a weird angle. His left arm was painfully distended. *'The guy must be in shock,'* Jacob thought, as he began to recognize what looked like a disguise. Edmund had grown a bit of a beard. His salt and pepper hair was now dark and cut very short: his horn rimmed glasses were gone. Jacob wondered how he had recognized him so quickly on the deck in the storm. Looking at him now, he realized he wouldn't have been able to so quickly on the street. Maybe it was his voice. Jacob raced into the salon, grabbed some extra line stashed there and quickly returned, cutting off a slice and tied Edmund loosely to the bunk.

Jacob could hear Smithy periodically kicking at the locker door. It seemed that maybe he might be giving up on the idea he could get it open. Against his better judgment, Jacob walked past Charlie, and braced himself for the boats movement. He retrieved a bottle of water from the kitchen and twisted it slightly open.

"Charlie, I need you to move yourself away from the door over here so you can cover me," Jacob said.

Charlie moved, looking anxiously up at Jacob as he untied the line securing the door. As he put his hand on the lockers catch, he said "Ready Charlie?" The boy nodded, putting both hands on the guns grip, pushing his back against the cabin wall to brace himself.

Jacob pulled the door open. Cabin light fell on Smithy who was now seated upright in a corner, looking in some pain.

"How's your head?" Jacob asked.

"Better than yours is going to be," replied Smithy, more quietly than Jacob would have guessed. The man's eyes seemed dull and heavy. "You are going to pay for this. Hank will be around to pay a visit."

'Sure, we are counting on it," Jacob replied, hoping to sound as full of bravado as he could. He hoped Smithy didn't notice that the thought of Hank returning didn't exactly thrill him. "Here, this may help you feel better." Jacob quickly put the bottle of water next to Smithy's hand, hoping the next roll of the boat didn't cause him to smack his head on something.

"I got to pee," Smithy said.

"Go for it," Jacob replied, closing the locker door. He quickly made the line on the door secure, glad to have that over with.

Standing, bracing himself, he asked Charlie if he wanted to take a break from guard duty. Charlie did, and Jacob took his spot with the pistol aimed at the locker as Charlie lay on the bench. *Pearl* rolled again and Charlie sat bolt upright, but kept his eyes closed for awhile.

Now all Jacob and Charlie had to do was get through the rest of Hurricane Danielle. They were both feeling exhausted. Jacob could see Charlie's eye staring to droop. He urged him to lie down on the bench for a short while. There was no argument from the boy.

After a time, the weather seemed to be calming a bit. The screaming sound of the wind passing through *Pearl's* rigging was lessening.

Charlie woke after a short nap and came over to Jacob. "I'm alright." he said, reaching for the gun.

Jacob got up and sat with Edmund for awhile, watching him until he regained a bit of consciousness. Jacob had retrieved the bottle of Irish Whiskey, as well as a small container of Percodan he happened to have on board. He lifted Edmund so he could drink some whiskey, and then put several of the painkillers in Edmund's mouth, before helping Edmund drink some more of the Jameson's. He knew Edmund wasn't a drinker. An idea suddenly occurred to Jacob. Satisfied Edmund was feeling somewhat less pain, Jacob went back to check on Charlie. "Are you doing OK over here? "

Jacob sat next to Charlie on the cabin floor facing the locker containing Smithy, putting his arm around Charlie.

"I'm so proud of you Charlie, and so glad you are here.'

"You were so brave Charlie. Your Mom would be so proud of you too. She trained you well. That dude in there is a very bad one. I don't know where his friend is. When the wind slows a little, I'm going over to the *Bronx Cheer.* That's the boat they tried to ram us with. We were lucky, somehow they just nudged us, a wave or something knocked them off course at the last minute. I don't know why they tried that but they did. We have to deal with this and I am counting on you, Charlie. You are doing a great job. Stay focused and awake. I trust you completely. The situation is that our mast is down, that's what that big crash was, but everything else is OK. We can motor out of here after I get the mast secured later. We just can't do it now. You feeling alright, your stomach OK with all this motion here in the cabin?"

Charlie nodded.

"Are those the guys you saw on the island, Charlie?"

"Yeah, dat dem. I ain't believing this shit Jacob. Who dat other dude?"

"His name is Edmund Capers. I am not sure what exactly is happening, Charlie. Edmund is supposed to be dead. I just looked in on him, he is sort of awake but in serious pain and I don't know how to help him. I gave him some whiskey and he fell back asleep."

Jacob didn't believe he could hear any sounds from inside the locker. "Charlie, I am going to take a look at that guy in there. I want to be sure he is alright for now. I need you to be ready is anything happens. If you see him you shoot immediately, aim for his chest. You ready? "

Charlie got to his feet and backed into a crouch while bracing against the cabin wall. Holding the pistol with both hands, his eyes focused on the locker door, he nodded to Jacob that he was ready. Jacob had the other gun ready, praying he wouldn't have to use it. He undid one of the bungee cords and quickly pulled the door open. Some of the cabin's light spilled in on Smithy, still in a sitting position in the corner. His hands and feet were still bound. Smithy's eyes blazed with fury.

"Get me out of here, you asshole, I can't breathe in here. I'm getting seasick."

'"No way, man. You are staying put until we are out of here. I will open the door from time to time, but we have a big ass storm out here. Don't get any ideas. There are two guns out here and we are a little on edge. You try anything and what happens is on you, not us. Got it?"

Jacob re-secured the locker door. Smithy kicked at it briefly, and then stopped, apparently realizing it wasn't going to break open.

The wind screamed for another hour or so, and then gradually, began to dissipate.

25

As the storm began to mellow, Jacob went back on deck. The night was beautiful. Stars shone brightly between fast moving clouds. The breeze had calmed some was still blowing steadily.

A sense of exhaustion seemed to have fallen across Osprey Creek. The forest was still, with occasional sounds of limbs falling. Lightening continued to flash much further to the Northeast. The *Bronx Cheer* was not immediately in sight. Using his flashlight Jacob could see it was further down the creek, wedged into the fallen pine. Jacob turned his cell phone on and quickly saw there was no service.

Going back below, he fired up *Pearl's* engine. Thankfully, it immediately roared into life. He attempted to make a radio call for help, but all the channels are jammed with messages. SOS seemed to be the norm. Jacob realized he may well have to wait for daylight in order to motor out to find medical help and the police.

He could not believe everything that had happened. Jacob was dog-tired but alert.

He knew Hank was out there somewhere and could reappear at any moment.

Back on deck, Jacob sat staring at the sky. He marveled at how the storm had been so violent, so magnificent. He thanked God he and Charlie have gotten through this experience alive and in one piece. Jacob started to think about Jody, and decided that no, he was not going to do that. She was gone and he was moving on. He thought about Peter Madison and Hamilton Brothers and knew he was done with that as well. He hoped his house on Sullivan's Island made it through the Hurricane in one piece. He didn't know what was next. He thought about something his mother used to say to him, that he needed a big bang on the head before he got the message. Jacob couldn't imagine a bigger bang on the head than Hurricane Danielle.

Jacob went below and found Charlie asleep on the salons bench seat. There were no sounds coming from Smithy.

Jacob went back to check on Edmund, who was awake and in agony.

"For a dead guy, you really look like crap, Edmund. Here, finish off this whiskey. It will help you feel a bit better."

Edmund opened his mouth and Jacob helped him get the whiskey into his mouth. Edmund swallowed deeply and then gulped down some more. *'Pretty amazing for a guy who says he doesn't drink.'* Jacob put the empty bottle on the floor next to him and turned to face Edmund.

Jacob looked at him closely.

"You want to tell me what this was all about? I don't get it."

Groaning, Edmund tried to move and couldn't. "Why am I tied up, Jacob?"

"We weren't worried about you running away, Edmund. Do you remember the Hurricane at all? I didn't want you to roll off this bunk and get more injured. Now tell me what this is about? Who was the guy they found out on the Island that everyone believed was you?"

Edmunds words were already becoming increasingly slurred, but he seemed eager to talk.

"Some homeless guy Smithy found near Myrtle Beach. He was built like me. Goldstein really put all this together. He's a pretty smart dude. Did you figure out that wasn't him you met on his boat?"

"What??"

"Yeah, that guy works for him, he's an actor. Maybe he was a lawyer once, I don't know. He sort of looks like Nathan G. But, it wasn't him."

"You see Southern Shipping had a number of investments. One went really bad. It was organized by Goldstein. We ended up in the hole. We lost a lot of money. This wasn't the only bad deal we made over the last couple years. We had to use a lot of the retirement money to keep our ass solvent. That Broad Street Bank account you wanted so badly doesn't have half of what it used to, not that old Joey Browne would have a clue about that. Then Goldstein made us general partner on a deal. That one suddenly looked like a Ponzi scheme and our name-alright, my name, was all over it. I figured I'd think of something to get us from out and under. I thought about taking the company public or something but didn't want the SEC to figure it out. Dear old cousin Buddy didn't know anything about any of it. He would have fried everyone's ass, the prick. Anyways, I knew Smithy from Key West. You never asked me if I had ever been there. I used to run dope with Smithy down there and then through McClellanville. It was a kick. My ancestors were all smugglers and bootleggers so I figured I could do it too. We made lots of money. Just not enough. There was never enough.

"Damn, Jacob, my leg is really hurting; can you move it at all? Thanks.

"I met Nathan when he was here about Harvey Ross. Goldstein has a lot of specialties. One is making people seem very dead as far as the law is concerned. He's the best at it. So we stayed in touch .He put me onto some deals that did really well. So when this thing came along we went in big. I just kept moving money around. But it all went to shit. I really wanted to find a way to land all this on Oliver Marshall, and that's where you came into the picture. We want that place he calls Whistling Dixie. Eventually, you were going to lead him straight to Nathan Goldstein. I would do anything to finally pay that prick back for everything the Marshalls have done to my family. But somebody needed to be the fall guy, and I decided it had to be you, Jacob. Nothing personal, you're a good guy, but someone was going down and it wasn't gonna be me. We figured if we couldn't directly burn the Marshalls then a friend of theirs would do just as well. Maybe tie them in somehow. It was nothing against you, it was just everything. I had one of my friends in town give the police some crap about how you were screwing Julia. We set up an investment account in your name with a bank in the Caymans. You have over a million dollars in it, you dumb shit. How's it feel to actually be a millionaire, Jacob? You'll just never get your hands on it. You are just screwed is all. Smithy got that street guy; they filled him with liquor before they killed him with my propeller. Then they towed him across the harbor. It was supposed to look like I got drunk, fouled my motor and didn't think to kill the engine when I pulled it up and got pulled into it—Do you have any more of that whiskey?-my arm hurts like hell-- They wanted him to wash up on Oliver Marshalls front doorstep. I was going to get out of town, my ever lovin' dumb ass of a wife would get lots of insurance and then I would show back up at some point. But this flippin' hurricane came along and screwed everything.

"I saw that kid on the island. It took me a little while to recognize what shirt he was wearing, what that was. Charleston's #1 All-Stars. What a name for a bunch of half-assed kids from the East Side. With his hair-I figured we would find him. With all those stories in the paper about that place, we knew right where to look-—oh, oh man, my arm, do you have anything? --Then I remembered you were pals with that football player over there. So the plan was looking good. We were following you all week out on the island, ever since you left your dock. We put it together fast. We had Smithy watch where you went after we passed you out there on the river. Then we came into the creek watch-ing you with night vision binoculars through the trees. It wasn't anything personal against you, Jacob. We just needed to get rid of that kid. He saw all three of us out on Castle

Pinckney that night. We were going to do you guys in during the eye, but a flipping pine tree fell across the damn boat and slowed us down. We didn't want another boat to show up so we waited and made sure no one did. We would have figured something out if someone did show. But damn that tree. So we got here late but figured we'd be done in a few minutes. Smithy is pretty good at doing this. You know how many people he has done in, Jacob? Lots! Hanks a lot worse. You got him too? But you know something, Jacob? This is all my word against yours. Unless you are going to dump me over the side or something, but I bet you won't. Ronnie Bolt, my lawyer friend in the upstate, is real good at figuring something out on deals like this. You'll just be screwed again. We own the police here anyway, you know, like we own everything here in Charleston. So I'll make you a deal. You get me out of here and I'll get you $100,000 cash. Today, no problems, no questions, $100,000- make it $150,000 in your hand. Good pay off for you. What do you say? I know you need money Jacob. I can even get you in on our next pot runs. The Wind of Fortune will be back next week and she always has a special container aboard. That's another $10,000 for you every month, tax-free. Good deal for you, low risk, and big pay. What do you say? Want to get rich, Jacob? This is your chance. Just get me out of here!"

"Let me see if I've got this straight. You guys killed that poor guy. You got yourself into all kinds of financial fraud. You are smuggling pot through Southern Shipping and have been involved with other murders. Now, you will pay me a lot of cash so you can just walk away from all this. Is that it?"

"Yeah, so what?"

"So, fuck you. I think the police will be really interested in this tape Edmund," said Jacob, pulling his handheld tape recorder out of his shirt pocket. "I got the whole thing down. While the tape is still rolling, let me add that, just for the record- You really are a complete asshole, Edmund, and deserve every bit of the crap that is surely headed your way."

Jacob turned off the recorder, got up and relocked Edmunds door. He put the recorder in a plastic sandwich baggy, which he made sure was sealed extra tight, and then returned the recorder to his backpack.

Jacob suddenly felt really tired. It had been a long, draining night, the hurricane, nailing Smithy, and dragging Edmund in here and getting the story. He was glad the storm was headed elsewhere, that *Pearl* was reasonably intact and that Charlie was with him.

'*The kid has been great.*'

Charlie was still sitting on the cabin floor, the pistol still pointed at the locker holding Smithy, but his eyes were starting to sag.

"How you doing, Charlie?"

"I alright, but I gots ta pee," he said, looking up anxiously at Jacob.

"Ok, give me the gun, I'll take over, you go ahead and I'll keep an eye on things." Jacob said as Charlie quickly closed the door to the head.

One of the cabin windows above Jacob suddenly shattered, the sound magnified by the quiet that was just settling throughout the boat.

Jacob didn't know what had just happened, but in a flash he grabbed a nearby flashlight and leaped up the steps towards the deck. He thrust the cabin door open, but hesitated, knocked backward by a sway of the boat. A large tree limb smashed down onto the opening before him, just missing him.

And then Hank suddenly leaped in front of Jacob. With the cabin light, Jacob could see a wound that still oozed blood which covered half of his face, a huge blood red smear over his white t-shirt, and crazy eyes above a nose that seemed to have been broken, and then broken again long ago.

Hanks hands were outstretched coming right at Jacob. The suddenness of the attack was unnerving. Jacob took a half step backwards and down. He grabbed the muscular forearms and pulled Hank towards him. Falling, twisting, the two men fell, crashing onto the salons deck.

The pistol flew from Jacob's hands. The flashlight dropped as he went for Hank. His wind knocked out of him, Jacob turned sideways. Hank rose up before him, his huge fist crashed down on Jacobs face, stunning him. Jacob kicked up, catching Hank and Jacob lunged at him, knocking him back down. Hank's head bounced off the floor. Jacob tried to push him back down. Jacob was looking directly at Hank's face, covered in blood, splinters of wood protruding in several places, including his almost closed right eye. There were many days' worth of stubble below his nose with a large scar running across it and down one cheek, his eyes the color of the sea under short brown hair. A tattoo of a deaths head with wings was centered on his throat.

Hank suddenly lifted Jacob's chest and arms straight up. His remarkably strong arms flipped Jacob unto his back. Jacob looked up and saw his flashlight in Hanks hand, beginning to descend straight at him.

26

"Freeze or I will blow your fucking head off," shouted a voice above Jacob. The sound of a shotgun ratcheted for action emphasized the command. "Put your nose into that deck right now or your sorry ass is grass. Do It!"

Slowly, a drop of blood landed on Jacobs face. Hank stared down at him, his eyes dead like a shark's. He was motionless for a moment until he slowly rolled off of Jacob and lay face up on the teak flooring of the cabin.

Jacob was also stunned. He looked up to see Randy slowly descending the steps, a shotgun aimed directly at Hank.

But that wasn't Randy's voice.

"Get your hands behind you. Do not try some half assed move here now, man. I will not hesitate to put you down. Jacob, get something to tie him with."

Jacob looked up, disbelieving his own eyes as Matthew Marshall pulled the thick wig and beard off of his face.

Jacob slowly got to his feet, feeling unsteady. His jaw ached, but he was glad he didn't feel any loose teeth.

"How's it going Jacob?" Matthew stood before him, his blond hair shorter than Jacob remembered. Half a grin was on his face, although Matthew didn't take his eyes off Hank.

Matthew was soaking wet under a red rain slicker."Who's your pal here?"

"What the fuck kept you?" Jacob asked, laughing in relief.

"Well, you motherfucker," growled Hank, his black eyes glaring at Matthew.

"I didn't say you could speak," Matthew snapped at Hank, before smashing the shotgun's butt into the side of his head. Hanks eyes slowly shut as his head fell sideways,

"Matthew, man, I am so glad you are here-but where the hell did you come from?"

"Long story, Jake-but I trailed behind these guys while they followed you. I didn't know what they were doing, but I had your back." Matthew turned to look at Jacob. "You alright? You look like shit."

Just as Matthews eyes moved away from him, Hank moved like a huge cat. Despite his injuries, he leaped to his feet and snarled, charging straight at Matthew and the shotgun. Matthew reacted just a little too slowly. Hank smashed into him. The shotgun fired, knocking out a cabin window as Matthew fell backwards towards the floor. Hank ran right over him and was back up on the deck in a flash. Jacob went right after him, but got to the deck only in time to see Hanks feet as he dove into the swirling darkness of Osprey Creek. Jacob rushed to the spot he last saw Hank, but could see nothing of the guy, only black water rushing past *Pearl's* stern.

Matthew and Charlie joined him on deck. None of them had any idea where Hank was. They each wearily sat on the gunnels looking about them. The rain had stopped and the wind was easing. The sky to the South was clearing.

The storm was moving away from them.

27

"How are you doing, Charlie?" Jacob asked.

"I couldn't shoot. I didn't want to hit one of you," Charlie answered sadly as he handed the pistol to Jacob.

Jacob stopped him. "No, Charlie. You did great. You hold onto that gun. I hope you don't need it but that dude is out there somewhere. He probably won't return, at least not today. I trust you as much as anyone I know. You hold onto it. '

Jacob moved so he was sitting next to Charlie. He put his arm around the boys shoulder. "I am really proud to call you my friend Charlie. You were a man when I needed one. Thank you."

Charlie slumped slightly, leaning against Jacob for a moment before sitting up, shoulders straight. "Thanks Jacob, I'm proud to be your friend too."

And then Charlie looked at Matthew.

"Charlie, this is my very old and good friend Matthew Marshall, who has a habit of showing up at just the right moment. Charlie-would you go down below and bring up some flashlights? We need to all be on watch for awhile until daylight and I want to get Matthew up to speed on what has been going on here."

"Jacob... can... Can I'se pee now?" asked Charlie, not waiting for an answer, hurrying below.

"Matthew. You are unbelievable. Where did you come from? What are you doing here? I can't believe how happy I am to see you. So what has been going on?"

"I've been watching these guys for a while, Jake. I got back a few weeks ago. I was able to finally send Randy home to his family. But, I didn't want anyone to know I was back. I just wanted to chill out for awhile. It's a long story. But the day I got back, that dude and another, a tall guy looking something like Blackbeard, were at the house, walking in the yard with the late great asshole Edmund Capers. I don't know why they were there .So I pretended to be Randy. I actually had impersonated him at a Halloween party once so I still had the wig and beard. I wanted to see what weird stuff the Capers might be up to this time. I figured if they just thought Randy was the only person at The Point they would feel free to do whatever they had in mind. You know, thinking maybe that was Edmund being the jerk off he has always been and they weren't up to anything at all. I didn't know. I thought about surprising you but figured we would catch up sooner or later. You saw me one night on my bike-actually Randy's beach cruiser. Remember that night you drove up to me while I was riding? I thought for sure you'd recognized me even when I tried to imitate his voice. Anyway, I was out riding the bike last night and passed these guys sitting in an old truck down the street from your house.

It seemed like they were watching you, which I thought strange. Then, I was getting the Grady White secured when I saw you coming on Pearl with Charlie here and I knew you were taking her someplace safe. But a little later these guys came by. It took me a few minutes, but I suddenly remembered who Smithy was from the Key's. He was one scary freak. I thought it was weird so I decided to follow all of you. I left the wig and beard on to stay in character. It actually helped me stay a little warmer and drier during the hurricane. I rode that storm right behind them. Then I got all screwed up with a pine tree I had trouble getting past after the storm. Really tough to do that in the dark. I'm glad I got here when I did. And when I saw this guy up close, I also remembered him. Where is Smithy?"

"You won't believe what has been happening, Matthew. I've got Edmund Capers—yes, Edmund Capers-down below all locked in a cabin, and this guy's pal is down there too. Smithy is down there locked in the sail locker" Jacob said pointing. "And Edmund Capers is in the cabin." Jacob added. "I think he's been looking forward to listening to his own eulogy."

Now it was Matthews turn to be amazed.

"You mean to say Edmund is really not dead? Then what the…What has been going on? You sure know how to throw weird Hurricane parties, Jake. Keep me off the list for the next one, OK"

Charlie returned on deck.

"Charlie, you are officially off duty. You have earned a long nights rest, but not tonight. We still have plenty to do but you go sleep now while you can." Jacob walked over to him. "Charlie, I am so impressed with you. If it weren't for you and how brave you were, I don't want to think about what would have happened. I know you had that gun pointed at that guy when he was about to whack me with the flashlight. Thank you Charlie, I owe you big. You are quite a man." Jacob then shook Charlie's hand.

Charlie seemed almost embarrassed and looked at Jacob sheepishly.

Matthew approached Charlie. "Good to meet you, Charlie. Thank you for being there for my old buddy. I hope we can be friends too." The two shook hands, and then, Matthew gently embraced Charlie, embarrassing him further."You look good with a TigerSharks shirt on, Charlie. It suits you. Is Jacob recruiting you to come to Tech?"

This was all too much for Charlie. He lay down on the bench, his eyes closing before his head reached the little pillow.

Jacob and Matthew alternated attempts on the radio, but there was still too much traffic, Maydays, missing boats, friends checking on friends. They decided to give it a rest. Through the windows they could see dawn starting to reveal whatever damage Danielle had done in Osprey Creek.

"You want to go back up on deck, Jacob? I'll keep an eye on everybody down here." Matthew offered.

28

Dawn finally broke. Stepping up to the cockpit, Jacob inspected the damage to the hatchway caused by Charlie's pistol shot at Hank. He noted how splintered the wood was; a huge section of it was missing and he thought of the damage done to that assholes face.

The sunrise was glorious. The sky was streaked in shades of red, yellow and deep purple. A cool breeze was blowing through the forest, bringing with it the strong smell of pine. The tide was flowing into Osprey Creek, bringing with it lots of after hurricane debris. Matthews Grady White was lashed bow and stern to *Pearl's* gunwale.

Jacob could easily see the *Bronx Cheer* further up the creek, lodged amidst the limbs of a huge pine that had fallen. The marsh grass across the creek was flattened. There were many downed trees in the forest. There weren't any birds flying, but a few gators made their way up the creek in the direction of the downed tree. *Pearl* was covered with debris; and a layer of pine straw covered everything. The boat seemed in pretty good shape over all. She was floating nicely. As he leaned over the sides, Jacob couldn't see any major damage to the hull other than some gauges in the fiberglass. The mast and rigging would be easy to secure before they motored back to Sullivan's Island.

Jacob was exhausted. A long day still lay ahead. He was trying to figure out how he was going to find the energy to get the little life raft inflated, paddle around the creek and undo the lines attaching *Pearl* to the oaks when he heard the sound of an outboard motor getting louder and closer coming up the creek. A large skiff rounded the bend in the creek with a really big man at the wheel. Tadpole had never looked so good to Jacob. With him was Smalls.

"Have a pleasant evening?' called out Tadpole as he pulled up to Pearl.

"It was just great," replied Jacob. "How was yours?"

Tadpole took a puzzled look at Matthew's Grady White, lashed to one of *Pearl's* cleats. Rafting up to it, he and Smalls found their way across it to board *Pearl.*

They were amazed at what news greeted them, especially after Matthew came on deck, followed by Charlie who grinned from ear to ear.

Tadpole was using his Uncle Rufus's crabbing skiff. It had a CB radio aboard, which they used to communicate with Jaybird. He was able to get the county police and medical EMTs to the site within an hour. They had arrived on all terrain vehicles coming through the forest. Smithy and Edmund were taken into custody. An All Points Bulletin was sent out concerning Hank. Jacob had never seen Tadpole as completely wide eyed as when he was listening to the story Jacob, Charlie and Matthew told him and Smalls.

Smalls had brought with him a hand held video game of some sort. He and Charlie settled into the skiff, having fun with it in the skiff as the police and medical people tended to Smithy and Edmund.

Tadpole, Matthew and Jacob sat together in *Pearl's* cockpit, enjoying the morning together and the sense of peace that the ending of the long night brought with it.

'Matthew, man, I am so glad you were here. I don't know what would have happened if you hadn't shown up when you did.'

'The truth is that Charlie was on the verge of pulling the trigger on that gun he was holding. I don't think that he wanted to. I do know that he was about to anyway. He is quite a kid, Jacob, but I guess you already know that. I don't know how good a shot he might be, but I suspect that Hank was on the verge of going down. You know Jake, we are all in this together. Always have been, ever since when we all first met up. Nothing has changed. Friends are friends, no matter what. I didn't do anything you haven't already done. Remember that night out near Camden when you saved my butt? Same thing. Those rednecks thought I was about to be the life of their party. Then you jumped in and put your ass on the line. It's just like the way y'all looked out for Randy all these years. He was our friend. When something happened to him, no one turned their back on him. Y 'all were doing what needed to be done. What these guys-Edmund and Smithy never understood was it's really the same for all of us on this getting smaller all-of-the time planet. It's not about me. It's always about us. But that's just me think-ing' and what do I know."

"Check this out," Matthew said, as the police brought Smithy up on deck. His head was wrapped in a bandage. He never said a word, but his murdering black eyes bored into Jacobs with a rather clear message. They would see each other again one day.

Edmund was brought carefully up on a tarp acting as a stretcher. His arm taped to his side, his leg in a tempo-rary brace. Edmund had nothing to say. His eyes searched the sky, probably wondering how he had ended up here, in police custody with several severely damaged body parts. Edmund remained calm. He was, after all, a Capers. There was no way he was actually going to take the fall for this. His family connections would save his ass. The EMTs secured the men in the county police boat that had finally arrived. The police took custody of the men and their boat turned and headed back downstream towards the Wando.

Jacob, Charlie and Matthew were each interviewed sepa-rately. After a short conference, the county police officers had told them they were free to leave. They offered assis-tance in securing *Pearls'* mast, as well as untying the lines securing the boat to the oaks.

Finally, after such a long and remarkable night on Osprey Creek, Jacob and Charlie were able to head back home.

The day was glorious with sparkling bright blue skies. A fresh clean feel was imbedded in the air as if the hur-ricane had flushed all the bad air to somewhere far out to sea. *Pearl* was secured by a stout tow line to the stern of the large crabbing skiff. The trip back to Sullivan's Island began. Matthew trailed behind *Pearl* to be sure there was no concealed damage.

As they were just a short distance down Osprey Creek towards the Wando, a puppy was swimming towards them. Tadpole stopped the engine and Jacob found a crab net, holding it by the pole ready to pull the little dog aboard. But Charlie just reached over and scooped the puppy out of the water. The wet, brown dog quickly found a spot in Charlie's lap and started licking his face over and over

"Looks like you've got yourself a new pal there, Charlie," said Jacob.

Charlie held the puppy, looking at it with curious excitement. "You think I can keep her?" he asked.

"Unless someone comes looking for her, she's yours, if you want. I can't imagine how a little girl like that got way out here. She must have been on a boat out here somewhere, maybe, and got lost. But now she is found. She's like us, Charlie. We all went through Hurricane Danielle."

Entering the Wando River, they saw many boats scattered around. Most were underway, but several were aground in the mud on the far side. The forest had been damaged, but not seriously as it had been with Hurricane Hugo. Matthew motored along side, shouted he'd see everyone later. He sped off back down the Wando to the harbor. Watching him go, Jacob was struck again at Matthew's arrival, how perfect it had been. Jacob knew he was mighty lucky to have a friend who would show up in the middle of a Category

Three hurricane to help him deal with the most intense night of his life.

Tadpole kept looking over at Jacob. His incredibly huge smile grinned widely on his face. He shouted over the engine noise "My man is back. Those dudes were hurtin'. I can't get over it. Mr. Edmund Capers is alive and well, and gonna rot in hell. Who'd a guessed it?"

They all fell into the rhythm of the ride. Jacob felt especially at peace. An eagerness to get on with his life surged through him, despite his extreme exhaustion. He knew in the next few days he would be resigning quite happily from Hamilton Brothers. He was very fortunate to have had the five great years at that fantastic house on Sullivan's Island. But now it was time for him to move on .He was going to complete the journey he had started all those years ago. He couldn't remember the last time he had felt this relaxed about his life.

Several hours later, Sullivan's Island began to appear. As they approached the island, they could all see The Point appeared to be relatively undamaged. Continuing down the waterway, they saw the effect the hurricane had on Sullivan's Island. Although there were plenty of downed trees and a wide scattering of debris, the damage was much less than Jacob had feared. National Guardsmen were already on the island, securing it from further damage. Several of the men must have spotted them approaching and were waiting for the boat at Jacobs dock. The guardsmen apologized, but said the island was temporarily quarantined and no one was allowed back on for the next few days.

Tadpole said, "No problem, Jake, you guys can come with us up to the big house in Awendaw. We got plenty of room for you."

Through his binoculars, Jacob saw that his house appeared to have also come through the storm in good shape. It was standing and the roof looked intact. He hoped the Honda was alright.

Jacob tied *Pearl* securely to the dock. Before rejoining Tadpole, Charlie and Smalls, he inspected the boat a final time to be certain there were no un-detected leaks and that everything was as ship shape as time allowed. Finally, his work done for now, he sat for a moment on *Pearl's* deck and reflected on all that had occurred. He wondered why he was not completely exhausted and was, instead, feeling somewhat energized.

His eyes fell on the water, and he was reminded that, just days before, devastated at the loss of the Southern Shipping deal, an unexpected voice had come across the water to him. He remembered the words it said. 'Don't be afraid. Put your mind on your work and everything will be OK. Just don't be afraid.'

He looked at his friends waiting for him. The little brown puppy was asleep in Charlie's lap. Next to him there was a big grin on Tadpoles face as he looked at his son, Smalls. Jacob was grateful to have this people in his life.

Jacob stepped back aboard the skiff. Tadpole had turned the helm of the skiff over to Smalls, who beamed as they got underway. As the bow towards the Intracoastal Waterway, Jacob settled into the bench between Charlie and the Big

Guy. Jacob was suddenly very tired. He closed his eyes for a moment. Images flashed before him. He would not forget the image of Hank's feet as he dove off *Pearl's* stern into the darkness. He saw again the eye of the shark, as well those of Buddy Capers and of Captain Capers. He thought of Jody's eye looking at him that first time; her eyes as she was drawing, her calm intensity and focus, very much like the coyotes. The image of his own eyes appeared to him as he was tackling the Alabama running back. The primal intensity he could still feel as he had smashed into Smithy.

A surge of adrenalin flooded through him with those memories .He felt his life force flowing through him, from deep within his heart. It spread throughout his soul.

Jacob opened his eyes. Massive dark clouds up the waterway were moving away to the northeast. Bright sunlight began pouring through what remained of the storm. Beautiful shafts of light illuminated the relief that came with the passing of another hurricane.

Jacob put his arms around both Tadpole and Charlie's shoulders and held them tightly. Tears silently filled his eyes. The puppy climbed from Charlie's lap on to Jacobs, and, while licking Jacob's fingers, the dog peed. Jacob laughed and laughed and held his two friends even closer.

Everything was as it should be. Nothing was ever going to be better for Jacob than loving the imperfection and delight of his life shared with those he loved and trusted.

He turned his back to Sullivan's Island, to the harbor, to Charleston; to all of his past. He knew Hank was out there somewhere. Nothing could be done about that now.

It was time for Jacob O'Leary to get on with his life, to find his work, to listen to the whispers from God.

It was time for him to find whatever awaited him around the next bend in the waterway.